NICHTS

All and Naughts

Kirk Shellko

Attic Spaces Publishing

What is and what is not are not merely
linked. They are the same.

NICHTS

Hip-trop, trip-pop they spread out along the now-tawny grass. No ocher did they produce – though some suspect it – crawling up hills along the inclement plain they stood heavy in the urban soil. Rivals and mates of is, they assembled where what comes. Tiny, intimate of each element, they let not the minutest of particles escape and they were enormous, no collection of is escaping. They rode along the sliver of gold that crawls through rock and terra beneath the surface of the plain; they made electricity that guides thoughts which produce psyches of erect beings walking atop prodigious hills with flocks of wool-producing bleeters. They rode in iron trains along dark mountainous paths in masses and within bunches of anything. They have no number and cannot be taken as one, fraction or many – though one counts their species. They marched and did not move, made glory and produced earth and were none of these things. When talking they produced descriptive sounds that gave presence to the light of things, but they themselves cannot be described. Just so, they cannot walk or run, and so they did not crawl, did not die, and one cannot call them immortal, them having no life ever-undying. They did nothing and unified with death, life-giving portion. They glided in proportion and shaped the whole of a man with sable features, penetrating eyes and raven hair. They partook of his making and did nothing while he changed one state for another. Wrapped around his presence, they kept wood from being glass and bent the shapes of words in the mouths of counselors.

APPEARANCE OF A NON-EXISTENT MAN

Xenis observed the man who stood before him with scrutinizing curiosity.

"Am I thinking correctly?" he asked himself. "Have I been acting in the wrong way?"

He tapped a finger on the long, wooden table before him as he listened to Dietrich Wright. The talk lasted an hour or so, and the gatherers disbanded from the wooden table and re-gathered at another where coffee and sweets awaited. Xenis ate one of the chocolate-custard donuts that appeared to be recently baked, and as soon as he had consumed half of the pastry, cane sugar overtook him. Unable to eat the entire delight, he placed it on his plastic plate. So too with the orange soda. He wanted only water, he realized. Walking out of the building into the clear, mild evening, he noted what looked like corn on the ground. Curious, he picked up what he thought was a corn's ear, but immediately dropped a severed chicken's foot. Shortly, he was summoned to the Davis family auto by Daniel – he and the crew about to depart. Those who had gathered exhibited the most pleasant agreeableness, tolerable homotheria. A mere instant of unkindness was summarily chastised – and unreserved kindness unceasingly exercised – by the majority. Xenis once witnessed one of them receive a slap in the face, and remain calm. An aggressive thought not only frightened them, but compelled them to repent.

The Davis family had agreed to take him into their home when he was for all practical considerations homeless, giving him the means of support when he seemed able to carry his self no further. All generous to Xenis in a way unexpected. Remarkably, these same personages maintained an attitude of kindness and altruism. Xenis found himself in a farmhouse room -- this large, simple group whose roots extended deep into the tradition and whose family had been in the Americas as long as whites populated the land. Their family welcomed him and his curiousness without much anxiety; yet a few logistical considerations complicated Xenis' entry into their comfortable, immaculate home. He was in the care of two odd-looking dogs and a tortoise-shell cat, all of whom he refused to surrender. The central authority of the farm and house being unavailable, no-one was able to determine whether or how completely the stranger and his animals were welcomed. The family patriarch readily agreed to care for a outsider, yet barred animals from his property.

"Everyone has their own private double standard," Xenis muttered.

One of the girls looked at him quizzically.

"It's a farm, so the dogs can run around the yard and play and when they want to come home, they can come back," Daniel said, addressing all.

"Does your husband have a phone?" Xenis asked Brenda.

"We're a simpler folk than you're used to, I guess," she replied. "He ain't got no cell-phone on him. He don't like those things neither."

"He doesn't own one?"

"He owns it. He just won't put it on, don't like to light it up," she continued. "He'll get back down in good time, and then he'll say 'Yay' or 'Nay'."

Xenis proceeded home with most of the Körper family, and once again at the farmhouse he immediately tended to dogs and his Dora. His two jade-collared and hairless beasts leaped up at him as he arrived, performing every-day dog-dance. Licking his face in bits, they jumped and occasionally batted him on the nose and chin, receiving his attentions with dog-smile all around and about his person. At the same time, they turned their attention towards the expanse of green that beckoned. A large range over which to run and explore had occupied their attention the entire day, with them examining the boundaries of land and creatures. They left for further exploration soon after a given welcome while Xenis stood and watched them quietly.

"When they get good and hungry, they'll come back. You'll see," Brenda said, watching with Xenis.

Daniel asked what kind of dogs these were. Friendly, hairless and initially somewhat skittish – their ears oversized just enough to give them an other-worldly appearance – gazes most-oft directed at their friend and guide. Xenis explained that this breed was one of the oldest domesticated canines, that they were gregarious and lively, if odd looking. The following days watched Xenis and the four children work as they awaited the return of the patriarch. The two girls guided the stranger-guest as he tended horses.

"You need to talk to a horse," Joy advised.

"Yeah?," said Xenis.

"They listen real good." The girls turned a glance toward

one another, smiling.

Xenis patted the three-year-old mare on her side, walking into the horse's line of vision.

"I don't know any of your commands, my friend," he said. The girls exchanged another glance. "To the barn!" Xenis said as he raised his hand, pointing to the barn.

The horse lumbered in the general direction of the barn.

"To the barn no longer!" he said as he held out his opened palms. The mare stopped. Xenis grabbed the reins and tugged lightly left towards a patch of grass.

"Let's walk in the grass," he said.

The powerful mare walked left onto the tiny, moist blades. He took hold of the reins and tugged this time right.

"Wait a minute! Let's walk on the path!" he said.

The horse turned right toward the dirt path on the right.

"Hold on a second!" he said, again with opened palms.

The mare stopped. Xenis patted her on the neck and wished he had some kind of treat.

"Apparently, I knew some of her commands."

He smiled as the horse nudged him with her nose. He pulled the reins, directing her toward the barn. Daniel, who had been sitting nearby unobserved, no longer contained himself.

"Bla-ha HA, Ha!"

"Shut up!" said Joy.

"You thought you were gonna punk him, but he punked you!"

Xenis' olive-skinned complexion stood in direct comparison to the bright and light-blue day, his impression striking the other others around him. His close-cropped, raven-black hair along with what looked like a tiny, golden earring on the right ear caught childhood attention. He employed a serious tone, with stern voice, and he commanded his dogs curtly.

"He seems a little angry all the time," Joy said to Daniel.

"He ain't angry, I don't think," Daniel returned after a moment.

"Don't get too near him," Rapture advised. "You might have ta get a switch."

"I won't get no switch," Daniel answered curtly. "He ain't dangerous. Just odd."

"Dad'll smack you," Joy said.

The *Xoloitzcuintli* joined with the other animals, brown and black weathered fresh environs and smelled brand-new scents, snatched and enjoyed. Xenis watched the dogs carefully, only reluctantly let them out of his sight. The three children watched as he peered around the corner of a shed near the black canine. He waited just so long as the animal's attention arose and dropped his head back around and out of sight. A few of these maneuvers caught dog's-eye and a few more brought sound from his belly.

"Woowoowoo Woaargh!" said the black as he smacked his tail on the ground and stared.

Xenis popped his head around the corner of the shed once more and again disappeared suddenly. The canine wagging trotted over to the shed-corner and observed the other edge of the edifice where Xenis once again showed his face.

"Woowoowoo Woaargh!" offered the black.

Xenis bolted toward the other end of the shed, disappearing from dog-sight. Having caught on, the black followed him, more strenuously tail-wagging. Again Xenis peered around the corner and ran again off, across a field toward a low, wooden fence. The black pursued and easily overleaped the ligneous obstruction. Xenis darted to the Davis house and into the garage, hiding behind a truck. The confused black sought and easily found him crouching, sniffing here and there.

"You know a bit about animals," Daniel said to Xenis as he walked out of the garage with the black.

"Just a bit. This one likes to play," Xenis said, patting lightly the grinning black. "You play with your animals too, yes?"

"Sometimes, but not like that. We don't have no dogs like yours here. Most of 'em are work-dogs."

"They likely enjoy playing," Xenis said.

A few days later the two met again. Both hid behind the shed and peered around the corner.

"Woowoowoo Woaargh!" quoth the black.

Gabriel Davis pulled the pliable and motionless slump of deer by the antlers out of his truck as Xenis watched. Gabe, at last arriving home from hunting, found the strangest of dogs attached to his children. He had not seen them play with animals for some time, farm-work having overcome them. Being a generous and empathetic man, Gabriel wanted to take in Xenis and his animals, but at issue was the place where Xenis' cat would reside. There were many felines who came and went at that farm, and ordinarily one more presented no concern, but Xenis insisted that the animal stay in his room.

"She won't harm nobody," said Joy.

"Xenis says she can stay in his room," said Rapture.

"She's a good cat. She doesn't scratch anything; she's too old," Xenis explained, his tone like Joy's.

Gabriel pondered a moment, observing the look on his daughters' faces.

"They can stay for a trial," Gabriel said with reluctance in his voice. "But the cat stays in the one room only."

Daniel approached Xenis cautiously and watched the stranger, who sometimes spoke quickly and curtly - expressing some frustration with those around him. Xenis explained things in detail and quickly, sometimes angrily, and Daniel sensed...pain or...something. The new stranger always appeared confident and used again an angry voice now when his animals needed direction, yet he petted and rewarded affectionately when the time seemed appropriate. He and his animals recognized when to do what with each other and how, retreating and approaching at times and other times. Daniel, like his father, grinned at this man in person and smiled inwardly when Xenis came to mind.

NICHTS

It, or they, are not numbered – cannot be counted, not even one altogether or no – though they are all the same. Their substance unsubstantial, nothing. They are neither prior, nor present, nor about to be, but they come to be. Nor are they illumined, not dark, nor even lacking, since they are lack, but they come to be. No space occupies place around them, no compression nor expansion, yet they are. There is no there for them; they are not even nowhere – cannot move. Yet, they are ability. Exuding no color, they cannot be lit, they are not absent; they would need to be present in order to be absent, and they are. There is no being-a-certain-way for them, no being in them, yet they are. They are what is missing, truncating, and in that way they are, yet such a characteristic is not. They are-not.

HIDDEN NOTHINGS

"Can I show Xenis around the farm?" Daniel asked.

"He needs a tour?" asked Gabriel.

Daniel stared blankly for a moment at his father.

"I don't know. I just thought it'd help."

"Go ahead," Gabriel returned, jabbing his son playfully with a fist.

"I want to show Xenis things too," pleaded Joy.
"Can I go?" asked Raven.

"There's no-one left to do any work. You'll all be wandering around with Xenis."

The wide eyes of children assailed their father.

"Go on, go on."

Xenis cleaned animal feeders with Joy, trimmed hooves of

smaller animals with Raven and washed cars with Daniel. The four organized tools in the large barn, Xenis asking many questions about tending to animals.

"He gets things quickly, but he doesn't know anything," Daniel observed.

"You don't know anything," Joy rasped.

As the weeks passed, the children and Xenis regularly moved hay and fed animals, carried water, specifically tending to particular animals at specific times of day.

"You sponsored by my dad?" Daniel asked Xenis.

"Did he tell you that?"

"He didn't tell me nothin'. Just wanted to know," Daniel continued as he worked.

Daniel walked to the other side of the barn, occupying himself with nothing. Xenis gave no response to the question and Daniel wondered if he was still there. Having returned, he found Xenis in the same place, performing the same task.

"Yeah, he sponsored me."

"I thought so," Daniel said. "He does that kind of thing a lot."

"He brings a lot of guys home?"

"He hasn't done it so much these days, but he used to invite all kinds here in order to make 'em straight and bring 'em into a clean life."

"What happened to them?"

"Not sure, but most clean up."

"Really?"

"There's at least two guys who still come every Sunday. They been sober for a long time...but some guys..."

"There are exceptions?"

"Yeah. Will Mayers is OK now, but he had what dad calls a 'long journey.'"

"Really?"

"He used to beat his wife and get so drunk he'd black out."

"Oh."

"He'd never remember it the next day."

"Sounds pretty bad."

"Yeah. That guy was no hero, but he came through alright."

Xenis met many friends of the Davis family, men and women who never harmed anyone; never fought with anyone; had no desire to deprive anyone of anything; became angry seldomly, but privately. They owned homes and ate well, or at least they ate what they pleased, and they had enough money and presence of mind to relax themselves into beer on Saturday or hobbies of various kinds: volunteer fire-fighting and poker. Most of these humans seemed to Xenis quiet and mild, and to these Xenis did not always relate. Some few others broke out upon the world in a sort of mania, wanting and chasing; they needed and labored; they immersed themselves in what they thought. Some of the males wanted women and others wanted money; others wanted and did not know what they wanted, only that they did not want what the others desired. Some of the women wanted men and security – comfort and stability – desired more material and some sort of recognition, but did not know their desire. Xenis thought he related to these men and women most. He met them on a weekly basis, discussing his present, most personal, dilemma.

"My name is Xenis and I'm an alcoholic," he said sitting at that same solid, comfortably blond wooden table. Gabriel listened as Xenis described his sometimes desperate need.

"When I was able to afford such things, I drank wine, sometimes absinthe," Xenis said.

The prioority of his former self Xenis felt more intimately at the reference to his prior ways. Coming from a low point, he wondered whether he ought to trust these persons; he listened to men and women talk about their beliefs, their lives. They, like most others, did not agree, but the ones who wanted the most dominated the conversation, pressing their thoughts upon others. These others listened and moved the conversation slightly.

"Hunger," Xenis said, mostly to himself.

"What?" asked Daniel.

Having always possessed whatever vim and vigor he required to perform a specific task or to accomplish an end he desired, Xenis recently experienced a unsettling diminution of energy. He had been compelled to abandon his home quickly, and for not much return, and he then relocated to Wisconsin.

"I ought to have recovered by now," he thought to himself on more than one occasion.

Xenis had almost no resources with which to pay for a medical examination, so he asked for a loan from Gabriel. The family doctor examined Xenis and drew blood, tests revealing a perfectly healthy, vigorous male. Frustrated yet not surprised, Xenis continued his work and became more accustomed to the Davis family, the children in particular – growing more at ease – his priority that potent uninvited visitor. The sale of his real estate had provided him with some funds, but legal costs had consumed them. He had a lawyer who was unable to help him, a period of former indulgence to occupy him, and other thoughts arising from his priority. He was well-educated and the desire for drink and conversation possessed him; the desire for ascendancy accompanied him, long known. Priority pushes.

"I can't say I'm made or maker," he muttered as he baled hay with Joy.

"What?" she asked.

After some time, Xenis began to work alongside the farmhands. One among his list of chores was attending the livestock, since disease and injury were dangers to the milk-cows. Hector and Juan were the settled farmhands, both raising families nearby. The Davis enterprise operated year-round, which meant that the cows contented themselves inside buildings most of their lives. The plot of land on which they labored was not enormous as other corporate plantation-farms were, but they possessed some three-hundred and twenty-three cows along with the occasional bull. The herringbone had been a state-of-the-art milking parlor, but its age and constant use each year accelerated a creeping obsolescence. The cows entered the building in rows single-file, and were led into a V-shaped platform that arose to about shoulder height. Each line stopped while Xenis or Hector attached a suction-cup to their teats from below, bovines in a line of eight to twelve at a time. The machine drew the milk from each cow simultaneously and thus only two farm-hands were employed. Xenis' appointed task was to assist Hector in monitoring the milking of the cows, he employed on one side of the V-shaped parlor and Hector on the other. The herding of the animals into the structure was a task assigned to farm-hands and the gates keeping the animals outside required tending as well. Xenis noticed immediately that should the equipment be shifted so that the animals entered from the other side of the building, entrance to and from the edifice would proceed with greater facility; the animals would have a greater degree of freedom to roam about the feeding yard.

"The cows need no more room than they have," Hector replied to his suggestion. "They are fine as they are."

Hector regularly smelled of the good drink though he appeared to be unaware of how easily one sensed his bourbon. He invited Xenis to partake with him and his friends, an amiable opportunity of which Xenis never availed, again that threatening priority. Hector and Juan were well aware of the influence and the position that the Davis family held on drinking and the use of drugs, yet they felt no need to restrain themselves, both being functional and discreet. They tended their duties without complaint, or without overmuch protest, and respected the Davis' view on the vile liquid enough. They had lived in the United States for seven years each, both having arrived within its borders illegally. The Davis family took the two men into their home and gave them resources for living and dignity, and their loyalty along with their gratitude the men returned. Xenis and Hector fell into a routine, almost instinctual, both men trusting the other. Xenis developed a certain respect for this man who took his obligations seriously, who tended to his family and who appeared to understand the boundaries of others even without recognizing himself that he did so.

The hands and Gabriel ate together regularly.

"I was thinking," Hector said to Gabriel.

Gabriel turned to his main hand.

"If we move the equipment in the building so that the cows can enter from the other side, the cows can move around more, and they would be able to run around more free in the yard. The milking will be much faster."

"...maybe you're right."

"The cows will be more happy and more healthy and better cows make better food."

"Hector, you have given us yet another good idea. I'll make the plans and you and Xenis can put things together next week."

Gabriel had a first-rate farmhand. Hector looked at Xenis and spoke.

"I must say that the idea to move the equipment was not mine, Mr. Davis. The idea it came from Xenis," He said.

The older Davis paused for a moment, looked at Xenis and nodded. The month that followed witnessed Juan teaching Xenis where the digging tools resided, asking him to fetch them; he permitted Xenis to move dirt and carry the wood that replaced broken posts on the fence, nothing more. Xenis watched him operate the baler and the tractor.

"Juan, he likes his tractor, and baler," said Hector.

"Can I rely on you to show me around? I learn very little from Juan."

"Si, you can," chuckled Hector.

The major challenge for the men was the maintenance of healthy livestock. Sick cows had to be contained or eliminated, depending on the malady, injuries had to be observed soon after their occurrence and tended quickly, sometimes in isolation. Some animals, particularly most bulls, were ornery beasts with entrenched dispositions; most farm-hands knew what animals to avoid. Xenis was able to develop a way of determining what creatures were perilously bestial and what more docile, the signs of an impending mania in a particular animal being discernible. He noted an irascible ox whose behavior regularly amused farm-hands, the enormous old bruiser tied to a post by a thick, heavy chain in order to contain him. A wrathful Bacchus often visited Juan, and he customarily squatted, reached out his arms and waved a white cloth before the bruiser, occasioning rapid anger. He would lean towards the animal while walking by and abruptly throw up his hands. Xenis attempted to keep the bibulous Juan away from the brute when the man's intoxication exceeded his reason and when he drew dangerously near the volatile and massive – frighteningly strong – animal.

"You are Juan's mother," said Hector, laughing.

Xenis frowned at the suggestion. "What ought I do?" he asked.

"Leave him be. He'll stop."

Xenis thought a moment.

"And he'll get drunk again, forget how the bull almost killed him...and then the bull will almost kill him again..., or maybe will kill him," Hector again chuckled.

Xenis was unable to suppress a smile and laugh a bit himself.

"Chance is a parent to fools," he said.

"Maybe so."

The farm-hands tended dotingly to the animals, and those male hands patted and comforted certain of the herd. Hector's kind, strong hands gained the attention of many bovines. They provided nourishment and culinary pleasure, and knew what each animal enjoyed, staying clear on a bad day. They gave silage to bovines, a kind of cow-treat. His inoffensive grip and sturdy tap became more well-liked, even loved. One of the more affectionate of cows adored the treats, and once when Hector was about to distribute silage, she half-jumped up and over top of the unsuspecting man, a kind of lumbering twist of the cow-spine displaying her excitement. A full sixteen-hundred pounds, the savage-loving cow knocked Hector about and down. Xenis distracted the loving bovine with a tap on the head. Out of breath and stunned, Hector gazed about him.

"Thank you."

This deliverance of Hector – alert and clean – unexpectedly intoxicated Xenis; the lightening of his mind and the release of tension gave him pause. Later in the day Hector, Xenis and the other farm-hands were taking their customary supper with Gabriel Körper.

"I was saved from the cow," Hector said, shaking his head back and forth.

"That cow she loves you a bit too much," one of the farm-hands jibed. And the others laughed.

"We have a love affair between Hector and his girlfriend," Juan re-laughed.

"The cow she's a good animal," said Hector.

"A good animal who would have killed you," Juan said sharply.

And the farm-hands largely became silent, with some laughs prevailing.

"Wise men prefer warmhearted animals to drunken fools," said Xenis.

"What?" Juan said.

NICHTS

Existence comes from is, and is simply is. Simple is is existence, that something or some act is there, and they are. That there is something is its act, and they do the act. There are horses. There are photons with strange nature. There are concepts of liberty and plans for the construction of a human state. There are states of animal communities. Philosophers have made clear that all these are. They act as existence. Humans call that being, and the act they express as is; animals do not need to name it, though they must sense it. All that is will show what it is. Nothing can do otherwise. Being is reciprocally predicated of being, and they are. They are in what the other and others do.

ADAPTATION AND INTEGRATION

Xenis abstained from drinking with the hands around him ordinarily drunk. He continued to remain in the Davis family's good graces, although temptation was a foe. Again that priority of his. As a result, Xenis came to meet with the teetotalling Gabriel more often, and Gabe liked chatting.

"A man has to take care of himself first. My father always used to say 'Look out for the big number one.'"

The words tired Xenis, though he liked the man. Regardless, he came to Gabriel when he was particularly fatigued, when he wanted or lacked – nowhere to turn – which at that time was frequent. He continued to experience the same thought.

"Have I been thinking correctly?"

Xenis noted in Gabriel the same clarity that he had encountered prior, a fixity of belief. He used to wonder at such assurance.

"Certitude makes lost those whom it occupies," he said.

"What?" asked Gabriel.

Xenis looked at Gabriel.

"Some adamantly cling to something vague or unclear. No-one is able to obtain assurance about such things," Xenis muttered.

"I'm not sure I understand."

Xenis used to believe that such persons needed belief in order to continue their lives, that such a fixity was necessary in order to determine or perhaps create a reference point. It had been difficult to live without a fixed belief, but Xenis did it – a vitality apparently fading presently. His way had been and continued to be a life without knowing, or at least without claiming to know. He returned to his room in the Davis residence where he tended to the his tortoise-shell Dora. Inside a laundry basket set against his closet wall. She emerged only when he returned and then crawled onto his lap or up onto his bed. Her plight and personality won deep his affection, years-long care and tending were hers.

"How the fuck you been, Fluff?" Xenis said. "I haven't seen you in...five or six hours."

A purr and a light butt to his hand with her head were a response. She was, along with the Xolos, the final concrete reminder of a priority now coming less real, now more illusion, a fading what whose influence refuses to abate. He thought about his friends Brazil and Leon, his old roommate Casper. On some infrequent occasions like this one, sobs broke out, and at times the animals that he now loved so dearly saddened him. He clasped the feline closer to him, then sleep came. The next day Xenis and Hector began their ordinary routine, Xenis moving the cows into the parlor as usual. He had been at the Davis farm seven months, abstaining and working regularly with his hands. His surprise that he enjoyed the attachment to the land continued; he was developing and even refining a sympathy for the creatures there and they in turn seemed to take joy in his presence, living the act of not-being-being-not along the land with its occupants. Some of the larger animals, the horses cows bulls, seemed to miss him when he was not present, and he enjoyed visiting particular ones, though he was uncertain whether their perceived affection was real or imagined. Xenis' dogs had taken to the company of the other animals, wandered about the stretch of bare land with meandering nonconstraint, delirious abandon in their trot. Initially, he tended to them, gave them the ordinary commands, but they appeared to be thriving and because of their good measure of health and because perhaps he noted something within striking at him, he met with and commanded his dogs less frequently. Joy, Daniel and Raven seemed to love the Xolos, and Xenis had never seen his canines so vital, immersed in that feral share that gave them ability and continued existence. His two animals were becoming a part of the pack of farm-dogs, ten in number, who wandered about and worked with the hands, living a hierarchy of their own.

As Xenis was milking a line of bovine, he heard strained voices. Outside. Overturning farm machinery or errant animals, men whose limbs become entangled in tractors or who perform maintenance on combines with grain heads might cause farm-hands to yell, but these sounds were a bit louder than usual, voices almost in chorus, dire strain. An animal had contracted something, a malady discovered. Disease is an old adversary to the farm, but this instance brought considerable distress. Juan had discovered signs of tuberculosis in one of the animals, which would not have been the cause of great stress except that such an outbreak of mycobacterium bovis remained uncommon in Wisconsin. The question as to whence arose this strain was the white-hot topic. Gabriel and Hector quickly acted when informed of the dilemma, removing the animal and investigating other beasts. When satisfied that no more than four cows had contracted the disease, Gabriel disappeared with Hector and a few sick bovines, including Hector's girlfriend. Xenis was unable to keep himself away from watching Gabriel cull a part of his herd.

"Juan has done a good job," Hector commented to Xenis.

"He does more than drink," Xenis remarked.

"Oh, don't be mistaken, my friend. Juan is a very good farm-hand. He just cannot stop the drink and he acts sometimes foolish, but he *is* a good farm-hand."

The topic of the disease was taken up at one of the breaks for lunch.

"I am so glad that Juan was there so that he found the problem," Hector said.

"We're all thankful that the disease didn't go any further," said Gabriel.

"Why is it such a dilemma?" Xenis asked.

"Some diseases are not only in cows. It can spread to other animals..."

"Like what?"

"Like deer."

"And foxes," said Juan.

"...and pigs," said Hector.

Other farm-hands looked one at another seriously, some turning down heads and eating rather than speaking. There was a considerable pause.

"Humans then." said Xenis.

"...humans too."

Gabriel concentrated on his lunch-plate.

"We have much to be thankful for," said Hector.

And farm-hands nodded as they ate.

A bit shaken and concerned, Xenis carefully looked after Dora inside his room, but he was not always successful at containment. She ate in the room, and most times the now-aging feline remained content asleep in the laundry basket of her diminutive apartment. The Körper children were not allowed into Xenis' room, and because of Gabriel's edict they were anxious to learn more. Both girls particularly interested, they waited patiently until all adults departed. The locked door certainly no match, the girls found their way inside, inspecting here and opening there – not much to see. No technological possessions, no drugs, some books and clothes spilled across the floor. During these investigations Dora frequently meandered out of her room and into the wider home, though the children often took pains to confine her. Most times the cat set herself free she became very difficult to find, the children understanding that should their father return and discover Dora wandering about, Xenis and his Dora would in all probability be asked to leave. In a regular panic, the diminutive Davies searched every corner and crevice of the old three-story house, sometimes not finding Dora for hours. On one occasion, Daniel delayed his father just outside the house while his sisters scrambled to locate the meandering beast. Always they relocated the animal before their father returned, but the feline desire to investigate all the more emerged. These two youngest of the children, Joy and Raven, deciding that they liked the diminutive predator, came to the habit of opening the door to Xenis' room in order to let out a prancing Dora. The girls captured and brought her to the living room where one was able to pet and play with the affectionate feline while the other watched for their approaching father, or Xenis.

"You better not keep doin' that," Daniel warned.

"Just shut up," they returned, almost in unison.

Daniel knitted his brow...

"If you tell, we got stuff to tell too."

As these clandestine encounters continued, Dora became accustomed to the front-room living-quarters kitchen as the girls moved or carried her. She discovered an ever increasing ability to remain at liberty. Xenis was at a loss when he returned to his room only to witness Dora dash out into the hall and down the stairs, at once into the living room. A bit panicked, he rushed after the cat only to find her enjoying prompt comfort on the lap of Joy, Raven beside the spry animal.

"What have you been doing?"

"She didn't do nothin'," returned Joy, petting the feline on the head – an indignant look on her face.

"I wasn't asking the cat." Xenis' angrily asserted, surprising himself with vehemence.

Joy and Raven locked their eyes briefly.

"She wouldn't bother with anyone she hadn't already met," Xenis interrupted sharply.

The girls remained silent, still petting the animal as she reclined comfortably on Joy's lap. Xenis tapped his Dora on the head and closed his eyes slowly at the feline who closed her eyes slowly and purred ever more.

"We didn't do nothin'," Rapture claimed.

"You must have entered my room."

The girls glanced at one another quickly.

"We didn't do nothin'," Joy repeated.

"You both are voracious liars," Xenis returned, still looking at and petting his girl. "But you're right. You didn't do nothing."

In the weeks that followed Xenis allowed the girls into his room. He thought it strange that his cat was the object of their affection when a score of felines waited outside.

"Those cats are feral," Joy explained.

"They don't let nobody nearby," Rapture added.

"You be good to her," he advised.

Some months passed as Xenis continued to attend AA meetings. He came more at ease among the family, and yet the thought of his former ability and great reach, that priority, remained inescapable. The most frequent contact with his former existence was that of his lawyer, Ülrich Geldsbaum, who wished to remain a friend and intimate, but the two men had engaged in enough strife that a close bond continued to be elusive. Though Ülrich had proven his innocence in the embezzlement, Xenis retained a mild and ever-present, unrecognized, aversion. Some reluctance guided him when they met.

"I am glad to see you..." Ülrich paused as the two men sat in the Körper kitchen, the customary but strained shaking of the hands quick and stiff.

"Xenis," said Xenis.

Urlich paused a moment.

"Are we safe to talk here?" he asked.

"No-one will bother us."

"I have some potentially good news, though there may be...drawbacks."

Ülrich felt that old angry countenance that Xenis emitted.

"What kind of drawbacks?"

"Well, should we discover some of your fortune that is returnable, your change of identity may present a... hurdle."

"We'll cross that bridge when we come to it."

"Yes, yes." Ülrich cleared his throat "As I say, I have good and bad news. The charge of complicity in the death of Kasper Thanatos has been dropped. The cause of death remains 'accident' as it has been."

"That's a relief..." Xenis nodded as he said this, but Ülrich did not appear to be in any way relieved.

"Still, the larger question is that of who is bringing these charges. There seem to be, as you know, charges emerging on a regular basis, and this is the essence of the bad news."

"What do you mean?" Xenis asked.

"Only that I suspect a single hand."

"...in order to bury me?"

"I suspect this, yes."

"Well, we both know who is doing that."

"Yes..."

"As long as the prince remains, the kingdom may return," Xenis said.

It was with these circumstances in mind that a weary Xenis continued his work on the Davis farm. His outsider status prevented him from ascending the ranks among the farm-hands, but what information he needed in order to perform his tasks well he obtained from Hector and especially from the children. Xenis' status in the Davis business, his priority, his need to work almost constantly, his recently-encountered poverty constantly thought over him. Solitary in his circumstance, he tended to the Xolos with greater frequency. They returned the desired affection, yet the brown and black busied themselves more now with their pack and they now had chores to perform. Some of the farm-hands had developed affection for them. Xenis thought good of these bonds, his animals' contentment meaning a great deal. Though he and his friends continued a safe and comfortable existence, his familiar state of isolation abided as well. He began to experience more physical fatigue, and the same thought plagued him.

"Have I been thinking correctly?"

NICHTS

The is of existence is the being of existence, that some thing or process is there. That there is an act, but it does not act alone; it acts with a hidden portion and with a material *eidos*. What is acts in context of what is. These acts are together; they make what is there. What is there acts in conjunction with what is there, and what is there is an act in conjunction with what is there. The act is the substance. This acting together is both part and whole of any act, which makes it exist. It is. What is there acts not alone as itself, being part and whole of any act. They act as their structure and substance. What the other humans and other creatures do is their act.

AN EMPTY
CONVERSATION

G abriel Körper was a thick man of average height, sporting a fifty-year hair-full-head of salt and pepper, and he was fit. Some perceived him as portly and thus not as healthy as he was, but Gabriel was vigorous, simply thick of frame. His physical constitution helped him manage his dairy farm. In his deliberations with his children he was average, communicating with them intermittently and attempting as best he was able to instill in them the proper – the only – values. In his demeanor he was gregarious, attempting to gather with others and to bring the larger family together, frequently wanting to lead poor families, convicts some prostitutes and stray souls. The claim that Gabriel was a commoner was not only no insult, but rather a decided compliment, yet his attentions collected individually an attempt to promote common cause. Gabriel decided that he would pay more attention to his new farm-hand, though he had already chatted with the peculiar, younger man. The odd, sable Xenis was a good worker, but Gabriel did not place him among the others. Xenis did odd things. He spent much of his time with his animals, which Gabriel thought odd, and he engaged in strange activity, such as climbing trees and sitting motionless in them, running his hands along the outer casings of corn or through tall grass. Xenis was strong enough for the work, but periodically he failed physically. Gabriel took to instructing the younger man in the ways of beasts and men as well as the dynamics of the dairy farm. Common sense would be best for him, grant to him social acceptance. Xenis learned things quickly, even Daniel noticed that, and he was not the kind of thinking man who remained incapable of performing practical tasks. Xenis had, after all, pointed out how the simple rearrangement of the herringbone parlor would benefit the cattle, which indeed it had. Gabriel enjoyed talking to the younger man, on one occasion moving piles of wood needed for mending fences.

"I am grateful for your idea about rearranging the parlor."

"You're quite welcome."

The two men mounted a small hill where the bulk of the wood resided.

"You have some good, practical suggestions."

"Thank you."

Gabriel directed Xenis to the lower part of the hill where he handed down to the younger man the planks. Xenis received and stacked them.

"I like to think, sometimes, that I have good ideas too," Gabriel claimed. He was now on the top of the hill the brilliant blue, sun and crisp-clear behind him. "Good ideas are all around us," he continued. Gabriel lifted one of the long planks, smiling.

"They're ever-present?"

Gabriel hesitated a moment.

"That's right," he said, a bit curious.

"I recall you saying something of that sort before," said Xenis.

Xenis commented casually without taking his sight from his work. Gabriel continued working, but paused his words as if wondering whether and when he ought to continue.

"You...do not sound convinced," Gabriel returned after a moment.

"Good ideas seem plentiful enough," said Xenis. "I don't doubt their presence, but..."

Xenis threw another heavy plank on top of the growing pile, but stopped his work, capped his knees with his hands and leaned over.

"You OK?"

Xenis nodded without making eye contact.

Gabriel smiled and said "I hope youfeel cofortable here. I like to think everyone feels they can rest and feel at ease."

Xenis cast a good-natured sigh nowhere.

"I don't know how to describe it," he said.

Gabriel continued standing at the top of the hill as he handed another of the planks to Xenis, silhouette flashing light around his shade in the afternoon sun.

"Describe what?"

"It's a sensation more than a thought, but it's a thought as well."

Gabriel cleared his throat "It's hard to describe many things, I think."

"I agree, but it is not something that I am able to discern clearly," Xenis said.

"Can you describe it at all?"

"I do not think so. But I am able to dericbe what it does," said Xenis, half-blinded by the light. He felt again more tired.

Silence again stood between the two men.

"I'm not sure I understand."

Gabriel wiped his brow.

"I do not understand myself'," Xenis said.

Gabriel again smiled good nature. He grasped three heavy wooden planks with strong arms.

"Describing its affects sometimes describes what something is, yes?"

"I agree, but it's something that is not there, but it is all around us."

"Does it destroy?"

"It is as if there is something I sense that acts, but is not there."

"If it acts, it must be there."

Gabriel pulled his handkerchief out of his pocket and wiped his brow.

One thinks that only present things act and produce," Xenis said, continuing as if Gabriel said nothing.

Gabriel cleared his throat and stood pensive for a moment, his method of delay in order to prepare.

"Now, son..." he began "...I...I can't see how something comes from nothing."

He placed his hand on the younger man's shoulder.

"That seems to be it. It is nothing that bother me," Xenis said.

"Not having something you need can be difficult," Gabriel stated firmly.

"That's true, but that is not precisely what I mean."

"You're talking about nothing?" Gabriel said almost laughing.

"I am not certain," Xenis said.

Gabriel thought for a moment, as if to ponder continuing once more.

"I have never experienced anything like that." He laughed and sat down.

"It is in the past as the past," Xenis stated, looking up at the sitting man.

"OK."

"But it is the future as well."

"It is time," Gabriel surmised.

"No. It is not anything, not anything clear."

"I am not sure what you mean."

"It is an intuation, I suspect. It surrounds everything and yet it isn't anything."

"You mean because it is not here?"

"It is here as well."

"Does it have any kind of quality?"

"No. No quality."

"Is it a quantity?"

"No amount."

"It affects you?"

"Yes. It tires me."

"Alright." Gabriel waited a moment. "We can rest."

zX"   "No, I do not need to rest. That is not the kind of tiredness that affects me."

"I'm not sure what to do to help."

"I do not believe there is any help that can be done."

"Well, if it affects you, it must be somewhere. If it is somewhere, we can locate it and help."

"I would not be able to escape, if I wished."

"So it's everywhere?"

"It's everywhere, but it cannot be touched."

"There is no past and no future and there is no here and there."

Gabriel looked away, then back again at Xenis.

"It gets worse."

The older man paid serious attention.

"There is no change to it. Not real change anyway."

"There's always change."

"That change is nothing. Just as the past, the future, and here as opposed to there are nothing. That is what I sense."

"This is what bothers you?"

"No time or space. No change. All in everything."

"I don't know what you mean."

"I do not know myself. Whatever it is that taunts me is everything and it is not discernable."

"It is everywhere?"

"Not entirely, but I don't know."

Gabriel removed some chew from his pocket, stuffed it in his mouth and began to savor the earthy taste. He placed his palms on the grass around him and leaned back.

"I found out a bit about you."

"You did?"

Gabriel nodded slowly in silence.

"Don't worry, son. I want to help, but...I know that someone or something is bothering you."

"Do you know who or what?"

"I wish I had some details. You describe some of it, so you must know a bit."

"No. I don't know. It's nothing."

Gabriel knitted his brows and cuppoed Xenis' shoulder.

"We get some rest now."

Gabriel assigned Daniel and Xenis together, working Herringbone parlor together. Xenis did not have much experience with children, but Gabriel trusted him. Xenis wanted keep his promise to the thick, gregarious patriarch; after all, Gabriel had no necessarily good reason to trust and to employ Xenis. Daniel accompanied Xenis when he played with the two Xolos, enjoyed their demeanor – especially when the black winked on command and the brown brought mail from the distant box. Xenis petted the animals almost constantly and embraced them, as he did with other creatures on the farm – amusing the hands. Daniel did what Xenis did. During the warm summer months the Xolos had been content to live and meander outside for as long a period as their sensitive skin would permit, but they had to sleep inside during the cold season. The boy delighted in assisting Xenis while he tended to his beloved creatures. And it was Daniel who pointed out to his father how this breed requires a warmer bed during the colder season. Not permitted inside the Körper house all night though Daniel-Joy-Rapture pleaded for it, the dogs were given a comfortable place to sleep in the edifice that housed the cows, a section of their own, and Daniel and Xenis met there, sometimes by chance, but many times the two planned an excursion.

"They're strange-looking dogs," Daniel commented.

"They're friends."

Daniel laughed.

"You think I'm funny again."

"You are," Daniel responded.

"Why's that?"

"You treat dogs like humans."

"I do no such thing," Xenis stated as he embraced one of his hounds closely, dogstail wagging more   rapidly. Daniel laughed again.

"You see? You treat a dumb animal like it's...not dumb," he said.

"You think animals are dumb?" Xenis asked.

"I know they are," Daniel said. "You think they're smart like people?"

"I think too much emphasis is placed upon the human kind of thinking."

"Dogs don't think like humans do," asserted a perplexed Daniel.

"No. They don't, but they do have a thought process, and their way of being what they are is neither more nor less than humans being what they are."

Daniel stared at Xenis.

"They're not our equals because they have a different is, that's all. But we're not their equals too."

"My mom says you're strange, but I know you're crazy."

Xenis laughed.

NICHTS

One was not-death and another was not-life. One was not-love and another was not-hate, the not-hate not necessarily love and the not-love not necessarily hate nor necessarily anything other than not. They wrapped themselves tightly around is, chased away all other, and all the other was completely all other, all times, all color, all texture, all motion, all. Animal was there, warm blood muscle-flesh and integument. Human was present as well, again warm blood muscle-flesh and integument with whatever else was necessary humanity. All else was there, with them breaking to pieces what is one and so not one. Neither angry nor content, not prurient nor satisfied they broke and sundered. The pepper-bearded man with the brown shirt and the thin wife they moved, broke open the girl and her animal with the long hair and parted the similarity between the raven-haired man and the tree that he climbed. They broke down the animosity between hands and compelled horses to eat. They wounded middle-aged men with awareness of addiction and provided the pious with a god. And they were unable to break what they continually acted upon because what they acted upon was motive illusion, a continuance of what that was nothing. Nichts. It was not any particular kind of thing that they assailed and still is was, was some kind of thing. Without being some kind of thing this that the they broke was not truly any thing. It was pure and complete, and yes the they opened it and broke it into pieces only to witness that this could not be destroyed, though its specifics changed. There were planes that sang as they landed and breezes that made blades of grass sway, and these things were what they affected, yet each was only structure, a kind of organized movement sometimes blindingly fast and at times inert – slow as stillness. This itself never remained the same, broken by nothing. The farmhouse shaped itself into a domicile made from wood, the wood from water and carbon-hydrogen-oxygen-nitrogen and these from the motive shape of atom-shells composed of electrons that circled charged centers. As the Nichts opened each into its what, they expected to find annihilation, but only more of this emerged, this that they opened to shape, organization, structure. What it was that they assaulted was, is, became, becomes, yet possesses no end, finds neither final form nor shape, no eternal structure. This had no structured organization, simply there. This then did not act, nor even move, was nowhere and did not grow old. This did not change at all, because they were no part of it, and yet this in its organization and structure, its shape and beauty, had no structure to which it fell. This was nothing without them to bound, break and open into what-is. It was something substantial that they separated, and yet its substance was not, as if what they made different was to them an utterly foreign intimacy. They made the structures that performed the functions for fireplaces and gathering-round women, and yet there was no substantial fireplace, no divine organization to structure, no element to elements. All could be separated and taken to be something other than what it was or mere form; all substance illusion. All elements minuscule movement, all movement vanishing, motive shape. Substance not substance, and illusion not illusion – being illusion and substance respectively. This it was, yes, it was nothing that crept into the head of the raven-haired man with the olive skin.

WHAT IS THERE

Spring, summer and parts of autumn found the four – Daniel Brown Xenis Black – walking the perimeter of the family's land, two Xolos enjoying unimpeded freedom. The dogs sprinted a circle regularly round and grass and hard land proved best release, breaking open energy, but November and January brought need for hairless dogs. Girls knitted black and brown vests, the black on brown dog, brown on black.

"I wonder how I'd survive without them," Xenis thought aloud.

The girls looked at one another and giggled.

None of the children intended to assist, yet when they saw Xenis laboring over the animals' amusement, a closer look took hold of them. The manner with which he scrubbed and rinsed and panting dogsmile summoned young ladies. Daniel began to assist, then Joy came and Rapture later. The dogs waited with seeming patience – more like playing – while the children rubbed towels around and about dog-frames. The canines kissed and shook, everyone thoroughly drenched in dogsmell and earth. The four of them tugged rope in the teeth of diminutive friends and threw plastic disk caught mid-jump, canine glee moving. Assured health and grace for xolos, demonstrating care that arose from need. The now so much a part of their all presented a grounding of canine-ness, what-is of dog, and when the diminutive homotheria washed and when they played and when gathered with animals what otherwise may have seemed labor was joy, and what tedious pleasure, what was what-is canine gave in turn, what communicated to any who perceived.

"Dogness of dog," Xenis said, not keeping back a laugh.

"It's the what that breaks upon the world."

Joy and Rapture coyly exchanged a glance.

He, his xolos and siblings – these children – idled and darted about. The young humans thought the play foolish, but Xenis' serious manner kept them nearby, all sitting floor dogside along cages. Daniel, and the girls especially, knew better than to ask permission. Knowing Gabriel would deny the privilege, they asked for nothing and simply slept near dogs with Xenis. The sun's wakeful simplicity, or the tap of paw on the cage-door cage negated coming trouble. Not-nothing remained with them as animals and homotheria breathed and when they ate and as they hiked hill and valley near the Körper properties. A touch upon a branch or the grazing of a leaf on leg gave assurance of continued existence; with each moment not-nothing became is of their what, Xenis now invigorated and healthy.

"Canine-ity," Daniel said, mocking Xenis.

So much came to them in these excursions, so great the indulgence. Negated negativity not fully expressed. "Canine-ity" brought out the is.

"You *do* have experience with animals," Gabriel pointed out at mealtime.

"My dogs are mid-level maintenance animals."

"Most city folk don't take so much time."

"You mean for animals? You'd be surprised," Xenis responded. "Dogs are two-headed beasts, like humans."

Gabriel knitted his brows and again asked Xenis to assist with the piling of wood. Xenis wondered why Gabriel himself performed these menial tasks. The older, thicker man claimed to contribute in a direct way, wanting to remember whence he came, not always so prosperous. Compelled to work hard save sacrifice, he felt the earth yield its resources to men who recognized their responsibility over it, and some men whom he met taught the mastery of things and animals and brutishness of creatures and humans.

"The boy has taken a liking to you, you know." Gabriel handed Xenis another piece of wood.

"Daniel's a good kid," Xenis said. "...and so are the girls."

"I wouldn't trust him with just anyone."

Xenis became silent.

"...like I said, I know a good man when I see one."

"You do?"

"I think so," Gabriel stopped handing the wood to Xenis. "...and I think you make a not bad influence on the boy."

"I am grateful for your generosity in so many things, but you don't know me," Xenis asserted in a forcible abruptness. "And the girls are good too."

Gabriel started a moment at the strength of Xenis's response; the refrain from alcohol had this affect on men. He had seen it.

"I think I know enough to trust you."

The men again labored in silence. Gabriel continued to hand down wood from the top of the mound where the sun shone behind him; his silhouette gave him the stout profile of being bull-like thoughts.

"I thought about what you said the other day."

Xenis stood, waiting, offering his benefactor an inexpressive expression.

"I want to help, but I am not sure how," Gabriel continued.

"It is a kind of madness from which I suffer. I do not know how else to describe it. No present, no past or future, no change..."

"There are coundselors who can help."

"If a health-care professional removed this experience from my life, I would no longer be living."

Xenis removed one plank from the pile of others. He was well within his tolerance though he had labored whole the morning long. Still, the younger man suddenly felt change and necessity's weighty, iron-ton hand compelled him to sit.

"You alright?"

"I...feel a bit tired."

"You felt that way before." Gabriel said with certainty.

"I experience spells of fatigue these days."

"I think you told me about these things."

"I did."

Gabriel dropped his weight of wood and sat next to Xenis, handed him some chew, which Xenis declined.

"You told me that you don't know where they come from, these spells."

"That much is true," Xenis said.

"We can rest as long as you need."

"No, no. I need to get back to work. If I rest now, I'll be unable to start again."

"That's alright with me."

"It isn't with me."

Xenis rose, then wiped off his pants and shook himself awake, willed to rousing what vitality possessed him. He stretched his legs, bent his arms and knees until they cracked. His priority would have been to rest the entire day, take advantage. Both men entered the truck, rode thirty yards to the next break in the fence and began unloading tools and wood, already sections of fence.

"I don't know how to get out of that dilemma."

"What's that?"

"What do you think is the cause?"

"Cause?"

"The cause of your spells."

"Well, if there is no not in things that are, then all that is collapses into being one thing."

"What do you mean?"

"It is a very old position that exists without nothing and difference. And I am meeting the difference."

"?"

"Predicates."

"?"

"I mean, that something exists is not the same as that it exists as something."

"A particular? I am at a loss."

"Yes a particular, but also a specific kind. It's a what. Like a dog."

Xenis smiled and thought a moment.

"Dogness."

"I don't follow."

"I'm not sure I do as well, but if something exists merely

because it is there, then a piece of iron, my   thought on justice, movement and a leaf all have the same being. The being of it is that it's there. That's Parmenides' topic."

"Oh."

"Yeah. And its being is not that it is there as something. If there is no not to existing things, then all of being must be and not not-be."

"I see."

"There would be no true distinction between things, no change."

"So, you are talking about different things?"

"Yes."

"How does that have to do with your spells?"

"Oh, well I sense the difference, somehow."

"Hmmm."

"It's...that something has an end."

"?"

"The end of something is the beginning of its presence."

"I'm not sure I follow."

"I sense the ends of presence. The end of something is where it isn't. Its not is there at its end, and its end is its presence."

"Oh, I think I see. You sense the...negativity that makes something a specific thing."

"Yes, more or less. And there is more to nothing."

"?"

"I think that not and nothing and negativity is what keeps being together."

"I don't understand this time at all."

"Being is a radically full emptiness."

"Ah."

Xenis raised his half of the plank to level with the fence, Gabriel raising his, fastening it to the posts. Now that fence section was again strong and the two men entered the truck once more. Gabriel checked his watch.

"Oh my. We need to get back. Lunchtime."

That night, Xenis felt vital, so much so that sleep would not come. He walked around the farm in order to tire himself, but was unable to shake the vigor. As he turned around the side of one building, he sensed a strange absence, a gaze. Unable to determine whence came the sight, he ran his eyes over tops of buildings and doors. Nothing. He knelt down and looked into the cornfield nearby in order to see someone or thing observing him, but was unable to see anything. The feeling of something nearby peering at him would not cease and he sat on a bench near what looked like a funnel affixed to the side of the building, a bucket resting underneath. An unexpected desire to smoke a cigarette came to him, quickly suppressed. The feeling of something watching was stronger here, he thought, but there was nothing... Suddenly, the stare became obvious. There beside him were two small eyes, dead-set against him, sitting inside a bucket filled mostly with severed chicken heads, but what looked in darkness like skulls of many other unfortunates, glaring blankly at him. Blood lie everywhere discernible – even in the darkness – fresh red put upon dried, caked blood, the smell like newly-baked rot. He felt the need to arise and find his way into bed. When he returned to his room, the vitality that had taken him departed, the occasional, stronger-growing weakness returning steadily. Sleep and forgetfulness arrived soon afterward.

THE END OF PLAY

L ater on a Sunday Xenis met Daniel, and they found the brown and black Joy and Raven – careful to walk dogs in the sun only briefly. Dog-crackers treated good dogs for proper behavior, canines embracing what-is dog. Daniel watched over them faithfully, sometimes arguing with his sisters over who would care for the xolos. The dogs enjoyed the chase of a ball thrown and back, thrown again and back and back. Raven tossed the ball into a coppice and it wedged within the manic, thin, wooden, upward-reaching fingers that touched the sun. The black xolo tried repeatedly to dislodge his toy, grasping with hopeful teeth and finding his attempt empty-mouthed. He sat a moment and turned his head back to Xenis; yapped.

"He needs help," Raven complained.

"No, wait," Xenis said. "Let him do it."

The dog turned again to the coppice and attempted to retrieve his joy, but again the same outcome. He circled the bush and yapped again, but no-one assisted. He then approached the place where the ball resided from a different direction, and instead of grabbing at it with his teeth he knocked the ball with his front paw once, twice, thrice a fourth time until the red and green piece of merriment bounded out of thick fngers, meeting again the teeth of the waiting animal. The dog trotted back satisfied to where these children sat and plopped the ball before them, ready.

"One plan wasn't working and he found another," Xenis said.
    "Not so dumb after all," Joy said, looking at her brother.

"Shut up," Daniel returned.

As the children played with the xolos and as the habit grew, what-is dog merged children with play and fieldworker with child. Xenis' dogs so commonly near to and a part of the house, they remained inside during summer evenings, expected visitors, then protracted guests. Still, many times Xenis' dogs slept in their cages safe within one building or another, Xenis sometimes digging with both hands as though they possessed front legs; periodically climbing to the top of a barn in order to sit at its apex. He never tired of hiking up and around the fields and the hills and within the forest nearby, repeating his same course.

"Everything is new..." Xenis said to Daniel.

Sometimes, Xenis poured salt onto the kitchen table only to sift through its grains, occasionally licking them from the tip of his finger; he slid his palms along flower-papered walls and he perpetually gathered rocks, weighed and observed their shapes, examining crevices. Horse-riding was particularly exhilarating, the immense vitality of the equine beneath. And children followed.

"Xenis says that he likes our place because of the 'is that is not what it is.'" explained Rapture to Brenda.

    "Because of the 'is...'?"

"The is that is not what it is."

"Well, what on earth does that mean?"

Raven frowned.

The creatures that surrounded Xenis, homotheria and all, drank deep his attention, and a vigorous energy emerged, the young farmhand now strong the young family potent. Whatever the animal-presence gave to the homotheria was that which bound them to one another, something prior. All emerged more brightly joyfully while these creatures in their simplicity paid attention to what was there, a priority breaking out abound upon within around. Such a priority was not merely the what has been of the homotheria, nor was it the sum of experiences of creatures, but rather it was something other than the now and something other than the here, still here still now. A foundation ultimately inexpressible arose, except in that time when living was accomplished well in leisure without strife, almost never. Xenis called this priority the "what-is" or at times he called it simply "is." And the Körper children laughed at first, grew curious second and adopted his words third, teasing him.

"You and my dad get along," Daniel said to Xenis.

Xenis pondered a moment.

"I like your dad."

"He's alright, I guess."

"I think he's a strong and generous man."

"You and him work together, right?"

"Your father and I work and talk with one another, yes."

Daniel snickered.

"You think we're funny?"

"I think that *you're* funny," Daniel grinned.

"So...your father does this kind of thing regularly?"

Daniel nodded.

"...he helps others in the same way?"

"My dad helps everyone in the same way."

"He says he doesn't dominate others."

Daniel laughed once more.

"Again you're laughing at me."

"What does dominate mean?"

"It means 'to control the behavior of others.'"

Now Daniel reflected for a moment.

"My dad says he doesn't dominate, but he does," he stated at last.

"He does, huh?"

"When he says that he's doing it least is when he's doing it most. My father is always dom..."

"Dominating."

"Dominating. Everything he does is dominating. I'm here talking to you because he's dominating." Xenis laughed and then Daniel shook his head and turned his sight downward.

Though he was a guest in the Davis home and though Xenis had lived with the children for some time, he had not shared with them much of his past. Other guests – some who had remained with the Körpers for a protracted period – at some point confided in the family, or some family member knew some semblance of history about them. Xenis shared almost nothing except what remained in the immediate present. His was a joy to children and to parents in different ways, and they all benefited from the mutual now, yet he and what appeared to motivate him remained distant, especially the progressively longer moments of fatigue that plagued him. When Gabriel asked him how he might help relieve his spells, "They're nothing. There's no reason to be concerned," he explained.

Xenis' apparent strangeness only drove interest higher. Daniel in particular, but also his sisters, now adored this odd man, and Brenda pointed out to her husband that one of the girls experienced a moment of fatigue very similar to Xenis' own.

"But she's healthy as an ox, don't you think?"

"She certainly is," Gabriel said.

Xenis made now-regular walks into and around the farm where the trees and the hills offered simple, tireless pleasure and seeming retreat. While they walked or hiked, the children observed new things. No color, no texture, no scent escaped their pleasure, all worthy of note. What most brought out the children's' interest was Xenis' strange words.

"This is a what," pointing to a tree "...and that's a what," pointing to Daniel "...each is a what-is," Xenis said.

They thought they understood immediately what Xenis meant, and immersed themselves as he did. Yet, when Xenis was not with them, the sensation grew shallow even as their desire for its vigor abided and deepened, an abyss opening. The need to fill it filled them. This desire made them wish to climb and brush their faces along the fur of horses and cows. With Xenis not always available to provide guidance or pass time talking, Joy and Rapture planned an excursion, wanting to experience "what-is" themselves, though they remained uncertain precisely what that meant. Their father would not understand, would give them the almost-ubiquitous "no."

"You won't be able to do it like he does," Daniel said.

"Shut up," both girls returned.

"Won't be able to do it."

"How do you know?" asked Joy.

"Because I seen you try it. It isn't the same...and you know it."

Unwilling to admit it, the girls recognized that Daniel had a point. Mulling over how they should go about going out on their own, they thought how it ought not matter that Xenis was not present; it ought not matter what experience they had as long as it was there. Xenis said as much. Still, though they walked about on their own, the girls could not yet evoke the same moment in the same way. Again thinking about what to do, they thought the most precious moments of their experience with Xenis were those with the Xolos, and so the pair Joy Rapture decided to take one of them, the golden brown or the black green-collared dog, on an excursion of their own. During a day when Xenis and Gabriel busied themselves with moving wood and repairing parts of a building, they quietly unlocked the door of the cage that encompassed the golden dark-brown Xolo, so glad to see them. They were careful with the animal, and knowing him they brought along one of his jackets they themselves had made, one they kept for walks with Xenis. Having stolen away from the house and quietly disappeared into the woods, they walked along a familiar part of the valley where a creek flowed flat along a rocky course down below the foot-path far from and away as a deep defile. The green-collared Xolo excitedly led them down the now-favorite path where they together had walked their what-is numerous times. The girls kept the Xolo on his tether diligently and watched as the animal sniffed here and there; rolled about on the grass; chased smaller creatures and chewed on putty roots and little goblin moonworts. They looked at one another and grinned. Joy Raven recalled moments when at home Xenis played for them some of his music. Mendelssohn the girls had never thought they would appreciate, but when they were with the Xolo, they played it on their pads and enjoyed the Gondola song op. 19 no. 6.

The Xolo smiled glad dogsmile all around, looking to the girls for approval and listening intently to stern commands. They used sharp words occasionally and made demands, and the dog enjoyed familiar mastery. They unleashed him in order that he enjoy his freedom, an overjoyed and puzzled Xolo dashing about in new-found liberty. The day passed quickly without their knowing, the need to concern oneself with schedules and time of day having evaporated – only the present what existed – none of its consequents yet arrived. When Joy and Rapture had faded somewhat from their excursion, the three creatures realized they had need of return, and began their diversion from their own to the mundane and tedious repetition of affairs arising to the surface of their what-is. Near the end of their trek back to the Davis house, while walking along the highest path far atop the creek with its deep rocky decline, the sweet brown Xolo, trotting as if he had just begun the day, slipped from the path and in panic disappeared clutching bits of earth and root with his nails down a hole into the suddenly growing darkness -- at the time when perception is fading and the ascending pitch of black does its primal best to cover the eyes. Suddenly, the girls wandered back and forth searching, Joy and Raven having arrived on quick at that harsh "not" of what-is. Had he been tethered, he would surely have choked. The girls were unable to determine where the dog had gone, and he surprisingly made no more sound than a whimper while he vanished – as if to slip quickly into some hole in their excursion and away he was. Joy lost herself and, afraid for the canine more than for herself, disappeared along the same decline as the Xolo. Raven had no idea what she ought to do, and so she too losing herself and feeling the dread called out.

"Where are you? Oh no!" she cried more to herself than any other. Raven attempted the same route that her sister had gone, but as the darkness covered everything rapidly and more quickly then covered complete all the whats there her fear had not grown sufficiently accustomed to the new light in order to navigate safely. She panicked and Raven lost herself.

"Where are you?" she again pleaded.

Raven waited until her fear adjusted, and it did so quickly, though not enough to possess her. She wandered about and looked where the two had gone, a black space flat upon the earth where they seemed to have fallen. She reached her head down into the hole, aware of her lack. Yet, the empty space into which the Xolo had gone was not deep, not a precipitous fall. The dog had slipped onto a former pathway situated near the one on which they tread.

"He fell a pretty short distance," Joy said to her sister.

"Is he alright?"

"He seems OK."

Raven took the hand of Joy and the two delicately moved the Xolo back up onto the path with the most light upon it; the two girls then tethered their animal, checked him once more.

"He's fine," Raven stated.

The girls took the higher path towards the house, grateful that they had averted that little nothing. As they drew near to the Davis house, they saw a number of indistinct forms of men and hands and movements in distance meandering about the area. One sighted them, but turned back towards the house, then paused. He seemed to talk on his phone, and then suddenly a disturbed Xenis emerged, coming toward them. The girls looked soberly at one another.

"You have the brown!" Xenis howled.

"He's here," said Joy, attempting a calm she did not feel.

Xenis embraced the animal as he fell to the ground, the dog tiredly licking his face.

"I'm so glad," Xenis said. The girls said nothing, expecting a reprimand. Gabriel arrived soon after Xenis.

"Where were you two?" he asked.

The girls looked at one another; neither said a word.

"You're both in serious trouble," he continued.

But before Gabriel was able to continue with another word Xenis interrupted.

"He's safe," Xenis said.

The two girls stood straight in panic, neither understanding. Gabriel glared at Xenis a moment, but quickly his countenance softened.

"What happened?" Joy asked, looking back at Raven – the two girls emptied of themselves.

"There was an accident," Xenis explained, looking at Gabriel.

Gabriel paused one moment, and then he hesitatingly explained.

"There was an accident in the storage building." A pause followed.

"Where the dogs sleep?" Raven asked rhetorically. Another, more pregnant, pause followed.

"One of our hands died..."

"Which one?" asked Joy.

"Hector," Gabriel said finally.

And the two men were once again silent as Joy and Raven gazed at Xenis who held his friend.

"...my black was in the building," Xenis said with some difficulty.

NICHTS

The part and the whole of what is there are both what is there, yet they are not. The whole acts through its *integritas.* It is a whole demarcated from other things or processes, which are the acts in the order of things. The part of a whole is a whole that is a part, always. It has a separation-from that acts as; it is the whole and it is the part, but it is not the whole in that it is part. Part and whole act together in this way, which is to say that they act as whole separately and in unison. Everything is separate from itself in its union. The act of union is an act of separation at once and same. Separation is a negativity. They are negativity. They bind their offsrping to their friends and bring great care to their living.

EVENTIDE

In the days that immediately followed the accident and the death of Hector, an unwelcome, un-restful and discontented calm spread out upon the ranch-grounds. The building had fallen on top of the unfortunate hand and more than a few of the animals therein, but an explosion also opened up a large section of the wooden building. Those outside felt the rumbling of earthen clods and body parts smeared into the heavy, merciless push of pitiless noise. The remnant, a tottering and fragile mass of useless edifice, had collapsed and because of the heavy debris spread about Gabriel and a crew of men were not able to determine immediately the cause. Busy hands continued to unearth corpses of animal and man-fragments alike. Blood and truncation of will spread everywhere – fresh fatigue put upon shriveled, evaporating autonomy. Several weeks after the explosion one might have found an ear of some animal or a section of hoof; chicken heads, viscera and gullets rested on rooftops, automobiles and in fields until eaten by crows or other scavengers. The building itself had been sound overall, yet well-used and in need of repair; Gabriel immediately set his employees to work bracing and restructuring the edifice. The residua of Hector was taken with great care to the morgue where pieces of man loosely reconstructed his physical state of living. The farm-hands set out the body of the black Xolo next to other animals beside a mass of rubble.

"It's good that it wasn't worse," one said.

"That much is good," Gabriel said.

Xenis again felt the weakness spread upon him as he walked toward the accident site, seeing one he had no desire to see.

"Get out of the way, Juan."

"I know what I'm told," Juan said. "I'm supposed to keep people away, even family."

Almost hearing the warning, Xenis hastened past towards the storage building. Juan initially remained where he was, but then rushed past Xenis, stood in front of him. Xenis paused for a moment.

"Juan, let me pass."

Xenis had been quite successful at the Körper ranch, working with others, playing with children, abstaining from alcohol. Consistency of affection and some imperceptible innocence being novel in his life, he did not wish to regress. He needed the Körpers and their compassion, and he felt a belonging at the ranch that he had not often felt during his lifetime; it had been an unexpected and unintended surprise that he liked these persons, that he played with the children. He had possessed a new arena of possibilities when he arrived, in the form of what was there - the background and character of the family. These things had not before been present for him. All of that was determinant for him. Now, he once more considered what was most important. Juan smiled, saying no more but continuing to obstruct Xenis' passage.

"Let me pass."

Juan did not move, again presenting Xenis with a wide and confident grin. Xenis again attempted to walk around his fellow farm-hand. Juan clutched his arm, hoping to pull back the stranger. The two men grappled with one another – the more experienced farm-hand confident -- but Xenis twisted the arm of the hand that had held him and, using the weight of his body and a twist, reoriented their center of gravity. After throwing him into fall, Xenis pinned the drunken man-boy to the ground.

"I have no interest in harming you,...but I will. I may enjoy it."

He held down Juan as he struggled in empty effort. After a time, Juan ceased his efforts and became still. When Xenis was relatively certain that his path would not be impeded, he resumed his walk.

"I'm glad you're here," Gabriel said as Xenis arrived at the storage building.

Xenis at first gave Gabriel a perplexed look. "Glad to be here," he said as he patted the shoulder of his benefactor.

"...I need to retrieve my animal."

"Of course, of course."

Gabriel pointed Xenis in the proper direction; the dog lay covered with a black tarp, which Xenis jerked off of the still body. He had hoped the dog could be saved, that somehow the animal lay barely conscious, still breathing. A vision of taking his black to an emergency room came to him, one where with difficulty and time animality once again returned, but the heaving of breast and twitch of ears – the stream of life-flowing iron hemoglobin – had ceased. His black drew breath and suffered life no longer. Strangely, the animal seemed unharmed, as though some god had simply removed his breath. Having gathered up the animal and covering the black in a white sheet he had brought with him, Xenis carried the corpse to his room where he remained, waiting for his dog's chest to rise and hoping to hear a familiar whine or a pained half-bark. The veterinarian was unable to arrive immediately and later informed Xenis that his arrival would be delayed until next morning. Xenis wondered at first what to do, but resolved to remain in his room with his friend. Knowing that Xenis was in distress, Joy Raven and Daniel each in turn knocked at his door.

"I'm well enough," he said to each of them.

He placed the animal in the corner of the room atop a small wicker bed, and the black-haired friend accompanied Xenis one last time in sleep. The veterinarian arrived early in the morning, but Xenis had arisen long before the sun. Once more he patted the animal and listened to his chest, pried open his eyes. More than twice Xenis arose from his bed during the final parts of the night in order to perform this odd and distressing ritual. When the vet examined the dog briefly, Xenis was possessed of the desire to explain to him how the black needed clothing for cold temperatures, that he enjoyed a particular kind of food, that he obsessed over a specific toy – one whose location he was unable to recall. A kind and pleasant thought continued within, thinking over an occasion when he had brought both dogs into a bar in Chicago. They howled at clumsy inebriates who applauded the animals' song, and the memory of the occasion compelled Xenis to recall that his Xolo was relatively strong still, older but vigorous, Xenis all the time watching for an inhalation or a whimper. The veterinarian took the corpse still wrapped in white and Xenis patted the black fur.

The next few days unfolded one apparition after another. Xenis found another place, ostensibly safer, to house the brown and insisted upon sleeping nearby, until Joy and Raven convinced Gabriel to allow the brown access to the house. There the dog would remain for the duration of its long life – though no-one at that time realized the change. Xenis returned reluctantly and with some heavy but powerful will to his labor. During the days initially following the accident, he assisted other hands in finding pieces of flesh and disposing of them, which meant swelling up the ever-growing mass of blood – fresh red put upon dried, caked blood. The hands joked about the body parts, especially the chicken heads, but Xenis was unable to laugh. He attended no AA meetings and received occasional visits from farmhands and children, weakness first leaving then returning. He and Gabriel resumed their work repairing the fence. The pair worked vigorously, and it was during his laboring – hauling heavy machinery or solving logical problems – that Xenis felt again the vigor and energizing vitality that brought out what he made of himself. He needed nothing more than participation in living to feel strong, and his care for others grew more powerful.

"I was hoping to resume our conversations," Gabriel began one morning.

"Conversations?"

"We had some good talks, I think."

"Oh...yes." Xenis' speech remained slow.

"You seem like an educated and intelligent fellow, so I may be telling you what you already know, but I like your words," Gabriel laughed. "And I wanted to ask you about something."

"Mmmm."

"Hector is gone, and we need to replace him as foreman. I was thinking maybe you would like to stay on in his place."

He handed a heavy board to Xenis who took it now with an ease noticeable. Xenis tried to bring to mind their former conversations and to ponder what Gabriel had said. He was carrying nothing, exerting himself not at all when suddenly he realized that he was lying on the ground – the weight of himself seeming to fall upon him suddenly. Gabriel quickly pulled him up to a sitting position.

"You alright?"

The following morning Xenis slept late, Gabriel having insisted that he not work that day. Xenis did not sleep long by habit, since he had the tendency to awaken around five am during the warm months, without alarm but rather along with the sun. His internal habit was to sleep only around four-hour increments and then suddenly awake he was. On this occasion he rested far into the late morning and was immersed in a deep, death-like slumber. He awoke with foggy concentration, moreso than an ordinary early-morning grogginess. Xenis decided to clear his head with a walk around the ranch, fetch his Xolos, only to recall with pain and in bits that the solitary brown remained. He and the dog meandered, ruminating. As they walked around the perimeter of the ranch, he shook off his thick-headedness, but it returned almost as soon as it departed, never completely evaporating. He patted his Xolo and there he experienced a familiar bond, but somehow his sense was not present...or not present as completely.

"Have I been thinking in the right way?"

Xenis sought out one of the members of his AA group later that day, thinking he might dispel doubt or at least give him some direction. His fellow members encouraged him to make use of his sponsor, which he had not done. Xenis thought that his abstention from alcohol was his own responsibility, that it was his will that was needed, but perhaps not. His sponsor was an older man who had assisted others in their ascendancy. The more experienced encouraged Xenis to attend the next meeting, scheduled for the following Wednesday, one full day away. Though Xenis was relieved a bit, he felt as if he needed immediate solace. There was nothing present, except a longing.

"There's no sense in waiting here," he thought.

He was at that time unable to concentrate, so his ordinary reading habit was out of the question. He paced back and forth in his room, listening to music, occasionally playing with the brown. When he had spent about an hour moving about without aim or end, he received a visit.

"Have you thought about replacing Hector?" Gabriel asked.

NICHTS

The part is completely a whole in that it is *integritas* to itself. Possessed by parts, the part itself exists as possession. This possession is what that whole is. It exists as. The part is entirely its own in that it exists as wholeness that is portion or part as well. It separates from the rest of the whole as it is a whole itself, yet its whole is parts. It is and is not what it is, being whole and being part. Its act moves it away from itself, by virtue of being a part. The wholeness of the part acts as the wholeness of the whole, but the wholeness of the whole does not act as the wholeness of the part in the same manner. They did their work in secret, kept hidden their ways. That was their nature and they adhered to it for countless eons, fortunate that time did and meant nothing to them. Something in and around nothing-being, something about being a share in nothing, made wrangling constant. They opened the space that moved creatures from one place to another and fought wars, gave birth. They were present, so to speak, when every creature died and that motion of what is not is what. They gave weakness to limbs and potency to vocation.

DISINTEGRATION

Xenis experienced more weakness in the mornings and as he went about the ordinary routines; when he walked his dog and roamed with the Körper children, his failing continued, and the occasions when he was unable to carry the weight of his job became more frequent. His thirty-nine years longed for his weakness to end.

"Let me know what you think of my offer," Gabriel said regularly.

Sometimes when he was especially fatigued, Xenis no longer worked. His labor made him feel better somehow, if temporarily, but at times he was unable to bear it. He had come to an appreciation of physical contact that labor made, the result of one; he was able to see the consequences. The what-is that presented itself to his hands remained there while he labored, but there was something else. Unable to say what it was, Xenis simply participated in it. He felt and touched it, thought over it and it seemed to be a part of everything. Whatever it was, it came only when he and the children were walking, or when he interacted with an animal. He was able to ask nearly anything of these persons. He enjoyed these moments nearly as much as he did with his friends, Brazil and Leon, yet the sense that he had possessed of presence and vitality, the one he had provided to the Davis children, diminished still. At the same time, Daniel and Xenis regularly worked together on the Herringbone parlor; Joy and Raven now practically lived inside Xenis' room when he was not there. He refrained from telling his host family of his doubts, and when he was alone, instead of calling his sponsor or talking to one of the group, he explored more the climbing of trees and the watching of animals; he drew within the brisk, comforting air about him and hands ran along marble statues, the spines of growing leaves and the living bark of trees.

"You're not like the others," Juan said.

Xenis looked down from his branch of oak.

"Don't you agree?," he said. "The joy and suffering, yearning and strife, it's beautiful. Terrible and beautiful."

"These things, not all of them are beautiful," Juan replied.

"You limit yourself, my friend."

"If I'm limited because of that, then I'm glad."

"That's another limitation."

"You're not just strange-looking, you have a strange way."

"You may be right," Xenis said finally.

"Come down and act like a man."

Xenis did not react at all. Juan drew near, cigarette glaring. Losing his balance slightly, he nearly tripped over himself.

"You're drunk."

"You will come down here, little boy in the tree. I know you...you may...fool the Davises...but I know   you. You are no good for...anything and...I can tell."

Juan's slurred words interrupted his loss of concentration. Xenis ignored him still, but Juan lingered, smoking and alternately attempting to climb the tree, but missing branches he fell to the ground, arose again. Filled with an angry attempt at another climb, Juan reached the branch on which Xenis was sitting, grasped it and pulled himself up, then let drop, pulled himself up and again dropped, the branch shaking violently.

"What's wrong with you? My guess is that I am talking to someone who is blacking out" Xenis said, curled up knees-to-chest.

"The thing...is wrong is you. There's something that you do not tell,...something wrong...for the rest of us," he said. "I don't know...what it is, but you're not right."

Juan finally ascended the section of the tree that led to Xenis's safe-haven, and again shook the branch every bit as savagely. On this occasion down came the stranger onto one of his feet, twisting his ankle. Juan jumped from his branch and darted towards the devil from the tree. Without hesitation or word, he lunged. Unable to gain traction, Xenis fell back and the two men struggled for moments.

"Playing with children, acting like a boy...there is nothing innocent about you. I...can see you," Juan said.

"I don't want to hurt you," Xenis said. Juan laughed.

As the pair struggled, Xenis recalled a moment from his childhood, a name, and his need. His necessity grew confidence, his frustration fueled movements, and having locked his fingers around Juan's wrists he bent back his assailant's arms, wrapped them round, limbs a straight-jacket about the body. Unable to restrain himself, Xenis lifted Juan and smacked his head against the tree not once but three times until he stilled. Vitality now full and plenty; strength as it had not been for some months.

"Have I been thinking correctly?"

Xenis tread slowly back to the Davis house. As he walked, his temper changed. The Davis family and their intimacy were what he had not yet known and he felt a part of them, and yet...the feeling of separation and difference renewed itself. He was unable to continue, no closer to clarity. When the family gathered in its entirety at dinner, he asked to speak, countenance saddening.

"You've welcomed me and given me a home, and for that I'm grateful. I want to thnk you for this period of my life."

"You're part of the family," Brenda interrupted.

Xenis gathered himself nervously.

"We welcome you, we'll always welcome you," Gabriel said.

Xenis then awkwardly sat again. The remainder of the meal was not tense for Xenis, but his usual free-spirited banter and jocularity departed. Xenis did not know what to do with himself afterward. He felt somehow jittery when he ate, nervous interacting with the farm-hands suddenly, more anxious in everyone's presence. He performed his usual tasks, read and wandered as usual. He and the children performed their regular tasks, hiked and camped.

"When are you leaving?" Joy asked.

Daniel with Raven stifled their sister with quick gesticulations and angled brows.

"I'm not leaving," Xenis said.

The children exchanged a solemn glance.

"If you leave, will you let Dora stay with us?" Joy asked.

Her question startled Xenis. He had no intention of remaining with the Davis family indefinitely, and yet he had no reason to leave immediately. He had not thought about his financial state for the longest time, perhaps as long as a year. He recalled then what he had been seeking, and Xenis realized a second time that the one whom he had sought so long was now no longer needed; he no longer desired to make that odd and complete encounter.

"If I leave, then Dora can stay with you."

Joy and long with Raven could not help but grin.

NICHTS

The whole closes itself off from the parts. A thing or process is the whole and the apparent command of the parts. That whole exists as the parts, but the whole in its wholeness takes primacy over the parts, still all existing as the whole. The whole is a kind of thing, and there is no end to an ever-growing whole; all wholes become still parts. The whole is the whole of the parts and the whole of the whole, while the parts are wholes that are not completely wholes of the parts. They are not the whole. Water and blood can be a dog playing ball or a man climbing to the roof of a barn, but water and blood are themselves water and not anything else and blood and not anything else. Animals perished and children sundered. Together they made a young man who feared the loss of a friend, fathers present in that they may depart, cultivating neglect. Here they come.

EXODOS

The next weeks made pleasant work, the season tolerable for human flesh. The two did not see one another as often, but when Gabriel and Xenis worked together, they did so in silence, or concentrated on their present task. Gabriel's manner had not changed, nor did he cease helping Xenis, but no longer did he invite the younger man to his section of the table when hands ate. He no longer asked Xenis to watch Daniel, or drive with his son to purchase supplies. Xenis wondered where he ought to go and considered how tolerable change would be this time – practically no possessions no obligations no-one asking after him. A light mist of guilt spread upon him, yet his thoughts were clearer and his moods less dour. His step came lighter and he meditated upon the shape of a comely female, drove away Juan with greater vehemence. Something chose him, he suspected, or perhaps he had been chosen by Xenis. His verve, such as it was, lifted itself evenly and high, and vitality became norm – all things were open to him once more. He had not imbibed alcohol in years, and to his astonishment he found no Bacchanalian desire. More robust. Yet, as before, he sensed a need for something else, and only a vague comprehension of it emerged. He grew distracted and tended to his chores on the ranch, but found solitude more gratifying than the company of others, he and his remaining xolo walking sometimes late at night. He tapped the ribs of the brown lightly, smiled. One crisp morning, cool to the skin, Xenis arose after a best night's sleep. He was prepared and eager to expend vivifying energy that day, finished his work quickly, pleased with labor and cleaning the Herringbone parlor when Gabriel summoned him. As he entered, he noticed that the other farm-hands noted him.

"I wanted to talk to you about something."

Xenis nodded.

"I'm told that you and another farm-hand had more than one confrontation."

Sitting in an old wooden chair before Gabriel's simple desk, Xenis weaved his fingers together and placed his chin atop them. It was not unlike ranch rumor to meander about "cutting up", but Xenis had considered the conflict to be between Juan and him, at rest. The official policy of the ranch was that anyone creating conflict between the hands was subject to disciplinary action, yet conflicts between hands occurred with predictable regularity. Almost always ignored.

"That much is true."

Gabriel paused and drew a long breath.

"I like you, Xenis..." he began. "...but complaints have been coming in from many places."

"They have?"

"Other farm-hands have been concerned about the disruption that an ongoing...feud may cause."

"They have?"

Gabriel set his eyes upon those of the younger man, eyes bright but fixed and raw.

"Is that all that you want to say?"

Xenis shifted himself in his chair, a sable countenance.

"Not long ago you told me that you know a good man when you see one. You claimed that I'm a good man, good enough to influence your son."

"That opinion has not changed."

"I understand you need to demonstrate care for the needs and concerns of your employees…"

"That's not the only thing at stake. Problems…need addressed."

Xenis again nodded.

"So?"

"You're causing a disruption."

"I am? Have you called Juan into your office?"

"You're causing a disruption on my ranch."

Xenis was again silent.

"I thank you for your help, but I don't understand. I'm no danger to anyone, certainly no more than a drunken, brawling child."

Here Gabriel was about to speak, and, rising, Xenis held out his hand and stopped him.

"I defend myself, that's all. Your farm-hands have no legitimate complaint. If you consider my presence here a danger, or some kind of hindrance, then decide what to do for yourself and for your family, for your business."

Xenis arose calmly and walked out of the office of Gabriel Davis, Juan and others watching without looking. The next few weeks grew new-ordinary tension like shoots in a well-watered field; Xenis secluded himself in his room often. Joy asked after him and the Davis parents explained that Xenis may decide soon to leave.

"But mom...he said he wasn't leaving," said Joy.

Juan and the other farm-hands avoided Xenis and he was relieved, but at the same time Xenis felt a empty when he talked with them, as if their amicability were sucked into a tiny, imperceptible but exceedingly potent singularity.

"I suppose it's no wonder," he thought.

Xenis at first continued to hike and talk but without the children, except on rare occasions.

"It's not the who that has done something for you, or given you a thought, but the what," Joy said to her mother.

Over the course of two months the children grew less accessible. Xenis asked if he had done anything wrong, besides his altercations with Juan.

"It's time they learned the way of things," Gabriel said.

Encouraged by Xenis, Joy started piano lessons, needing a goal for her strong, quick hands. Raven ran and trained herself physically, making use of a new set of weights and athletic clothing.

"You're not to take such things from him," Brenda stated firmly.

 "Why?"

A startled look emerged on Brenda's face in her eyes. "You must beware of gifts from men," she said.

Gabriel called Daniel to assist with the overall management of the ranch. Absorbed in its regular affairs, he vanished from Xenis' side until he one day appeared at the Herringbone parlor.

"We need you to sweep the porch and hang laundry," he said.

Xenis did not react, continued working with the parlor.

"We need you to sweep the porch," Daniel repeated a bit louder.

When he awoke and during the day Xenis felt a presence, or rather...something. Something came to him,...but...it was a strange visitation. It slipped around his alarm clock and his table in the mornings. It was near his toothbrush and in his soup, even inside his xolo's quiet howl. It was there, or rather...not there, and then gone very suddenly. It was not something graspable, nor was it the weakness that had dropped over him. Its seeming absence was a present element and...odd and novel, one that continued. He sought it. He knew – more than he knew anything else through an intuition – that his seeking was imperative. He wanted not to meditate upon this thing, but rather he desired somehow to find what was already present, to become what was already there, found.

"It isn't an object," he thought.

"It isn't material."
"It isn't a god."
"It isn't the god."
"It isn't fully transcendent; it's immanent."
"It isn't an idol."

"Xenis!" Daniel shouted. "Did you hear me!?" The boy seemed anxious to depart.

"I heard you," Xenis said vociferously, a lament filled him.

"I heard you," he repeated calmly.

Xenis reluctantly left the Herringbone parlor and walked slowly toward laundry and porch. He had not expected that Gabriel would put him in this position. Daniel had been closest; the girls not distant, but their boundaries rose higher. He had been careful in that way. Whatever seemed to call him was already a part of the Davisies. The farm-hands as well were a share and they knew whatever it is as well as anyone else, yet they were in another sense completely ignorant of it. It was strange that Xenis recognized this...whatever, but also he was unable to express it. If someone should ask, he would be able to say nothing.

"Maybe I'm imagining things," he thought.

The children less and less granted him credit, kept their company from him. The thought that they would forget about him until later in life saddened him, but there was nothing to do. It was just as well. Stricken at his loss and enraptured at his gain, he thought to himself he must leave, but his animals concerned him. Dora had long since availed herself of the company of Joy and Raven, and though the girls had contact with many and different animals, they enjoyed her most. The cat had taken to sleeping in their rooms, only occasionally appearing in her little apartment. They dressed her up in socks and clothes that she quickly removed; played with her; gave treats; reclined with her as cats enjoy. He sought out his old friend whom an accident and an old woman had given to him. Sleeping inside the girls' room on their bed, she recognized him with a slow closing of her eyes and moved very little when he sat next to her. He petted her on the head and along her body. At a start, Dora raised her ears as if she heard an alarm and darted out of the room, down stairs around a corner. Slowly, he followed and found her beside Joy enraptured with the sounds, smell and sight of the food the young lady prepared. Xenis stopped at the top of the stairs and watched the animal and the girl.

"Have I been thinking correctly?"

While he entered the kitchen, Joy and Dora greeted him with quiet and grins. Xenis suddenly realized that he had spent two and one-half years with the family Davis.

"Do you still want to care for Dora when I go?" he asked the young women.

They nodded.

"She's yours, if you want."

Joy wasted no time asking her mother, and over the next week, there again arose a particular sensation for Xenis.

"It's no concept," he thought.
"It's not an abstraction."
"It's not an intellection."
"It's not a material substance."

The same dearth Xenis needed presented itself. He wondered

where he might find what he sought, if it was discoverable. He felt strong and worthy of the search, and one night in the middle pitch of black when only animals sensed his movements, alone he stole his freedom under the darkness that shrouded his stay with this rattling, simple family – mourning the joyous change.

NICHTS

The part and the whole act as not themselves but as each other; they are wholes and so they are whole of whole or part of whole. They are part even if they are the whole; the whole never ceases to be part of another whole and the whole is part because the part is a whole of the whole and the whole is not whole without being the part; they part makes the whole. Their very being is not being what they are. Their being lies elsewhere, not in themselves. The whole and the part exist because of their being that is a non-being of their being. Here is context and nothing can exist without this relation to itself and to things that are other-than, which is the same as being part. The Nichts, nothing or nothings, emerge so very often and make what-is not only not what it was, but sometimes altogether other, making possible always a lack exists as what-is, part not part whole not whole.THe other-than acts in this way, a species of nothing. Nichts are unable to refrain from breaking, sundering things and concepts, even emotions, and continued efforts continuously; the what was the not in common with all species of Nichts. Not was still the not-other and made parameter and so was still what-is, no escape from being for not.

NICHTS OF MIND

All arrived at once, as if a sudden rousing. It certainly was not a box, and then it was. No, it was not not a box, nor was it box's other, but it was opposed to box, against box-ness. It was connected to unconnectedness, or not; it was certainly not uniform, yet it was one and different, and it was not alone, lacked not other...what? It lacked no other things, but was a something in itself. And there were present circular squares and triangular rectangles, isosceles ellipses and oblong – perfectly-squared – ovals.

Wait.

That was not quite it, no it was...then again it...was what it was. What was it happening, this dance of circumstance around and about was the question. The chair was there against the wall as it ought to be, but it was not quite right, tight chair there by that stretch of hard, that surface-horizontal obstruction. The legs were all staggered, neither there nor here, and the seat of chair was on the floor, no good, not possible to use – no end for me, for her – it sitting on the floor, chair-like, but no purpose for me my being there. It was soft all around, a metal useless-incapable of being chair proper. Yet, yes, it was a chair and useful and there and upright and standing as chairs do, oh yes it was. Not all staggered, nor thrown about, not useless at all and he sat there in it wondering about it the chair, and stared hard at cement. Yes, it was a concrete floor and up did it hold him who sat on that not-chair with its chair-like abilities. Old it was and dirty with tar on it and rubber and probably blood and then it had been cleaned, smelled of inescapable carcinogenic fumes. What was happening was another question. The floor was beneath him and over against the wall and atop every-thing that stood in the room in the gathering and one breathed the floor as one would breathe air, but no that was not quite right, or...yes it was. Now wait, the door was the floor and the chair stood staggered and the floor was the air in his lungs...

No-no-no.

Yes, the floor he breathed in, he knew that, but it made little sense to him as he sat on the chair. Yes, that was it! The chair was there and useless and he sat upon it euphoric and that was the starting point. Yes, he sat on the chair and it was there that he swam through the floor and one walks out the door, and the persons seated beside him knew not what had happened to all what was around them...how did they not notice the oddness and careless manner that these things – these doors, floors, wind-air, chair-like vending machines, all these – were the same again same and the different, the now through the then; what was happening, this was not correct – not proper at all – and he knew it.

Yes-yes-yes.

The persons around him were no exception, if there was a guiding principle here; their heads were the size of peas and similar to the most immense shape that ever existed. They were minuscule in shape and cone-shaped in size, and when he looked upon their forms, they existed as they always had. They walked well and talked gibberish, but recognized what each other meant. Their words were legs the sound of blue, and because they formed well their size and shape. Because they were proportionate and cruel-smelling, they were consistent, and he saw their thoughts; read their gaits and smelled their colors and height all at once, coming to him without restriction. When he perceived all of these, he thought he received in the widest way, loved and raged in the profoundest manner, empathized and heard moment upon moment after width after depth. No, this was not correct, nor did it ring true, not sensible, nor capable. And yet it all reached him as if a moment were all that was needed to see every and more corners of the many objects that hoped for him to be with them; they were he, and when he lifted his head, he saw again as he had seen. Yes, he was awake and he had not dreamed; he again saw the chair on the floor and the air he felt through the door, the walks and the sizes of men, their wives and women and their children were more common and proportionate and talking now consistent. What just happened he was unable to comprehend, but now he was able to speak once again and he recognized his new friend beside him.

"I had an encounter with a young man who was an African-American woman, an older woman...."

Xenis paused, his mind a bit disoriented.

"He...or...she was also a bee made of stone and diminutive men who assaulted me."

He waited a moment.

"And I think he was me at one time..."

He reached the grogginess and confusion inside his pocket and withdrew his vibrating cell-phone.

"Excuse me."

Xenis answered the call from Ülrich Geldsbaum who had left a message for him two hours earlier. Head now clearer, his voice upbeat, excited even, and Xenis was anxious to hear. He had heard neither good nor bad news since he left the Körper house, and he hoped Ülrich was able to oblige with something pleasant. He had taken a bus out of Wisconsin, not headed in a particular direction, except that he was traveling south-east. Xenis had always wanted to live on the east coast; when he had more resources he had planned to buy real estate there.

"Hallo," a friendly German voice answered with a warm tone.

"Ülrich, how are you?" Xenis asked. "I only just now saw that you called."

"I am well, my friend, and I fear that I have little news."

Xenis sat up straight in the carpeted and slightly uncomfortable bus seat.

"Nothing yet, but soon I expect."

Unsurprised, Xenis ended the call. "Strange, how I miss the animals more than the humans," he thought.

His attention then returned to the man who sat beside him. The two had met waiting for the bus, and Xenis, taking a liking to his rather mild person, felt a comfort and presence that made joy of him. Dean Fromm was unremarkable, certainly. He puckishly declared his love of burgers and potato chips, his like of specific shows on internet-television and his disdain for certain others who wore yellow-white shirts; he wore white-yellow shirts and plain blue-jeans, smelled of soft-drink syrup, yet he appeared fit and healthy. That Dean moved with a sudden adroitness and alacrity was apparent even in Xenis' initial observations. He opened a box that sat waiting beside him, pulling out a thin, elongated chocolate bar and ripping open one of the ends, as cavalier as all that. One-third of the bar unceremoniously disappeared as Dean locked his eyes upon a small video screen. He stared at it one moment and pressed his face nearer the blinking graphic, seeking a specific document, but the reception in the station prevented a comfortable download, and made necessary a sturdy apology for his new acquaintance's wasted time. Deciding the document was not needed, he squirmed around and about in his seat uncomfortably, recognizing that he offered no chocolate. He again apologized and presented a long, thin bar – eyes wide and brows lifted in an offer upon his face. Xenis refused. A kind and gentle manner pervaded the offerings and generosity of Dean but Xenis sensed another, different, emotion in the man. That feeling made him appealing.

"The ride is long and I don't know why I'm leaving,"

Xenis blurted as they claimed seats on the bus.

"No?"

Dean Fromm thought it odd, someone not knowing why he left home.

"I didn't get along with all of the farmhands, but that wasn't it, or all of it."

"Something else. You needed a change." said Dean.

"Yeah, that's true but that's not all of it either."

"You could've stayed and made a change there."

"I could have, but…"

"It sounds like there were many reasons."

Xenis watched the bus driver fuss with luggage and argue vehemently with a passenger.

"I felt this weakness. And I simply needed to leave."

"A physical problem?"

"Not sure. The work was hard, and dangerous…but manageable."

Dean leaned over, looking in his bag. "Farm-work is hard, I hear."

"It's not too bad, once you get used to it, but there was a lot of…death."

"They do kill the livestock on a regular basis, don't they."

"Yeah, among other things," Xenis said, his voice trailing away.

"I'd imagine that cows would be slaughtered almost every day."

"And culled."

"Isn't culling killing?"

"Yes, but one culls in order to prevent the spread of disease or some other problem. One kills for resource, like meat."

"Right. So, there must have been a lot of killing and culling."

"Too many chickens were kept in tiny coops, then killed. Chickens everywhere, they lay cramped in their own excrement. Eggs were taken from the hens, roosters beheaded routinely. In some places the blood was everywhere – fresh red put upon dried, caked blood. The smell was constant, like newly-baked rot. And there were accidents. It's a dangerous place."

"Farmhands have a tough job."

"True, but I mean for the animals. There was always some problem with one animal attacking another, or mistakenly trampling over each another."

"More death."

"And I felt this weakness there," Xenis said, paying half attention to his new friend.

Feeling strange, Xenis suddenly rushed to the back of the bus, into the bathroom where he leaned over the blue-stain commode and brought up the sandwich he had just eaten. He arose and comported himself, stared down on the floor for some moments, then cleaned his face, thinking about his xolo and Dora. He felt only a bit better as he looked over his portion of a mottle-colored and stained cushion.

"They're better off," he muttered. "No-one'll kill them."

"What?"

Xenis sat again beside Dean Fromm.

"Just thinking out loud."

"I can sympathize."

"Really?"

"I can't bear to see something die, no matter what it is."

"I guess I can't either," Xenis said. "Not anymore."

"Anymore?"

Again, Xenis felt the beginnings of wretchedness.

"Let's talk about something else."

"We could talk politics."

"*That* isn't risky."

"We could talk religion."

Xenis looked out the window.

"I've had my fill of that."

"Fashion?"

"Goodness no."

Dean laughed.

"How about music, social trends, the internet."

"Not right now."

"A good, sound and healthy feeling?"

Xenis laughed, liking this man.

"Let's talk about all of them."

"That will take some time, but I guess we have it."

"There's something that keeps slipping away."

"Slipping away?"

"Yeah. It comes and then disappears, and I hold it in my hand."

"I don't follow."

"How can I explain?"

"I don't know," Dean smiled.

Xenis looked around him, seemingly for an example: his water, the thought about the water, the bus, the light from the sun, Dean'sn dark green shirt, his own confusion.

"Parts are strange things," Xenis said after another pause.

"I suppose so...not really."

"It isn't strange that we think of something as completely itself that must be made of other things that are completely themselves?"

"That might be a little strange."

Xenis again looked out the window, the same field of horses

and open farm-field seeming to pass him. The denuded land let off a pale but bright yellow color, some scent of demise.

"We call something an ecosystem, right?"

"Yeah."

"But each element, the vegetation, animals, minerals, etc. could exist on its own."

"They could, but an ecosystem means that each thing thrives on each other, I think."

"Or is necessary to one another, right? Minerals don't thrive on animals."

"Right, yeah, but isn't that a division we make?"

"We do. But, we didn't create the system. It arose and we noticed it. We divide it along natural partitions: animals, plants, rocks, whole sections that operate in unison."

"Why's that so amazing?"

"That there isn't just one thing and not many."

"Maybe there is."

"One thing?"

"Yeah."

"That's my problem. There isn't one thing and there aren't many."

"There isn't both?"

"I don't think so."

"How's that?"

"If I say there are some bananas that are fruits and there are some oranges that are fruits and therefore oranges are bananas, then someone will say that I'm not logical, yes?"

"I'd say so."

"But in that oranges and bananas are fruits they are the same, fruits."

"And?"

"In a sense these things are one, yet they possess an obvious difference."

"Oh. Yeah, but you've really just broadened the category."

"I've broadened the category, but how is that possible?"

"You just did it."

"Isn't it what we call a 'natural division'?"

"I suppose so."

Xenis again looked out the window, still more of the same yellowing pasture.

"I didn't really do it. I noticed it."

"What did it?"

"Ought not one of these categories be no other category?"

"No."

"Why? We just made that distinction."

"They're not absolute."

"Not absolute in what sense?"

"Categories don't prevent other categories from being a part of one another."

"What is it that allows that lack of exclusivity of what is also exclusive?"

"I don't know."

"If I were to say 'either X or Z' and 'If not Z then X', I'd be saying the same thing, right?"

"I'd say so."

"What allows you to say that?"

"Logic I think."

"You're right, but then, is saying that one or the other exists precisely the same as saying if one   doesn't exist, the other does?"

"You're not using the same words, but the form is the same."

"Then the words carry no different meaning?"

"In this case a difference that's...the same."

"That's what I'm talking about. Why are those categories not completely exclusive? How can we say, with some confidence, that there is a 'difference that is the same'?"

"It's a pair of opposites that work with one another."

"You mean against?"

"Against too."

"I'm not sure it's merely opposites."

"'Same' and 'difference' are opposites."

"But they're only categories we use to describe and discuss things. They aren't ontological categories. There's no eternal 'Same' and eternal 'Difference.'"

"Why not?"

"There's something about an existing thing that's not. That's what makes difference, not 'Difference.'"

"Then you're talking about another set of opposites: being and non-being."

"There's another pesky couple, but non-existence is myriad as far as it is existence, it isn't absolutely not."

"I'm not sure what you mean."

"I'm not either, but it's a thought I have."

"Yeah? It's more interesting than I thought, but weren't we

were going to talk about politics, religion, fashion...."

"...music, social trends, the internet, and a good, sound and healthy feeling?"

"Yeah, all that."

"I think we just did."

Xenis laughed an old, oily welled-up laugh.

"You're interested in many things."

At this Xenis chuckled. "I'm not sure what it is that interests me, but it's...there."

NICHTS

These parts and whole are the what, the kind. The kind is a particular thing or process or happenstance; its *integritas* is the whole that can be discerned, but not an absolute whole. These acts are patterns that arise again and again. The what is a particular that acts as a universal; it happens again and again, but perhaps not universally. What humans know to repeat itself is what humans can perceive and what humans can predict through calculation. What humans can calculate and predict, they can control. They find a what in being, and more fundamentally they find being reciprocally predicated of being. But the what is a whole; the whole is a part and they exist outside of themselves. They exist outside themselves because they are not themselves in some manner or other. Everything that is exists in this way. This way is becoming, and they make it happen.

NEW FRIENDS
FROM NOTHING

Xenis felt good, his new friend and conversation buoying him. He and Dean bore a hole through their ride along the mid-west. He had no particular destination, but wanted to find a familiar place. He lifted his sack from the storage compartment beneath the bus and looked around the station. Xenis had never seen this place, though he had lived here. There were older men and women who appeared tired and worn, yet who continued as though the alternative was to be no longer. Their clothing wrapped a worn hue around them with beaten fabric that appeared to be as used as they. A comfort resided in their raiment: jeans, old leather, flannel and sweat-shirts all about. Xenis owned the clothes on him and a few more located in his sack, no more. He wore hiking boots and jeans, a medium-weight jacket. His clothes layered in order to present a lighter burden and stave off the approaching cold of winter, he meandered about the station, wondering what to do – where to go.

"It was a pleasure," came a new-familiar sound.

Xenis was not disappointed when he turned to see the man attached to the voice.

"Same to you," he returned.

"Where are you heading? ...in the city I mean."

"I'm not sure. I think I'll head north."

"Well, if you need a friend, or a place to stay," Dean said, handing Xenis a slip of paper with an email address and telephone number on it.

"Thank you."

Xenis looked down and observed how little charge remained on his cell-phone. He had no way to earn money, and what funds he possessed he needed to preserve. The comfort of Dean's apartment was enticing, but Xenis thought of the Davis family and the hospitality that they offered.

"I think I'll visit some friends," he said.

When he departed the station a clear, cool night met him. He had emerged on the south side where the buildings and streets, colors of things unfamiliar to the point of anxiety, jutted against the emerging dark blue. The sun had fallen some time ago, and though Xenis had no fear, he felt the need to move to a more familiar part of the long stretch of concrete, asphalt, metal and glass. Some familiarity spoke to him, as if the same calling he had felt when a very young man; he had sought after someone, or...some thing. Xenis did not believe that same thing, or person, or whatever it was, called him now. It already held him, had held him, and yet the summons continued in a relentless pull. He wanted to move north, but having counted his remaining cash, realized that he ought not relinquish his only means to sustenance. He was compelled, then, to walk the distance from the south side north, and then long-walk northwest and perhaps a bit longer might take him where he believed his friend Brazil now lived. He may be able to stay with her for one or two nights. The trek seemed daunting for one walking; urban uncertainty and darkness with which he had not contended awaited.

He was unable to extract himself easily from this part of the city with a taxi ride, or some other form of transportation; he was compelled to remain diligent, the city stretching out ubiquitous, questionable and occasionally affectionate hands. Xenis walked a kilometer or so, becoming less confident. He continued north and he noted that some sections of the neighborhoods through which he walked were wrapped in the darkness that begets fatuity and selfishness, drives away shame and erases conscience. He came across a small grocery store where he purchased water. The clear, rejuvenating fluid took away some amount of money, but out of a habit that he had never been able to break he purchased carbonated water of the more expensive kind. The taste was fine, sparkles gliding down his throat. As he passed a drinking fountain he once again counted funds. Not much. As he continued north, Xenis realized that his coat, while sufficient for many climes, was unsuitable for the now cold-coming hours. He worked with this same, old covering at the Davis farm and it breathed well, which was good while he pounded out sweat and bull heat, but now that he merely walked it covered him insufficiently. Avoiding the eyes of employees, he entered a restaurant; walked into the bathroom and piled many of the clothes that he carried onto his frame, layering more the sweatshirts and sweaters until the clothes on his body beat off the chill. He recalled the frigid city wind as he continued, and soon realized that his walk might consume the entire evening. He needed sleep, and Brazil would not answer if he arrived early-morning.

Xenis thought that he might profit from purchasing a card with which he could ride the transit. He found that the fare for a single ride on the train was now over three dollars. Even if careful, the city's need would pitilessly take his twenty-four twenties and two tens. He felt even more compelled to be careful, especially because a living wage in Chicago was only a surviving wage. Still, a transit card would prove useful. After purchasing the week-pass on his Ventra, Xenis decided to refrain from using   it. The death-like cold seemed to have abated some as he walked, or perhaps he was acclimating, yet it bit into his face. He wanted to see Brazil as soon as possible; looked forward to their reunion. As he passed along Polyalgia avenue, he watched constant goings-on vending riding and movement of urban homotheria. He was less than most of them; had no livelihood, and once most of these persons determined that he had so little, they would, in all probability, refuse his company. He lost the notice of anyone who might be glancing his direction, and mixed with the company of amblers and the occasional wandering dog. As his legs swayed forward and back along the concrete, Xenis felt more at ease with his surroundings. Noises lurked all left and down, behind and right – irksome pressing utterances. As Chance had it, he noticed a bicycle had been left untended-unheeded unchained near the entrance to a townhouse. Small and rundown it sat as bicycles do, with foam exposed from within the seat, and one saw immediately it had been well-used, badly maintained and sported verdant manner in a green color. He glanced around furtively, grabbed quick-handed the bars and immediately burst into bicycle-sprint. After he had put two or three kilometers between himself and where he met the bicycle, he slowed a bit, observing the neighborhood of his old venue new. Much transpired around him, not all good. These persons there and there-nearby and here and up-close, he thought over what was probable for them. That they had moments of satisfaction, that they were content to a certain extent. Not all was perfect; there was something about what they were and what they did that was not what they were, some...he did not know what...he grasped, had been sensing. Maybe not "grasp." It surrounded him, though he had little articulation to offer for it, if it was at all. This lack did not disturb him, though it seemed anxiously indistinct. No action or character of those around him was bad; such was a different species of absence. At the same time, Xenis seemed to sense the kind of contentment he sought as he pedaled, slowing the bicycle in order to observe. Strange, but his sensation was an impossibility.

"Am I thinking correctly?" he asked himself.

He had passed the city proper where the river wound through peril and treachery and where street signs and persons walking dogs imposed themselves upon their surroundings, merged and demarcated their what, as buildings, carpeting and cicada trills do. He passed up town, noticing the pawn shops and the laughing men on the street corner. They exuded the same sentiment that he had intuited, and he again caught himself wondering whence came this mindfulness. A mere feeling it must be, and nothing true, real, or proper. He had been incorrect in the past, and had thought that things were one way and they became something other; perhaps he simply wanted to possess that feeling; perhaps he desired that intuition and it was the desire that he felt, nothing more. He had, after all, no reason to sense such things, and he had every reason to suspect he simply knew only the most superficial aspects of the persons animals circumstances around him and about town. He needed much observation and years of thought to make a simple determination about one single person who presented him with this sensation.

"I must be wrong," he thought.

As he rolled lightly into Brazil's neighborhood, Xenis felt even more some kind of presence, an impossible admixture of things. It must be that he was about to see his old, longtime friend that brought about this intuition. Brazil had remained near him even when they had little contact, though she probably did not know it. He set the bicycle against a stop-sign as it had been when he came upon it. As he wandered about the area – near where the pair of red and black friends used to imbibe the ice-melt on lake's water – the sensation that he had been experiencing began to fade. He felt a lack of familiarity with the place, though he had spent time here years ago for years. The familiarity, the sense of having one's own, the general interest in that what surrounded him, his similarity to that what surrounded him, all of these were suddenly not, though he now found himself in the very place that he sought. Still they remained, or so it seemed that nothing had changed, but not as strong as when he first stepped toward the north of the city.

"Maybe my sensation was the novelty of returning," he thought. "Now another kind of familiarity."

He was not certain what it meant, but what seemed so near and clear, his belonging to what surrounded, was not so much any longer – not presiding. Perhaps it would return and perhaps not, but he already missed, indeed longed for, its return. It seemed as if he were not without it, a man whose vitality faded when such a...he did not know what to call it...diminished. Xenis thought again.

"I must be imagining things."

Though he longed for his original intuition to return, he had a task at hand, and his friend may or may not live where she had. Brazil, a sometimes difficult and unpredictable person, may sympathize with him and may not at any given time. She seemed to Xenis prone to sudden outbursts, conflagrations that arose from nowhere and suddenly disappeared. She refused to see him the last time, something about personal issues – difficulties that appeared to follow Brazil constantly. They lived together at one time, enjoyed one another's company, but berserkers and imps consumed both, grotesques that accompany the living. When he arrived at Damen avenue, where Brazil's last-known domicile was, a thought suddenly fell upon him.

"Why have I returned?"

He remembered that he had avoided this city in order to avoid whoever had been plaguing him, whoever had sent notes filled with accusations. Xenis did not want to endanger anyone by visiting them, let alone imperil someone who had been, and may again be, close to him. He wondered over these things, but at the same time desperation for the company of someone in whom he possessed trust remained. He had helped Brazil a great deal, he thought, and though his generosity entitled him to nothing, he believed she would be unable to turn away his need. Concerned over all of these things, he considered not pressing the metal knob when he arrived – alert that someone desires entry – but that he had already depressed it into the metal box on the side of the building came into his awareness. The door erupted in electric hum, loud and at once soft, giving him a surprised and much-relieved entry. He hesitated not at all pushing the door open, climbing the stairs toward the second floor. When he arrived at 2B, Xenis stopped as the door stood ajar before him. The apartment was alive with activity, and Xenis was able to hear a quick movement within, though the hour was late.

"Come on."

He pushed open the door and there a thick, voluptuous woman meandered back and forth, a movement not possible for the once-rotund Brazil.

"I'll be there in a moment. We're late."

Xenis smiled at the regular tone of Brazil's voice. Stranger still became the quick movements and sudden gestures; he caught glimpses. Looking about and observing the paintings on the walls and the many bronze figures standing everywhere, he noticed the works of familiar artists. Some paintings he had purchased for her and others by artists Brazil and he had known quietly hung in colorful abandon, demanding perusal. Familiarity with the place and what had been there for him arose again; a thing sought seemed to have arrived. He felt that same sensation of belonging and presence return, old friends.

"I have to go to the grocery for something..." Brazil said as she dead-stopped before him.

Xenis instinctively threw her a stern glance and placed a displeased look onto his face. Brazil seemed...confused.

"May I help you?" she asked, alarmed at the mistake of an open door.

"May I help *you*?" Xenis asked, mocking her with a smile.

A shudder ran down the back of Brazil's head, as it did when she became excited about a topic or when she was creating something that pleased her. Yet, this shudder lacked the comfort to which she was accustomed.

"I think you can," she said.

And a moment of silence fell while Xenis beamed.

"You can leave," she said.

The beam disappeared.

"You want me to leave?"

"What else would I want you to do?"

Xenis expected such a reaction, but a weight of sadness and a thorough pop of distress dropped into him whole.

"Still cranky in the morning, still the unhappy girl, I see."

Brazil stared hard at him for long moments that tasted bland, examining the dark-toned man with bright eyes and a seemingly pleasant demeanor. She was unable to place this person. His face was not recognizable with its sable features and the short, thick black mane surrounding his head. He had not shaved in what seemed a week. One was able to discern the chiseled and precise beauty of his face, a thoroughly male, familiar existence stood before her, yet she recognized him not at all. She sensed no hostility, but instead there came more contentment that came pleasant in its affect. He was no threat, though she had thought he might rape her, or kill her, or at least steal. She knew him slightly, or at least that was the message sent by his open body welcoming sight and clear expression, unassuming stance. She looked again at him, and, noticing the confusion, Xenis smiled and laughed, a risk at that moment.

"Are you still complaining constantly about nothing?"

"Oh my god," she said.

She stood quite still.

At this moment their reunion might have proceeded in any one of a number of ways. Xenis wanted to be his old self, but carefully, arriving without much pain or hurdle; they may take up as comrades they had been, his hope not reasonable. Yet, it was that, what he wished might happen.

"You don't look the same," Brazil commented, putting down her brush and keys.

"I don't?"

"No."

She again observed him for moments.

"You look as if you are a...well...a human."

"I am and always have been..."

"I mean one might mistake you for human, anyway."

Brazil smiled at Xenis in no manner, but she was capable of sardonic humor. Her humor proved grace, but that she made light he did not know. She would never reveal that the levity was primary. No. Her humor may mean that she yet cared for him, perhaps loved him in the way that they had done. On the other hand, she might simply dislike him intensely.

"I need to meet someone," she said finally. "You can wait here, but I won't be back for a while...tomorrow maybe.

"I don't mind. I need some rest."

That sensation came to him again.

NICHTS

A what is a particular thing or process; it has a specific way of being. It is a kind. A particular thing or process is a whole; a whole is a part; a part is a whole. They exist outside of themselves. They are a particular kind because the kind has its own what. It is a kind of act and so it has a particularity that repeats itself. A what has boundaries without which it cannot be what it is. Those boundaries cease being where the end of the what shows itself to others. The boundaries make a what other-than; other-than makes a what not some other what. The other-than separates the what from others. The separation makes not of the particular what. The making of not is the making of kind of the particular act. Not then of some what produces the what of the what. The not of the what they are, one may say; they cannot be in any way yet they are part of what. They fold upon themselves in the absence of existence, and where that is something-other-than-not is. The what comes from here, but first there is. These Nichts howled the dogs, made curious the girls and boys, alcoholed the drink, bovined the milking and co-workered the tendered relationshipss, manned the sable males with the disposition of nothing. And none perceived them. They were and will be thoughts and ideas, photons, particles and the complete act of all.

REJECTION OF COMPASSION

Dean Fromm smiled large and gladly at others, his voice the crunch of moccasins on colored pebbles. Tones of dark blue, welcoming and reassuring, wrapped themselves around his fairly well-cut frame, each word he uttered graciously floating onto ears of others.

"How are you?"

"I hope you're doing well."

"Have a good day."

He had patiently listened, but now grew tired with each passing minute. At last the meeting ended; he turned his attention to more pleasant things, a return home. He occupied a smaller space – his a more expensive neighborhood – but he attempted to save as much money as possible. He managed his finances with difficultly because he earned nearly enough to cover all of his expenses – composed of living necessities and one loan payment – and then merely a bit more. The "more" was not enough to save him regularly.

"I'll have to save irregularly," he said to himself.

His trail mix accompanied him everywhere, until it was nowhere, always there. The videos and social media chatter he consumed online was present as much as the health snack at least, his amusement there as well. Online entertainment made him smile while a quick pint of dark beer in the early evening and sometimes morning perked him. His mini-van lugged him around and about when his bicycle was inoperative or no jogging mood inspired him; the most welcome presence who came to visit besides his parents was exercise; they were good friends. Dean ritually ate his fruits and oat-cereals early-evening late-morning, during his waking hours and restaurant visits. Accounting occupied his thoughts mostly, but he read now and then. He possessed a full social life, that he had made and maintained plenty of full-bodied friendships, especially with his parents. Dean was an admirer of photographs and photography in general; he abided fully in that appreciation for virtual and electronic moments of brightness around and about loved ones or over beloved things, especially his mother. It was that light what he cherished, what made the photo, and he possessed all sorts of pictures downloaded from his entertainment station. Endlessly imprisoned seconds of living interested him effortlessly; he returned to them daily. He possessed the obligatory landscapes and animal pictures – he relished photos of animals, but that topic was far overdone – he owned photos of interesting persons in the city, eccentrics and college students, blues-musicians and business-players, political-movers and elegant buildings with the dark lines of homotheria flowing in and around insensate concrete. A whole series of building-photos was sold at the art museum, and he felt driven to procure the oversized, thick book of pictures at first chance. These were magnificent: a theater whose beautiful seats were occupied by smartly-dressed, cheerful observers. The stage lived, mid-performance of *The Magic Flute* production 1959, Tamino refusing ladies' temptation. Dean scrutinized that photograph, the bustling red-velvet seats and characters caught mid-act and animated. He liked particularly the slightly colorized photo of a living room. The walls were faintly yellow and a tired sixties-era couch sat middle-room – mother and son upon it – an ovular rug the colorful-most moment. The mother read to the son from a book with a black cover. Dean believed the text enlightened the child with widening grin and eyes, brightest moments. These photos he enjoyed intensely, basking in an image age. Dean adorned his desk, a deep golden-brown butcher's roll-top refinished by his father, with photos of his family. There stood his parents, center and close, who grinned large and mighty with Irish-Catholic bliss and discipline. They stood forever on a large, rented boat, not quite a yacht.

"That time," he said aloud.

Proud and lively parents, they dutifully ate and rested, sang occasionally; lounged and drove their autos, refrigerated the air in their living-spaces. They rented and then owned a home; raised three children; cared for and wrangled with one another. All the time they organized-ordinary their livingstyle and were guided by a single force of the utmost charisma and sureness. Dean's father once convinced a man to relinquish half of one paycheck to the policeman's charity, Alec's favorite. His uncle joked that his brother was able to charm life into a dead man. This odd phrase fit his father, and Dean envied his parent's natural way with others, wished to imitate it at least. Almost everyone liked his father immediately, but his most significant ability was an astounding talent for composure and gift for calming others in the midst of crises, why his work as a police officer was so valued. Dean respected his father's ebullience, manifest when he was confronted with the worst human-being offered. Strong as well and a picture of health, he enjoyed his way through life.

> "He's a good man," Dean thought, looking at
> his father.

He observed the picture of a man laugh-talking with his uncle, the two on a pier fishing in thigh-length bathing suits. Time had worn away most of the hues – a slight wash of Kodachrome on the lively males. Alec's head turned toward his brother, as if in the act of charming, and all around and about him seemed to agree. Dean cherished this moment, and it cherished him. The photo of his mother depicted him and her on the porch of their first home, roughly at the same period as the photo of his father, 1959. Candidly, she was occupied with her son, a well-fed lad who rested erect on her lap as she sat. She appeared to be moving her son's hands, directing them upward, and the boy Dean looked downward with the pointer finger of his right hand, its mate extended upward. Both mother and son appeared content and sad. She wore a long robe of sorts, something that one dons after showering, its light blue color never faded. As he recalled this moment, the two were stopped by Dean's father in the midst of playing in the pool. He seemed to be in the mood for a photo and commanded his wife and son to pose, a tight position. The pair dutifully smiled and worked their faces, bodies and thoughts into an arrangement correct for father. She fed and soothed them both, the father and the son, gave emotional succor. She cleaned with hands and legs, feet and back, scrubbed clothing and brought purity and order of place; she provided clear and translucent – virtually invisible – necessities and where she no longer remained, there they arose without her.

> "She's a good woman," Dean thought.

Dean entered Bane Accounting and sat down at his small desk jammed into a section of metal, carpeted dividers. He started his computer, leafing through a pile of numbers that sat before him. When he opened his drawer he saw more numbers, and when fully the computer had booted-started-greeted-loaded, he opened a file on the desktop and still more numbers met him. During the next three hours Dean moved the numbers from place to place, used Allie AI to analyze them and organized them for corporations that hired his company. He was one of the last remaining in his section; most had been replaced by artificial intelligence. Really, he was there to check the work of the AI. Sometimes, it did strange things and made bad caluculations. He was there to finalize what the articifical intelligence did. Dean recalled what he had seen known understood seen again for some time; the numbers on one side here were not the same as the numbers on the other side. He rearranged the numbers here and then nearby and over yonder in the ledger, and then, alas, he found that incredible balance. Relieved and elated, he decided to feel overjoyed with a cooler-drink. He wound around the desk and ambled speedily to the water where he snatched a cup and drank the too-cold, clear fluid.

"I have performed a service that connects me to no-one, except a computer."

Dean recalled this thought had come from him on other occasions in different ways, having limped its way back somewhere into oblivion. He remembered that he needed to tell Alonzo what he and his parents found; had promised to find counseling for his daughter. Dean's father knew of a service that provided free guidance and support for disabled children, performed the research Alonzo needed. Grateful for Dean's diligence and hard work, Alonzo thanked him.

"It's nothing," Dean said. "My father helped. He's knowledgeable about these things."

He remembered that he wanted to inform Teresa about the fund-raising drive for homeless animals that Dean's mother managed. Though Dean was not as fond of animals as Teresa, he wished that she be aware of it.

"Oh, that's great!" Teresa said. "Thank you so much, Dean."

She seemed excited, glad that she heard, amazed at what he did. Dean felt a satisfaction that he had not yet felt that day; he relaxed and enjoyed the moment, but after two hours some welling and churning sensibility appeared deep within, disrupting the glad moment that would have made a splendid photograph. He remembered a chore and found his way outside the office of his superior, shaking dreading cracking his knuckles. He tried to like everyone with whom he worked; they were nice, despite regular bad moments. He disliked conflicts and posturing, and resented how he needed to protect himself, stand guard. His parents agreed. His superior, Miles, boasted six feet and always kept things in place out of concern for the company. He was compelled to grant paid days leave for specific maladies, and he believed such expenses to be reasonable, thought himself quite reasonably empathetic. When one of his underlings came to him with a domestic concern, one which would necessitate his absence from a few day's work, he asked his employee what was it, this concern.

"I have a health issue I have to address," Dean said.

"I see." "Well, you have about a week's worth of off-time saved, so no problem."

Dean – his head shook and his mouth emitted a barely-audible trembling, angry grumble.

"I was hoping that it would fall under 'emergency time'."

"Emergency time off is for things like heart attacks and car accidents. Is this like that?"

"Not exactly..."

Miles stared hard.

"I tell you what. If you can prove that the issue is life-threatening, then I can help you. Otherwise, it has to come out of your off-time."

"Ah."

Dean grumbled and mumbled as he walked back to his desk.

"Mumble, grumble. So upset," said Franklin, as Dean walked.

"Not fair. Not fair," mumbled Luka.

Both men smiled to one another over the tops of office-stations. When Dean arrived home, he quickly balled up his work-clothes and jammed them promptly into the drier in the basement, still upset. He turned the heat to its highest temperature and the timer to forty-five minutes. Once the clothes tumbled, he was relieved and he dressed himself again, observed what lay before him. Prim dresser drawers and soda-bottles set straight in line all smiled at him, friends greeting him after another trying day. He smiled back and quickly bundled up his shoes and what remained of his clothes into a garbage bag, then waited. The room tidy, all-surrounding garbage-bags filled with more clothing than he recalled asked for deliverance from their gaol. Dean wished that he were able to put everything back in place. He checked his messages and a scowl overcame him; he dialed his roommate.

"I realize you have a lot to do, but I need some help," he said with firm kindness to a satellite somewhere.

He had asked his roommate to perform chores, like garbage-taking and cleaning, but Steven claimed his size prevented him from being able to carry the trash down the stairs, just as it prevented him from snow removal meter-reading, caring for animals and plants along with other living organisms, dish-washing and food preparation.

"I'm trying to understand," Dean thought.

There came the door-buzz, declaring the presence of someone. Dean asked who it was even as he let in the Arbeit's pest-control men. They entered his unit while he departed. He would return later, he thought – pests deleted.

"Such dirty, impure things," he thought.

As he wandered around the area in which he lived and ruminated over the day's events, Dean thought how rude and insensitive were his coworkers and his boss. They spoke with him infrequently and expressed little interest in his concerns, but Dean continued to drive their children to school, cover for them when late. He had, in the brief time he worked at Bane Accounting, patched up differences between workers; counseled some of the more distraught and disappointed underlings; almost constantly heard grievances and personal complaints from persons desperate for the smallest bit of attention. Yet, no-one listened to him, not anyone. Some of the persons whom he counseled had teased him on that very day. Dean ate steak and fries with a large beer, but that what buoyed him ordinarily did not now. He walked to the park and watched the dogs bark and observed the young women. He walked about in order to circulate the blood, felt drowsy, had nowhere to sleep. Two hours more passed and Dean decided that the Arbeit's pest-control men had departed. The next morning he dressed as usual and swallowed his coffee after a seemingly extended sleepless night. He washed himself and wrapped his mid-sized form in fresh-clean pants and a dress-shirt, mint-breath and unsullied walk. He made his way out into the wisps and push of morning air and slowly drifted down the stairs; he reached his car and entered; turned the key and up he ascended once more and he felt a weakness that pushed him back into his bed where he slept hours-long. When he awoke, he did not realize where he was or what had transpired. He had simply not gone in to work; he was glad at having abandoned Bane, but now very nervous. He considered calling Miles, telling him that he had been detained unavoidably.

"No."

He would find another, more collegial, place.

In the days that followed, Dean found himself considering all sorts of livelihoods, even the grocer across the way. Unable to imagine himself doing anything that was available, Dean thought that he would not think about it and continued with his concerns: clean house in evening, awake at 8am, dressed at 8:15am, out or up and about at 9am.

"There's nowhere to go."

On Saturday he met his friends at The League of Human Sufferers where they distributed food and drink to the homeless and working poor. He was ordinarily the soup dispenser, but he found Gladys performing this task.

"That's what I do."

Dean appeared suddenly before Gladys.

"Michael says he needs you in the kitchen," he said.

"Oh, OK."

When she departed, Dean gave soup to Alex and Jim, chatted as usual. He arrived just in time. As he pressed on, he became more content, though he thought again on the indignities of the past few days, needed more coffee. When he had completed the task of soup distribution, he sat next to Adam and smiled. The work was gratifying, if menial. Dean felt again a warm and satisfied sensibility like that which arose on his last day of accounting.

"I quit my job."

"You what?"

"I quit my job."

"Why, Dean?"

"It didn't fit."

"You were doing so well," Adam sighed.

"Two years. I was there two years. Something better will come."

"I can't believe another job is gone!"

"I know, I know."

The next week Dean found only menial positions, offering little compensation – certainly not enough. He suspected that he would again quit whatever position, should he find work simply anywhere. Another week passed and he grew more nervous. Dean distracted himself by jogging in the morning and bicycling in early evenings. He consulted Adam as he usually did; maybe it had been a mistake to quit. Adam listened and offered a sympathetic mind, but little assist. Somehow exercise made Dean feel better. His mother told him so; she also suggested he keep himself clean and regular, so he commonly tidied his apartment, cooking and cleaning for both him and his roommate. He helped neighbors by watching after their animals and sometimes baby-sitting. The presence of children buoyed him almost as much as his study of photographs. The third week that Dean remained jobless found him more sleep-deprived; a call to Adam every day. He continued: up at 8am, dressed by 8:15, eat at 9am, search for work from 10am until 2pm, clean house around 8pm. During idle hours, he delved most frequently and deeply into his portraits and photographs, especially those of his family.

"Dad knows what to do. Mom's comforting."

Dean fidgeted more and remained awake longer, talking to his parents and leveling the same complaint.

"Everyone's so apathetic and deadened. No-one cares," he said.

His parents explained that he needed to be patient; he would find something just right, but he was not convinced.

Dean arose on a Sunday morning intent upon enjoying his day; he tended to his parents, talking to and asking them what they needed. When Adam surprised him with a visit, Dean learned of a tolerable, possible form of employment. Nothing exceedingly difficult, care-giving for an older man.

"Really?" Dean said. "Thank you."

NICHTS

The what was a kind of order, or a structure. That structure is the aspect of what that allowed others to apprehend it. It was a shape, a relation of moving notes in a harmony, a combination of color among the other whats that had a concordance to them. Humans notice the harmony the concordance and that harmony is the shape of the repetition that made regular particularity of act. When the particularity of act performed itself, the humans called it a kind of act, thing or process. The Nichts lay waiting, hidden from sight. One was not-death and another was not-life. One was not-love and another was not-hate, the not-hate not necessarily love and the not-love not necessarily hate nor necessarily anything other than not. They wrapped themselves tightly around is, chased away all other, and all the other was completely all other. Animal was there, warm blood muscle-flesh and integument. Human was present, again warm blood muscle-flesh and integument but not-tiger, not-whale, no-other than human. All else was there, with Nichts breaking to pieces what is whole and so not whole. Neither angry nor content, not prurient nor satisfied they broke and sundered. The pepper-bearded man with the brown shirt and the thin wife they moved, broke open the girl and her animal with the long hair and parted the similarity between the raven-haired man and the tree that he climbed. Nichts broke down the animosity between hands and compelled horses to eat. They wounded middle-aged men with awareness of addiction and provided the pious with a god. And they were unable to break what they continually acted upon because what they acted upon was motive illusion, a continuance of what that was nothing.

MOTHER AND
FATHER KNOW

He was a tired and shriveled man whose years had faded him, his frame and color washed like the years-long spray of sunlight over a photo. John's friends and family were thoroughly impressed with the physical and mental abilities that remained strong and capable after ninety-four years of life, though they too had grown weak. Accustomed to having a share, he had earned well; managed his own legal affairs; repaired or built his house and directed his home. He had grown up in a Caucasian household that possessed servants, fairly well-educated – his family owning-operating supermarkets. John had done his growing in a fine place. Sundays brought sleep and laziness, Mondays new work, Wednesdays an extended-family meal, Thursdays minor worry and Friday-Saturday-Sundays lake excursions on the family yacht. He walked with the confident gait of a man whose years had given him much contentment, but even his children were growing old, and yet he remained relatively lively and comparatively strong. He cared for himself, and though his daily existence might have been easier had he allowed his children to care for him, John refused the assistance offered. His children, his friends, his subordinates inspired others, his awe of his beloved wife, his beautiful and dutiful children lovely-house thought-filled-compassion vacation-at-liberty late-sleepy-Mondays prevailed through his adulthood, but now not nearly so. As John came to be rather old, his mornings were tired, afternoons dim, evenings wore him to the edge of nothing – all of them demanding a nap here-there and slowing him seemingly each moment. Within the measure of his ability, John continued to fix things around the house and he tended to all of his financial affairs; refused to surrender driving his car, continued his walks in his latest and final neighborhood. He wished to continue the John who sledded and rode his motorcycle and his go-cart where time and his influence would allow, sometimes more than a bit extra-legal of indulgences.

He golfed at proper clubs and perused photos of himself lounging around a score of caught fish. His outgoing and generous spirit pervaded everything he did and his way of acting and commanding changed very little over more decades and more decades. His wife and he dedicated themselves to, found contentment and high satisfaction in the donation of their time to belief in compassion and charity. After the departure of middle age, he and his wife had moved nearer to one of their children, away from their much larger home – more comfortable at the ease with which they cared for it. Not a lot of the city now interested John, but that was no matter. He had immersed himself in his wife, the routines that were echoes of his more active existence and – after his tired days arrived more often – his television. Fifteen years of contented retirement having passed, his wife departed and his vision failed in most places except direct sunlight. His body slowed his walks; the diminished vision along with the weakening frame of old John barred him from most urban driving. Really, John had no reason to use his car, but he liked that he was able to dart about the city, always horns blaring always noise-making attention-grabbing. His inability to place himself in congested traffic and compel his vehicle to meander about block after block seeking parking occupied him. The steady departure of his what slowed him toward a displeasing stillness. Slowly, the whats that were within him became primary. Now he was more flesh than mind, now more water that walks than the what-John was prior. He awoke at the same time each morning, ate at the same time and watched the same television programs; these consistent acts and habits he always had kept – again as he had performed them when a child – surrounding his immediate person similar of same, a good for him. When he possessed more difficulty still, slowness making coffee and spreading blueberry jam on rye toast, alarm compelled him to ask for assistance.

"Not from the children!"

No, his children would not be supplementing him in that way.

Although he realized he needed assistance, only with severe and truculent reluctance did he surrender any of his daily activities. He trusted Chester, an employee who had tended to him long and competently, to care for things and to drive him about, but Chester earned his sixty-fifth birthday and sought withdrawal, left John to his tasks, and when a neighbor found John attempting to break back into his condominium, authorities informed the children. His boys knew nothing of any difficulties, nor had they inquired often, knowing John. The near decagenarian possessed many friends, some that came from the lonely gathering of older bodies and some continued the now seemingly ancient associations once thin now old-age thick. When his boys realized his circumstances, they united in an effort to assist and he finally accepted. Not much. The family possessed the resources to hire a care-giver, someone who was able to burden themselves, the old man's need becoming theirs. William knew Adam who knew Dean who arrived at the home of John Verdunkeln, eager to assist a diminished man.

"My kids want you to help me."

"Yes, yes. They care a lot about you."

John let out a grunt and cleared his throat.

"Come in. Take a look around."

Dean mostly agreed and chatted, visited the family, asking about old John and his habits. Even on the first day, Dean noted John's state, his walk and energy-level.

"There may be little I can do."

He offered to cook for this John, and John's character relegated Dean to visiting regularly and cleaning the large domicile. Unable to move about in order to extend his presence, John occupied only two out of the seven rooms of the well-lit, mahogany unit. Dean offered to play cards with the older man, but John showed little interest. He offered to watch films with old John and attempted to chat with him about what they watched, but after only a few such viewings Dean wearied old John. Occasionally, when a weaker John appeared, Dean spent the night, careful in his watch. He cleaned, washed clothes, assisted old legs walking. The gladness with which John performed menial tasks surprised the younger man. The old John ate almost nothing and when he did, he consumed chocolates, graham crackers, salted crackers and beer. Dean again suggested that he prepare meals.

"What, are you a woman now? Go get the pretzels."

Dean laughed at these interactions and continued, asking if John wanted some good, old-fashioned chili or barbeque ribs.

"No thank you , Mr. Housemaid."

"Do you mind if I prepare some for myself then?", Dean asked.

"I'm here a lot and I don't have time to prepare the best food at home."

"Be my guest," John said with a thumping voice bordering on loathing.

Dean found himself the best ribs in the city. He spent three days creating a vat of sauce, purchased a grill small enough to perch on John's patio. He asked John if its place was acceptable, as he assembled it.

"Sure sure, Yeah yeah."

After days of planning, Dean brought out the meat and prepared it, sure to leave on the kitchen counter ingredients as well as the spice-scented sauce. He repeatedly passed John when he took the meat onto the back porch. As the meat began to cook the savor and the steam floated periodically into John's unit, the back door open too wide. Dean's mother taught him precisely how to cook, just right and ever so minutely, carmelized then browned by flames produced by wood and not curious black rocks; his mother helped him choose the proper meat and the best ingredients. He basted his meal in the heavy sauce regularly, not too thick, savoring the moment when each set of ribs prepared to leave the grill. On each occasion when Dean brought another batch of animal parts into the kitchen old John meandered closer to the smoldering back porch.

"It smells like it's burned."

"Mom says you should brown the ribs ever so carefully. Carmelize, don't burn. But maybe a bit of burn will do us good."

When the ribs were prepared and the table set, old John Verdunkeln asked to sit with Dean who happened to have enough cooked meat for both. Old John ate ravenously, as if for the first time savoring. When he returned over the next days and weeks, Dean prepared new dishes: fried chicken, steak, corned beef, all preparation supervised by his mother. At her suggestion, Dean began to organize the routine of the household; awake at 8:30am, breakfast at 9:15am, lunch at 2pm. Between these predictable events were conversations.

"I have the best family. You wouldn't believe," Dean told the old man.

John nodded.

"My father is an ex-policeman and my mother is a saint. Actually, they're both saints."

"We need more saints."

John ate the well-cooked meals on almost every occasion, particularly fond of the ribs and corned beef. He insisted the graham crackers and the pretzels be ever-present in the condominium, but forgot them more often. Emboldened by success, Dean suggested John drink water, or tea, or maybe even seltzer, but geriatric John would not let go his drink. He demanded one pack of six "Stroh's" every night, though hardly able to consume one whole bottle on a sitting. When he helped John, Dean felt the absence of something, an odd perception of a lack. It seemed that something present had not been, but he did not conceive it well. Having perceived the old man and his care-giver, John's children invited both to their home.

"The old man seems much happier," said the eldest. "He moves quicker and talks more."

"My mother helped with all that...and my father. They know a lot about a lot," said Dean

John gained weight, and he was able to dress himself

more often. He walked around his home, needed less the wheelchair, even began to walk more comfortably about the whole condominium, peering out of windows unvisited in a year. John talked with thoughts clearer, did have some trouble with the meals Dean served at times, necessitating a pureed chicken, or an overcooked chicken soup. Still, on most occasions old John relished the what he had eaten the whole of his life. They shared. Dean explained how his father talked men out of doing the most horrible of things, calming raging domestic squabbles and relieving thugs of their weaponry.

"There is a history of cancer and Alzheimer's in our family, but mom and dad are in good health, I think. Knock on wood," he said.

John regularly felt strong and able enough to exit his home after six months. The older man did not stumble, but moved too quickly, excited over old freedom come new. On such occasions he tired quickly and Dean relocated him within safe walls. Departures from John's stagnation became more frequent, more often and still more ability returned, until Dean found him outside the building.

"John!"

An old smile returned.

"How long have you been outside?"

"About an hour."

Earlier yet earlier did Dean arrive in order to prevent recurrence of old John's dangerous independence. The pair walked around the block, and though the exertion initially exhausted John, strength gave momentum, new *vis*, greater brute spring. He felt more himself, his what, and the more what he wanted more. Dean took precautions to ensure John's security, but occasions when he found the old man outside walking or descending the stairs grew. Sometimes, John emerged in the afternoon, sometimes morning, sometimes evening. Dean consulted his mother who said that he ought to talk to his father. His father thought the old man susceptible to certain charms; the cooking had produced the desired effect after all, too effective. He talked John back into his home many times, but the effort came harder. Television, snacks, movies, conversation – none of these things now dragged old John back into his chair, but Dean's father had a good idea. He asked John why he was so determined to step out.

"Special project."

"What's that?"

John refused to say and as more days passed, John said nothing about the matter.

"So, what're you doing, John?" Dean asked on another occasion.

"Don't know altogether," John admitted.

"No?"

"Well, I do and I don't."

"What do you mean?"

"There's something missing."

"Oh."

"There's something that isn't there that should be...I don't know."

Dean was quick.

"I have that too."

"You do?"

"Oh yeah."

"What do you do about it?"

"I ah, I help you."

Abruptly, John began talking less frequently, roamed out of the condominium less. He ate with Dean and the pair talked at various times of the day, but John watched a bit more television and a nightly pair of brews or more consumed his strength. He talked less, now quiet rather silent more observant. During the times when John was unapproachable, Dean would text his friends and chat on social media. Occasionally, he heard from friends at Bane Accounting.

"My daughter did well at the school you recommended," Alonzo explained.

"I'm glad to hear it."

"But it was de-funded. When she returned to her former school, she became depressed."

"Oh my."

"She stopped working and the school held her back."

"I'm sorry, Alonzo," Dean said.

"Remember Teresa?"

"Yes."

"She quit her accounting job."

"Oh no!"

"She got fought with someone from a dog shelter, and it was bad."

"Oh my."

"She was hurt and she hasn't returned to work, maybe never come back."

"I feel so bad for her."

"She is missed."

What with all these things happening, it cheered Dean when he walked past the dining-room table, John talking to his friends Nick and Ruth. He smiled to himself and decided to talk with his parents again tonight. He had not heard from them in a few days. He asked his father and mother what he ought to do, and they knew.

NICHTS

These whats were nots and every moment they were able to bring the bit of naught out of the what that they were. The end of the what that limited its kind to what it was lay open to the other-than of alteration and change. Both species of nothing. The what and the not were not fused, but rather they were the same and the what allowed other what to redefine the what that it was. The what as whole and part was then not only not what it was, but the whole of anything continually reduced itself to other whats that were certain structures, themselves ever more reducible. Whats in most substantial form were not-substantial, a kind of empty essence. It was a kind of illusion of *integritas* that could within its own probability alter to something-other-than, which is being open to annihilation. There was not one what, not altogether collected into one. Yet, what-was continued in its presence spread along all of its differences. What connected this singularity to itself by separation and negativity. It ran along itself not as itself, but as whats – as what-is whole and part. Each of these manifestations of the same that were different, the emptiness that was full, were together existing by doing nothing.

EKSTASIS

Brazil was unable to suppress a smile when she awoke and hers was a more-vital step upon the brightening floor in the morning when she prepared breakfast. She possessed very little, and her living-space was comfortable with its yellow and blue watercolors and the brilliant, impressionistic paintings on the walls, one of a tree and another of a piano in the corner with a candle atop. Muralistic yellow-rust rugs kept her feet comfortable and figurines of cherry-wood and mahogany end-tables livened her space with a bright and glad vision. Two small rooms provided sleeping-place for as many as four cramped persons, two comfortable. A brass-and-wood ceiling fan circulated the heat and cooled a roll-top desk and its diminutive wood-carving occupants. Her space clean until a project of art occupied her attention more than tidiness, Brazil lived comfortably.

Xenis had been in her space for a month; slept only until 7:30am, his corner of her small space tidy and simple. He cleaned after himself; volunteered to perform chores and most surprisingly, ridiculed almost nothing. No obesity jokes, no provocation. Brazil did not know what to think. Xenis suggested that the two of them peruse some of the art in her small region of Chicago, and because the summer had come almost to a close the art festival neared, August's end. Brazil rented a space among the booths and Xenis assisted, carrying bronze statues giving advice where to situate each work watching for the best aesthetic. During the time they had already shared her unit, Xenis sugsested when she needed to adjust her hair but was unable to see it, or when she had worked too hard, when she can relax and cease worrying, all care done. His wanted but unexpected affection came as an unknown. Xenis sometimes prepared food and other times supplemented their idle time reading to her or taking amusement from word games or mimicking strange or annoying neighbors; she missed the dogs. He had somewhere learned how to prepare eggs and vegetables, a surprisingly good omelet consisting of green pepper, jalapeno, a bit of cheese and full-yellow egg. Xenis comported himself at ease, his manner came somehow softer in used, baggy jeans and dirty-white cotton shirts. That he remained quiet in the morning while she slept, that he cleaned up after himself and after Brazil, that he talked to her neighbors when Brazil wanted nothing of them, all surprised her, unsuspected. The pair regularly sat up late as they once did.

"Where have you been? Where did you live, I mean," Brazil asked.

"On a farm in Wisconsin."

She laughed.

"I know. It was odd."

"It isn't just odd. It's impossible."

"All that does seem far away." Xenis' voice trailed off.

"What changed? I mean, what..."

"What?"

"Well, you're like this..." She raised her hand, gesturing towards him.

"I was always like this."

Brazil frowned savagely.

"What?"

"You were never like this."

"No?"

"No. Never."

"How was I?"

Brazil's dumbfounded look surprised him.

"Abrasive and self-centered, demanding and impossible...to name only a few of your less-pleasant traits."

"I guess I mean that I was always able to be this way," Xenis said after a moment.

"Then why weren't you?"

"I was."

"You were not."

"I helped you."

"You helped with money, which is another way of doing almost nothing, or nothing at all."

"I did more than that."

"Occasionally you did slightly more, but mostly you were cruel, savage even."

"No."

Brazil glared at him. "Yes."

A long pause here occupied Xenis.

"I didn't intend to be."

"Didn't intend," she scoffed. "You didn't even think about it."

Brazil observed his quietly sad expression.

"It's alright...I guess. You seem...not the same. In fact, when we lived together, you were better. Even then."

"I was?"

"Still abrasive and cruel, but yeah."

The two did not know what to say for moments.

"What happened to your Xolos, and Dora?"

"The black died in an accident. The brown and Dora live on the farm in Wisconsin."

"Oh No!" Brazil's eyes turned down, her cheeks lowered.

"They're fine. They're favorites with the children and the family knows how to let animals be animals...certain ones anyway."

Xenis' present state in itself did not give him what his talking, reading, walking and other simple activities with his friend granted. Some kind of intensity to these conversations and simple company with Brazil produced a recognition in him, but he did not know precisely what it was. It seemed to be a present always, and it helped him, but the fullness was not alone. There was something else. He thought perhaps he had again found what he sought, though it seemed redundant that he once more found it. He had felt something similar at the Davis farm. Xenis felt as if he ought to seek more and when the pair came together, he discovered again the same thing, again he was unable to describe it, though he knew somehow that it was not the man, or woman, or whatever, he had sought. The pair looked to invite others into their state, wanted company. The art festival gave Brazil an opportunity to sell three of her statues, nothing expensive or large, but the rush of even this small success pushed her and so him into contentment.

Each time he left Brazil's home this seeming ubiquity followed to a greater or lesser extent, at least when he and she were together; they shared it with others and it came present for them as well. This continued sensation arrived immediately larger, coming ahead of him and pressing him further, and strangely he recognized it. Not definable, he knew it. Immediately present, it was something he continued to seek, not knowing that he could seek it no more than he already had. It was perplexing, yet now the feeling had changed and now the same it went. Again, it came and then was gone and again arrived. It was exhilarating, then absent. When he and Brazil performed simple tasks and ran errands, he sensed all of the things around him as he always did; he projected himself out and into, no will of his own except that what he willed. Out and into what was not clear, but evident at the same time. He thought over it for some time, and realized that it was as if this jutting out and into that he sensed was anything, it not a container of sorts, but contained itself. It was a part of any instance of pressing, as that pressing emerged. This jutting, this movement and continuance, was a priority, something coming before and part of whatever. Where this was he did not know or understand, but he felt that pressing moment each time he breathed, as if the breath of life were itself an indication of whatever it was.

"I get this strange sensation of pressing," he said to Brazil.

"That's odd."

"I'm not sure it is."

"Is it a bad feeling?"

"It's calming."

"Then why fight it?"

Xenis noted that same calm he felt when he returned to Chicago. He was bursting even when incomplete, yet the sensation seemed somehow full then not, again. He made Brazil dinner, or they read a book together, attended the theater, one of his personal favorites, and at one point during these excursions he found an intense desire to walk out of the restaurant, or rapidly exit the theater-enclosure, move about. So potent was the sensation. At times he had need to run when they walked together; he shook his head and stared when they talked. He felt at times overwhelmed – unable to articulate what. He suddenly recognized he as it and the pressing came loud – compelled him to where he was unable to say. Then, it was not only he. Then, it was not there.

"It's our mutual interests," he said. "It's the trust that we share and the kindness you express as well as the calm I return, but it's also stress and the carpet, your dog and justice."

Brazil frowned then grinned.

"I tell you..."

Just so intensely would his experience end; Xenis felt not just an absence, but nothing. The sensation just as powerful and enjoyable, but it was not at all. At times, Xenis bundled himself in as many clothes as he was able, though the day was balmy. Then just as suddenly he tore all clothing from his body and climbed onto the roof of her building.

"What are you doing?" she asked.

Silence was most-oft his reply, but occasionally

"There's nothing here."

On other occasions Xenis and Brazil played charades, or perhaps read, and he suddenly tore off his sweat-shirt and shoes, socks and undershirt. He waved his hands about, cried aloud something indecipherable. When his senses returned, he had little explanation.

"It must be broken," he said.

Brazil was careful with such moments, sometimes unsure of her safety. Still, she sensed in her longtime friend not the danger, as she had in the past, but simply otherness. He was capable of anything – especially if he changed so much and she became accustomed to his turns of behavior to a point. On their way walking to the fruit market, Xenis suddenly stooped down and stared intensely at insects gathering about a tree. He touched not one of them, but observed their movements and just as abruptly stood straight and threw a wide gaze into her, burst into a sprint around the park nearby. He wandered about back and forth, and eventually met her inside the fruit market.

"Sorry about that," he said.

The pair looked through the fruit.

"It isn't worse than what you used to do."

The two smiled.

"I can't get away," he said. "No matter how I try I can't leave it, and I want it never to depart, yet it gives me madness."

Xenis came free came quiet with this companionship, struggling to comprehend what he was understanding. He felt odd in his discovery and he wondered at the find.

"So quick?" he asked himself.

This state of affairs disturbed but at the same time satisfied him. As long as his moments like these continued, he felt close, near, maybe just a near-ness, but that made little sense. He needed to do nothing in particular; there was no ceremony necessary, no ritual demanded. He thought that perhaps he turned his attention toward and meditated upon an opening that had arrived, at least that was one way to describe it. He knew he would not discover it in a church, knew that he needed to pray to no god, no thing, no "higher power." No eternal parent waited to explain; it arrived through those moments. It must be recognized and grasped, or found wherever, and then it would come suddenly. Xenis began to wonder if he was able to discover its absence and where would that be. When Brazil worked, he cleaned and performed chores; he began experiencing that same sensation, a mere touch or sound a sight were all enough to bring it about, or perhaps they brought about only perception of it. Still, he had need of exiting occasionally; he felt as if his bursting must overtake all that he was, everything around him. Thus grew his habit of walking Brazil's dog in the park and there he met a woman who enjoyed his company. They exchanged the usual pleasantries and met twice in Brazil's space. Brazil said nothing, yet she came quiet and her eyes swelled with fat but tiny beads of circumspection.

"What's wrong," he asked.

She looked at him incredulous.

"Do you not want me to..?"

"It isn't that," she said dismissively.

"What then?"

"Maybe...," she said finally.

"What do you mean?"

"You're so different."

"I feel no different."

"You don't do the same things."

"You said as much," he said in a tired voice.

"I know, I know, but it's...confusing." Brazil stopped there, then continued abruptly. "I keep expecting some cruelty. I hear you're pursuing someone; I'm scared for them."

"Really?"

"Oh I know you're... You seem different. I think."

Xenis felt then again that pressing and jutting – the anxiety and rush of such a conversation intensifying.

"You can think of it this way..."

"Yeah?" a few tears she wiped from her face.

"There's something with me. The same with you. I don't know what to call it, but it fills me out and opens me. It seems to be me, but it's you as well."

"Yeah? Really?"

"It makes you and I the same, and in a sense we share it as same, we are the same."

"...OK, but what does this have to do with your cruelty?"

"Let me finish."

"OK."

"It's some priority, something coming before us, that's us. I'm possessed by it and you too."

"I'm you?"

"In a way, yes, but of course not."

"It's neutral. Not moral, not good, not bad, not even complete and yet it's full."

"?"

"...and it feels like it breaks me..."

"You've felt it?"

"I felt it in a way...and I feel it when I am here with you and.... Anyway, I think that as much as one can be cruel and ruthless, one can be caring and gentle. What allows both is what I'm talking about."

"I don't know what you mean."

"I don't either, but it's here, evident."

"It's all very vague."

"It *is* vague. I wish it were otherwise."

"Do you mean to say that you need to leave again?"

"Nothing of the kind. The opposite, in fact."

Brazil wondered. One who loses so much must be angry or resentful, but he treated others fairly; shared his resources; listened to and sympathized with her, most often. Her body and sadness recalled a very different man, and in spite of his considerateness and apparent decency, Brazil remained hesitant. Xenis had been caring for the chores and cooking for the two of them, but.... Each time Brazil attempted to talk, she felt a stiffness in her head and her spine straightened. When she brought up serious issues in the past, he had reacted badly, or with savage acuity.

"He would still do that kind of thing, wouldn't he?"

She asked about his former livelihood at the farm: what he did, how much did he earn. He explained, and she mentioned she always thought he would make a good instructor, or tutor. He again agreed, and yet thought nothing of it.

"I've been meaning to discuss something with you," she said to him finally, not knowing how to begin.

"I work in order to pay the rent..."

"Oh, oh. Yes, yes..."

"Let me finish. There are..."

"I know what you are going to say," he interrupted.

"You do?"

"Yeah. No, really. I'm trying to find something. Work-wise."

"Oh."

"Yeah. I need to find something that pays well enough."

"I see. Pays well enough?"

"And I need to get this thing out of my head."

Many different thoughts ran thundering along the vari-colored cotton of carpet on which they resided.

"What thing?" she asked.

"I can only explain it indirectly. It's part of what we were talking about."

"About what?"

"We were talking about cruelty."

"Oh yeah."

"I keep thinking about difference."

"You do?"

"There's some kind of absence that...comes. It stops what something is."

"It stops."

"Yeah. Where you stop and where I stop are our limits, yes?"

"Yeah."

"It's a...a kind of difference, a limit of something."

"Oh."

"It demarcates, makes possible. It's 'that a being not be all being', you know?"

"I think so. No."

"It makes. It's jutting out or opening. Nothing."

"Right."

"Existing, it escapes itself...it...not is part of it."

"Yeah."

"You know?"

"I know."

"It seems to be within itself presence and without itself as particular."

Brazil simply watched him speak.

"It exists without itself; that is, it's outside itself."

"And what has this to do with your getting a job?"

"Oh...I need to get that out of my head."

"And then you'll get the job?"

"Yeah."

"It's out of your head?"

"Not really."

"Then you don't plan on getting a job?"

"Oh. No. I do."

"Good. Good. And we can let it be without and outside and escape and all will continue as it is, except that you'll be earning money."

NICHTS

Nichts crowded loud and motion-filled cities and put them to plain sight. They put forth the what and then not; kept in place and not; drove aspect away and not; completed and kept from fulfillment. Nothing that comes from section of space to period of time was they, so to speak. There is no thing that is not made not, nor not made from not – the way not and Nichts brought part of what-is to any thing. It was not the Nichts but the what-is of something that made anything not what it is, but Nichts made what-is – Nichts have made something not quite what it is. Nichts propelled whats and made them clear; the whats were Nichts that broke them out but severed each what-is out and into, putting each thing in place to become other. Naturally occurring things – living beings – may be these; the what that grew into itself was possessed by a most clear principle, an acting in and endeavor inside. A body growing, a thought thinking, community gathering. The mere act of doing, the expenditure of time and energy for tiger to be tiger broke what of tiger out and into where it may come to be tiger no longer, Nichts. That a what was there made possible that what came to be other. Nichts that are what-is risked becoming, being the same, being the connection of becoming-to-becoming. Nichts as what-is and as presence were potent indeed. Here is presence for living and not.

NICHTS OF MIND

The black was tempting , its cool touch and tight pull keeping him. No wish to arise took him, leaden-eye warmth of nothing-doing. Some covering-not-he becoming him he wore clean on his face, covering a distinction not yet discerned. He knew he did not know what it was that covered him, covered what he wanted to refuse. Something was present of which he wanted nothing. No, he wanted none of this impending action, and he knew that he knew it must occur. It must come and it will envelope him, and he remained still able to say that no awareness arose in him of what it was, though it came to him familiar in manner. Something he would not enjoy; something he did not want, yet he refused to resist. Wait. Possibly there was no cover, nothing there; something else came. Sudden on sudden sluggishness did not overcome him, but the sluggishness became aware that lethargy surrounded him. He moved across the white and yellow and yellow again and flowered mass that folded him while he ascended full-through the fog.

"No. No," he said.

While he denied all that he wished to not come – it coming – the thought-thinking-he warned him. "No" was not correct, not the accurate reply. He wished this what to arrive with, come at him, and it was no stranger, not a bad nor unpleasant arrival.

"Oh, wait," he said to himself, mostly thought. "It's here."

His mind then adjusted and reworked itself, a configuration and active and driven moment, first recognition of understanding coming; one rolls in covers. He revolved again in the white and yellow sheet that embraced him with its pliant and slumber-coming grasp.

"Oh," he thought. "I'm...here."

His eyes opened to light.

"I always end up at her place," he thought.

He lifted his head and peered at the dog who returned the sentiment, dogness grinning dog-like what. Still slow from stupor of slumber he raised his head, again dropped, again rose, once more fell back. He believed something coming was not unwanted any longer, now realized its good. That to what he was accustomed, what was prior no friend, that movement of limb and stretch of muscle had appeared so vile and loathsome. He started this morning, that unhappy and beautiful movement of body gaining life and preserving vitality, and Xenis then lifted his form from the rest that engulfed him, shook out the drowse that continued. Water first companion. He recalled what the man in the center told him.

"You become a god."

This absurdity meant little to Xenis, yet he wondered at it.

"You become a god," he said in an accent that sounded like fine sand rubbed on glass.

Xenis knew the what the man meant, he thought. This person who granted him leave to perform daily labor performed himself the same tasks. He moved the dirt and cut the wood, carried the metal that transformed these entities. Something about this labor – this pain that made them nothing and bore profit for Others – brought forth a reality that had eluded Xenis long. Here was another what he sought, another version of vision and feeling that made actual what was already, not surrounding. The sensation of physical motion and the palpating of objects brought real what came present – open and protrusive. It was capable of change.

"Something is here," thought Xenis as he carried the metal frame for the old man.

This old one had asked him how he might demonstrate his ability, show his value, day laborer Xenis. Accustomed to the hardness and toil of farm-life, he easily bent his frame and moved the hard and pitiless material while the old man observed. Already, they perceived the recognition, needing nothing saying some what that was nothing. Geras looked to him and alongside of them and Xenis returned the moment just as the dog had that morning had done. This old man, frail and nothing, began working and toiling.

"Something is here," they thought.

And they knew it.

Both smiled and grinned as they performed the lowest brute tasks, but today was the day to see it again, whatever it is. Xenis would be for his friend and every moment no matter how small and seeming unpleasant made measure of pleasure and pleasant of moment until once more they do it again. At home and rested, he possessed a nebulous image of the work-day there in his head like the moment he arose covered in yellow and white sheets, but it had been there. It was something he had done, though the work was labored and the day gone, another coming. He returned to what made him larger, was able to see but little clearly, yet the pleasant exertion and suffering that would come to him that day now possessed him. Brazil, in no good humor, emerged from her room, frown in hand.

"You're working today?"

"I am."

"Good boy." She tapped him on the chest, open palm.

When Xenis arrived, old ever-present Geras awaited, realizing the seeking occupying Xenis. He sent the younger stranger to the distant end of the building, a place where work was most difficult and remuneration least. Xenis thought little of the distance and less of his earnings and, grasping the metal frame in vulnerable fleshy hands, he lifted one section of thick-steeled scaffold rigid-with-strength and top-heavy with the weight of dense metal. Configuring his body as comfortably as possible, he semi-buckled under the sudden strength of weight, hands, shifting-legs compensating for a fall barely avoided. Next weight he lifted confidently, yet part-way moving the strength shifted-weight lifted him and turned him around while the pull of earth pulled the scaffold from under his surety. The metal fell to the ground and clashed with the floor.

"Smack-pack!" spoke the floor and the scaffold, complaining.

Xenis, first surprised then angered, sought the eyes of the laughing old man. He felt suddenly the need to lash at someone or something, knowing the metal would take the punishment. He wanted to lift the scaffold and bring it down repeatedly onto the concrete and at once felt the shame of an urge given opportunity to come away from him. He did not recognize that part of him any longer, though it was familiar.

"Kill it."

He wanted that part gone, finished and departed. Xenis had thought it vanished and removed, but the anger waited.

"Try again," said Geras. "You need to find the center of gravity."

"I realize that!" Xenis surprised himself with the strength of his annoyance.

"It's the center that meets you and the mass of steel together."

"I know the physics."

Geras laughed no longer and the smile on his face departed, but still one felt the grin from his body come.

"Everything here and now is best."

"What is that supposed to mean?" Xenis said in a frustration that displeased him.

Old Geras, seeming frail, walked to the scaffold section Xenis had been carrying, propped it on end and lifted it easily, seemingly effortlessly carried it to its resting place. He seemed not to notice Xenis as he did so, and well did he balance on it. Xenis grasped another section of scaffold and balanced it as he had done the first, it waving slightly – weight bearing him staggering. When the body and his effort aligned the singularity of weight arrived, then almost with no effort did the metalwork cooperate.

"More like it."

The two men busied themselves for the first half of the day moving and arranging pieces of holders of workers. Xenis moved his frames less clumsily, and yet faltered thrice more trying to bring together the weight of the metal and his frame. Learned quick, then faltered and back again went the repetition of same as the labor and moment arrived. Nothing mattered more than what they did at that time, and the drudgery that would have been became a moment of unfolding for the what and not, not an unpleasant toil lacking in status and gain. These two continued the action and repeated the moment and Xenis brought his work to conclusion with hands-made-frame at day's end.

"I hired you with good reason."

Xenis each day did the same and again the same and the same again and once more differently same came and once more these men repeated the moment again and same and again. They performed this labor months-long and when old Geras asked if he wished to do any other kind of work

"No," said Xenis.

Adjutant to day-laborers, his was not the kind of work he imagined for himself, nor would an earlier raven-haired youth or rising man have considered moving metal back and forth, endangering his limbs. Still, he now longed after it, desired it to continue. Old Geras was able to refrain from such work himself, yet he continued to toil. Xenis asked why.

"Because it is" was the reply.

Xenis thought that he understood the spirit, yet he remained reluctant to inquire further. They continued to perform the same monotonous task, men rolling a boulder up a hill only to find that it rolls down another and up again lifted it.

"This ought to be tortuous. Why is this not horrible?"

He did the same thing, moved even precisely the same equipment, cleaned after the same men, and all for so wretched a compensation. Xenis expected to feel a sort of calm and a knowing, but there was with him the same pains in the morning and grievances. The days were as hard and unforgiving or comfortable as they had been, but he felt somehow closer. "To what?" There was no epiphany required. He lived this sense of what around him for long months and the satisfaction of contribution with hands, legs and movement occupied him. He possessed little and struggled mightily, and now suddenly the old one had need no longer of moving the metal back and forth. The work now not.

Surprised at Geras' lack of need for him, Xenis remained at home. He read and played like a child on the internet, believing he would take pleasure from the hiatus. He expected old Geras would call him, proving that this brief interruption was a test. He thought of merely taking another position or repeating some deed or act enough to fill that lack, and handy jobs in Brazil's apartment granted him some relief, but their number was finite. The closest approximation he found was that of cleaning, an endlessly needed task that remained incomplete no matter how often done. He performed this service for Brazil and found again the same moment. Still, again something came and then was missing once more. Familiar with the site where he and Geras had worked, Xenis surmounted the gate and having entered the building with the key he had retained, back and forth, forth and return he moved the awkward and unforgiving metal and again again-again. Brazil thought he was earning extra money.

"It's...a meditation I guess," he said.

"Where do you meditate?"

"The place I used to work."

Xenis edited for an online journal and tutored children; he educated illiterate adults. Some of his labor was remunerated fairly and some not, but every task he completed bore the same quality, a stamp that made his efforts pleasant. Each task repeated itself, Xenis made certain of that, and thus he learned quickly the parameters. Simple, but not as satisfying as his work with Geras. Another month passed and he received a message that old Geras again needed his services. Delighted, Xenis grasped firmly the opportunity. Again, he moved the high metal frames back and forth, and again Geras accompanied him.

"Something is here."

He appeared glad at Xenis' return and they took lunch together, talking of work and family. Old Geras fathered many children, grown now and wished to have someone with whom to talk. The two chatted about trivial everyday concerns, knowing something but not what. Xenis returned home and slept soundly, enjoyed Brazil's good company, yet a sensation came over him once more. It had been difficult to work through the few times that he had experienced it, and now it arrived strong, made stronger, came better. He wished to avoid it, but his desire greater was to embrace, although "embrace" was not quite precise enough to describe what he felt. He had once climbed stark naked to the top of Brazil's building and sat on its roof, not wanting to be there necessarily. He disrobed and climbed trees, houses, ladders and trucks more than a few times.

"They'll kick us out," Brazil complained.

Xenis felt these excursions were not enough. Something that he had gained from these odd moments he no longer found, but he did not know what might produce the same..."Release," he thought. "That's what it is."

Unable to prolong the same sensation climbing things, he paced Brazil's wooden floors, every so often vacuuming or scrubbing in order that they be clean and he immerse himself in a task. Pacing and tidying he looked through his belongings: books, pants, shirts, shoes and a few mementos. Not much hindrance, though he did not any longer enjoy possessing them. They were necessary, but many things around and about the apartment were not. Several toxins lived under the sink. "They can go." There were many bars of soap with the most disgusting of perfumes. "These *must* go." A rug that smelled of powdery perfume and insect repellent was not at all tolerable. Plastic cups, plates and bowls of all sorts did not need to remain, could be recycled. "Glass is best." Stuffed animals resided on shelves and porcelain figurines sat near the faucet and in the bathroom. He found decorative towels and magazines along with photographs and a series of bottles that simply lay around, no apparent use. Glass candles and wooden boxes too small to be of real utility with business cards inside; plastic boxes a tiny battery-operated fan large bowls that were never used unadorned hangers many seldom-used clothes and paint brushes neglected dog toys an old canine collar all these Brazil had not touched in the months that they had lived together.

"These can go."

He gathered these things together and looked at his pile of ragged clothing. ""I don't need these." These objects he rolled into several balls and fed three strong black plastic bags that he took out to the dumpster. When finished with this task, he felt an enormous gap of richness, a part of him relieved of itself – still there now lighter. Xenis then performed his daily routines, but he felt...buoyed as well. His step was higher and thoughts came brighter and with greater depth – not necessarily clearer – he sensed that he was able to recall more and when he napped and woke he recognized his quiet magnified his sleep – great rest death-like. Now born once more, now another, Xenis sat at the table in the kitchen as he pondered whether another such episode would give him greater birth.

Brazil arrived home tired and prepared for a relaxing evening. Her day had not been difficult, but not without frustration. Prepared for doing nothing and thinking even less, she observed several trash bags in the dumpster.

"Someone is moving."

When she entered her abode, she noticed immediately some things were out of place, a rug gone. Her space had been cleaned, and the lack of need to tidy it herself produced a grin. She entered her bedroom and changed from her more formal work-suit into loose-fit jeans and an oversized sweatshirt, art-habit. Relieved to be home, she went into the kitchen in order to retrieve a diet soda from the refrigerator. When she passed the kitchen sink, she did not see her porcelain Shiva. She took her drink from the refrigerator and looked around.

"Did you move Shiva?"

Brazil looked around more and noticed several not present items. The bottles she was collecting in order to build her glass arrangement were now gone and her magazines, the ones she needed for their paper, and some photos. Most likely in another place.

"Did you clean today?"

"Oh. Yes, I did."

"Whew," she said. "For a minute I was scared."

"Why?"

"My bottles and magazines aren't here. Where'd you put them?"

"Oh...."

"Where are they?"

"Outside."

Xenis picked up again his book as Brazil ran-walked out of the apartment. She jogged back to the alley where several bags of garbage hid inside a filth-ridden metal box with a plastic cover. After a bit of difficulty, she managed to find five thick plastic bags filled with her and Xenis' belongings, but she was unable to retrieve them, big girl. Thankfully, none of the bags had broken open.

"Get over here and help me take in these bags!" she screamed.

He rose from the table drowsy from concentration and walked quickly with Brazil. Calmly he climbed into the bin and unearthed two of the bags covered with dripping brown fluid. He brought them into the apartment, a dim realization beginning.

"What the Fuck!?"

She reached into one of the bags and pulled out sink-cleaning solution.

"Why was my stuff in the garbage?!"

Xenis sensed that he ought not answer as Brazil removed two porcelain figurines of Shiva and three paint brushes from one plastic gaol. One of the fire-segments from Shiva's circle had broken.

"You gonna answer me?!"

She removed more cleaning solutions and several magazines.

"Most of this stuff is mine!" she said as she threw two pairs of Xenis' pants across the room. She stopped removing items and glared at him.

"What's wrong with you?"

Xenis slowly widened his eyes.

"I needed to get rid of some things."

"You what?"

"I needed..."

"I heard you!"

"Ninety-per-cent of this stuff is mine!" she yelled.

"It's more like seventy-five, considering the amount of stuff you have."

She glared again.

"You'd find the sensation magnificent."

"What sensation?! What are you talking about?!"

"It's hard to describe. The sense of buoyancy is euphoric. You should try it. You'd like it."

"By throwing away all of my cleaning supplies? And personal belongings?"

She poked carefully into one of the thick, black bags.

"Throw away your own stuff!"

"Yeah... Maybe that was a mistake."

"Maybe?"

"You have to experience this with me," he said. "The sensation is indescribable."

"I've lived non-materialistically before."

"This is not quite the same thing. It's...a ridding that completes. You have the artist's sensibility. You know what this kind of thing is."

"It's a hard life, 'Xenis', living without any possessions. That's what homeless people do."

"No. It's not that. You need to remove everything."

"What do you mean 'remove everything'?"

"I need to be rid of something. I think it's perception."

"Perception?"

"Yeah. And prejudice."

"We all want to be rid of that."

"No. I mean the framework of perception. I want to be rid of that."

"Why?"

"I want to experience the kind of release I felt today, but in every way."

"By throwing away my stuff."

"I explained part of this to you already. I want to be rid of everything, even thought."

"How does one do that?"

"I don't know, but I want to find out."

"Meditate over a garbage bag of your own necessities, not mine!"

"That's supposed to be one way, but I'm talking about something different."

"Meditating over a garbage bag of necessities?"

"Just meditating," he said calmly.

"How's it different?"

"I'm talking about finding what's not there."

"What the hell does that mean?"

"I want to know nothing."

"You already know nothing."

NICHTS

Being itself moves but only into itself. Every thing or process is tied to being as a prisoner tied to a pole by being cylindrical, hard, and sturdy – immovable. Being continues because it breaks down being, being part and whole, which are and are not one another. Being is one more manifestation of any what that breaks down itself in order to be, the act of Nichts as what. The breaking down acts the cohesion of part and whole, and Nichts were the ends of the whats that gathered with other whats in fitting among one another. That they are different is that they brought themselves together. They then opened to being present for other-than, which was Nichts as limit that ceased where the beauty of a harmony arose. When once the whats came to be, they engaged in strife that moved being, a what prevailing. Humans are simply only one more manifestation of being that breaks down being as it is. What they break could not be made one, yet it was all the same: it was there. The strife moved being and there was not one what, not being altogether collected into one; they separated what. Yet, what was continued in its presence spread along all of its differences. Each of these manifestations of the same that were different, the emptiness that was full, were together existing. Now a man with raven hair whose temperament made him impossible, now a man who tended beasts and who loathes death, now one finding care for others.

THE STATE
OF POSSIBLE
DIFFERENCE

B razil sat at the kitchen table, her back slightly arched and head bent down, Xenis quickly removing all the belongings from five black bags. On each occasion that he brought out another figurine, he looked up at a Brazil, whose frame seemed to sag, as the wood planks of an aged ship droop and separate from one another. He quickened his pace and removed more items, each producing more anxiety than the last. Four of the figurines had been broken or chipped in some manner, and the magazine pages were no longer straight. As he perceived that practically every object was in some way damaged or disheveled, his breath drew in sharper – emerged in wisps. He placed the undamaged items where they had resided, hoping to have found their homes but not recalling precisely where they had been. At the same time he fought a desire to dash them against the wall, or to toss the larger objects out the window.

"I'm sorry. I'll replace anything that's broken."

"I'm stunned that you would do such a thing."

Xenis placed a Shiva and two dancers on the kitchen counter, their broken pieces spread about them.

"No wait...I'm not," Brazil said as she looked at them.

Each object strained him in some manner. When his eyes rested upon them each in turn, he felt anger rise. He wanted their absence, sought nothing from them, literally wanted that they be nothing. He attempted again to locate the original place where each object had been, and he feared asking where they ought to reside, somewhat terrified of the expression of Brazil's present mood. Brazil left her apartment and refused phone calls until late that night. Xenis found replacements for three of the porcelain figurines and immediately he returned to their rightful places the magazines, bottles and paper...he thought. He asked her about their locations only in bits and pieces so that she would not explode. She seemed annoyed continually and when she returned home from work the following week, Brazil looked under the sink and in closets and over the round-about places she often ignored, fearing abrupt absence of keepsakes. She talked after a time, but only out of necessity. Xenis once more apologized, promised to touch her things never again. He agreed to her suggestion that he occupy the smaller room in her apartment, a closet-like space with dingy, off-white walls. He would be able to do anything he pleased in that space. Xenis removed all of the nails from the walls and spread a sleeping bag across the hardwood floor. He wanted to dispose of his clothes.

"You need to work," Brazil said. "And you can't work naked."

Xenis thought it best to refrain from pointing out that certain jobs could be done in the nude, or even required nudity.

He labored during the day, and when able he occupied

himself with work that brought him close to that longed-for sensation. When he sat with himself and thought, he was not entirely certain why he had thrown out Brazil's belongings. He had wanted to be rid of them, certainly, but he also recognized their necessity and her strong reaction had reason to it. Xenis understood he needed senses, but there remained a beckoning, or something. He thought first of perceptions and then of the images of such perceptions and then he thought of the shapes of those perceptions and then he thought of the categories of those thoughts that formed the perceptions, something coming with all of them, and he rejected each of them consecutively – turned them away – attempted at least. Once he did so he felt greater what he sensed earlier, even better, though he knew it in no way. There he was and he was empty and glorious and not, attempting never to have, only satisfied with lacking. Bliss for a brief instant, though he knew he was still there, moment fading quickly. Disappointed that he was unable to sustain the sensation, he attempted again to find and then reject each of these things, these aspects of and around him. He again achieved the same sensation, short-lived, yet on this instance he recognized its simplicity, a necessary brevity. He removed his clothes and his perceptions his senses his thoughts once more, and continued the same sensation, and yet it came not enough as he repeated the ridding. He wished to perform another act that would further his elimination.

"What can I do?"

It occurred to him that many ways of ridding oneself of self are possible. Certainly, he did not want death. Though toilsome and intermittently insufferable, life gives great pleasure, its interests warranting continued interest. He knew nothing practically about what might happen – the future only relatively predictable – thus curiosity took him and no matter his material state he desired to remain alive. On the other hand, he was able to imagine some state in which he may willingly end his existence – pain too extreme boredom too long ability too short. Instead, Xenis sat in his solitary room at night, giving himself thoughts.

"God is meaningless."

"Music makes no sound."

"Eyes have no sight for depth."

These thoughts released him as before, still too briefly. He considered thinking these same things, or things like them, each night. His thought-not-thinking a regimen of sorts. As far as possible: no table was before him, no place-into-which the table occurred. He removed himself from that useful navigation in and among objects and found Brazil's butcher-desk and his correspondence with Geldsbaum. No sounds, not music, but poetic lines of Schubert and the mighty Beethoven. No spatial demarcation, yet he navigated the chair and bed in his room.

"Touch never tactile."

"Empathy serves no purpose."

"Decency is a species of violence."

The same sensation occurred to him, yet he thought that should he think these thoughts first and then remove his perception, his sensation may come easier and better, more full. He denied his eyes, removed his hearing and touched nothing.

"Harm is kindness."

"No human possesses thought."

"No creature has feeling."

He continued this practice late at night and in his bedroom for several weeks, all the while trimming and keeping neat his living-space; lifting heavy objects at work; reading and talking with – soothing – Brazil; looking after his body. As he continued this practice, his understanding of those creatures and things around and about him came loose and shaken. His thoughts came easier, made higher, gave brightness.

"All men are human."
"All women are human."
"All women are men."

Brazil gradually descended from the height of anger while Xenis kept his interests and possessions, such as they were, inside of his singular, diminishing space. He made Xenis calm, dressed himself properly and his words were kind and well-spoken. Most-oft. They dressed out of the ordinary: a long, oversized dark grey-and-almost-black gown and an inexpensive, second-hand black suit with barely perceptible pin-stripes. Xenis' short-cropped black hair complimenting his slender, steel-firm masculinity and the still ample figure of Brazil, they found their way to the opera-house. The over-large entrance-way opened space to attendees and the marble-lined walls – stately – marked solid gay solemnity. Theirs was an instance, an exquisitely beautiful silent piling of one here after another where art and beauty merge. The murmur of the crowd greeted the pair as they entered and Brazil's unwilling-unrecognized grin threw upon him an acceptance of a friend's apology. Cases lined with baubles and mementos waited as men in the broken colors of browns, greys and blacks moved their mates about the palatial space. She stared into one of the cases for a time; Xenis tapped Brazil on the shoulder, in sign to walk and wait. They slid past businessmen and musical politicians, came to a high stand of marble where a man in a red vest and bow-tie stood.

"What would you like, sir?"

Xenis passed to Brazil a questioning look, and she thought hard.

"You don't intend to?" she asked.

"Oh, no. Not I. But for you."

"You don't have the money."

"Go ahead. Please. We need this."

Brazil decided upon a German white wine, pointed to it with a question on her face. Xenis paid and purchased some water for his occasion. All near them seemed like them, smart-dressed, neat-fit, clad in tidy color. This "many" of the crowd were older of movement and slower of age, still-undiminished. Brazil walked along the gallery of costumes that lined the walls of the theater, each with its own photograph and exposition of when and who wore its habit. Xenis meandered alone through the thin-sequined gowns and the clacking shoes with the educated males inside and the jean-clad humans wearing sweatshirts. He had thought they were most like he, excited and vitalized by the coming-song and moving orchestra, yet not all belonged, video-games and small computers in hands. Nonetheless, Xenis found himself animated over his visit. He looked to an older couple, a pair who were not yet geriatric, but prime-spent. The woman wore a lady sport-jacket and matching slacks, smelled of the lightest hint of Jasmine; corduroy wrapped marble round the man in a brown and black hue. They conversed mostly with themselves, occasionally nodding to others who recognized them. Xenis nodded to the man who slightly nodded return.

"Good evening, " Xenis said playfully.

"And to you," said the man.

"I'm excited."

"Oh?"

"I haven't been here in years. I lost my place."

"I see," said the man, somewhat uncomfortable.

"My name is Xenis," reaching out his hand.

"Kent. This is my wife Marjorie."

Kent observed the dingy suit, dark eyes and skin color on Xenis.

"How do you do?" Xenis asked in what seemed like a genuine question. Kent raised his chin a notch.

"Are you a Chicago native?" he asked.

"I am native to earth."

"Ah." And Kent laughed as he looked at his wife.

"Why do you ask?"

"I'm not sure. You seem perhaps out of place."

"Always. I'm always out of place. I don't think I know my place." He laughed.

Kent and Marjorie quick-glanced at one another, excused themselves to other distractions. Xenis observed a young man accompanying two girls. A yellow, button-down shirt without tie black beneath made him sharp, and lively. The girls inhabited gowns, long – one rust one yellow – giggling in the corner and pointing in different directions. They noticed Xenis and laughed again, almost pointed. He moved toward them quickly in an aggression he did not recognize; the smiles ceased. He turned eyes toward them and talked as if they were long acquaintances, terrible friends.

"Fine evening."

They nodded, glanced at one another, seeming to talk only among themselves. They turned down their heads and began moving their fingers on top of their familiar flat, rectangular pads, laughing occasionally. They glanced up every so oft, observing him observing. They paid no attention to him otherwise, and Xenis was poised to ask the young man a question when Brazil arrived.

"What are you doing?" she asked.

"Nothing. I was about to ask a question."

"What kind of question?"

"I wanted to know if these young persons know what kind of wood makes a violin."

"You were not about to ask that," Brazil said in a low tone.

"I was."

Brazil turned to the young ladies who were preoccupied with

their tablets.

"Is he being cruel to you?" she asked.

"Yes!" said the petite and playful lady in the martian-rust gown.

Brazil extended suspicious and accusatory eyes at Xenis.

"What?"

"What are you doing?"

"I said...nothing, Nothing," Xenis claimed.

"Mmhmm. You asked them about nothing?"

"No. I did not even talk to them at all."

"Is that true?" Brazil asked Peter.

"Yes, ma'am."

"See?"

"Well...you don't have a good track record."

Xenis paused a moment, sagging slightly.

"I suppose that's fair...but I didn't do anything."

"OK. OK. Be sure to keep your clothes on."

NICHTS

Part of the activity of things, they move whats into themselves, breaking down what was and opening is into what that will be – sometimes painful. They are the act of the what that was not what the what was, being part and being whole. That act separated and united the part as whole and the whole as part. This separation is a motion that brought the what into its own *integritas*, but there was an opening-to that the Nichts brought to the *integritas*. The what opens to being other-than; it is the manner of the what that makes it more available to other. A change in energy; an alteration of form; a transformation from one life form to another. That act proceeded through what as moment to moment. Bringing moment to moment is the opening of the what as it is to what will be – sometimes the what as it was and at other times the what that arises from the kind that the other what was. The what is there as an affirmative act that proceeds through its act negatively. Humans call it difference; change; disintegration, *et alia*.

PLAYS GUEST VIOLIN SONG AUDITORIUM

The light mood that pervaded Xenis dimmed slightly as the pair again passed through the marble interior. Brazil tapped him on the chest affectionately, and he attempted a grin, un-succeeding. They found their way to another marble kiosk where Xenis adjusted his drab black suit. One moment passed when he thought again of the time when he had more resource than wisdom and gloom spread from spine to limb. Brazil ordered another white wine, taking two hefty sips quickly. She gathered the sights of the on-goings around her once more. Noting the lack of joy in Xenis' eyes, she took him away from the wine booth, neglecting to retain her glass. They took their seats. Lightness in limb and clarity of head returned to Xenis slowly as he settled into sitting, a state of mild and quiet mirth. There he put again beneath his mind the loss that had carried him long; they perused the brochure. Xenis removed his sports jacket and draped it about the back of his chair as they read and compared notes. He listened to the music in his head, preparing for the actual, and repeated the thought that had come to him.

"Music makes no sound."

Xenis noticed something, around-about, within and beside,

overtop. It was everywhere, yet he noticed it in specific things. It was there and impossible to describe and he wondered at it thoroughly. The words on the pamphlet were mere words, in themselves only words, bits of thought and then whole feelings, ink and lines, curves and shape. The same applied to his seat where the metal of the seat was not seat itself, only metal – something that could be a door a back-brace a farming tool. He fidgeted. The pages were pages in themselves and not the brochure. He thought then of himself and even he, his arms, were not he, but water and protein with hemoglobin. Still, he was whole, maybe.

"Now, this is simple," he murmured.

"What?"

"Oh nothing."

The thought of a violin came to him. The wood of the violin was not violin; it was wood. The strings were not violin; they were metal and animal gut, or only metal. The violinist was the violin because the violin played music only with the musician; it played the song that played the musician; the auditorium fit the violin into its play, and yet obviously the violin and the violinist were not the same; the auditorium did not play the violin; the song did not listen to the music. Yet, the audience did play the music; the auditorium sounded it to the audience. The audience, the violin, the violinist, the music itself all played the music.

"It can expand. Think of your *Truth & Method* here," he thought to himself.

One could expand more. The formation of the humans, a Bildung, directed their being in a particular manner. They develop a common sense, a *sensus commnis*, that directed their preference for a kind of music, a what, in a certain trajectory, and of course these humans develop a judgement from all of these things together. They express their preference of judgement through language that integrates their what into the playing of the performance during the evening.

"But Gadamer did not think of this."

The performance existed and acted in all of them; their being lay in each other. Everywhere he pointed his head he perceived similar relationships and connections: the curtains, the marble in the walls, the fabric on the seats, the parts of the play and the song and the singing. The concepts of the characters; the conception of the plot. The murmur of the gathering audience.

"Nothing?" he thought.

The hair on the men's heads and the thoughts in the women's minds were theirs and yet were not they at once, had to be, and the emotions of their heads were not their own, but they were the performance, the thoughts reaching their what in the play of the music. Xenis thought it strange that this thought occurs, and that elements must not-be in order to be themselves continued upon him.

"The simple nothing of difference leads to being residing in other-than."

The bow is needed for the violin and yet, it is not the instrument itself, and even the violinist is not the violin and yet is the instrument playing, necessary for the instrument to be what it is. They become, these whats, and make actual the possibility of other whats through being whats, but because of difference.

195

"It's only a part," he muttered.

"What?"

These primordial thoughts would not leave him, partness of part as some kind of not-ness. And then a thought terrible and distressing came to him. The lights dimmed and at last Xenis was able to turn his attention to the performance, playing the players acting the music. The sound's impending movement calmed him in ways that he recalled, yet even as Xenis listened, he became confused. He heard music, but also mere vibration then arrangement alone. He saw actors as actors and as costumes and as mere homotheria. He listened for the violin.

"Can you hear that?"

"What? The music?"

Brazil pondered her friend a moment, but looked on. When the music played, he heard hollowness and friction, not notes; he listened to wire and cat-gut, not fine gravity. The Count was a noble, but metalloprotein and a mass of water, and the water and the mere sound of the voice, and not the music of the sound and the character on the stage, came to the fore. He looked to the audience and the seats that were no longer chairs, the building and the acoustics were not the walls, but the reverberation came forward. He felt a touch of vertigo and during the last act was compelled to surrender to the washroom. He walked around the end of the seating and up an aisle; he noted that the carpet was fibrous plants, and the movement of his limbs was earth and the motion that moved him up the aisle was the aisle and the performance-with-him-walking was not the performance, but he was unable to bring himself to the end of the aisle. It was not as if the walk-space was long and slow, but again he sensed that all was happening and about to be at once, had already happened. The walking was he and the floor was not the ceiling, but the usher before him was not not a mass of protein, and protein alone. When he looked forward he headed south, but south was down and down was left when up was down, and Xenis was not moving at all when movement meant changing one place not another, yet another space came closer and there was obvious change. Somehow he arrived outside of the theater and he attempted to set correct his certainty once more where a straight line there made easy the perception that directed him from day to week and back to the same day and within the year that made up his life. He was able to balance himself upright, had been granted that favor by fate at this moment. While his thoughts seemed to have remained what they were, and not become other than what guided him, he feared that again this destruction of what-is around him might befall him and undo him as all seemed becoming, becoming seemed undone.

"This cannot be," he thought. "How did I lose it?" he asked a man beneath a captain's hat.

He found that he did not recall what was there and the what-is he was supposed to recall. His thought was on the act and then upon the song and a bowstroke, and then it came to him that his thinking was outside the theater and then he found himself beside a kiosk in 1933, June 22. The moments of his mindfulness came to him slip-slap side aflicker in rushes and pieces, and when he attempted to take hold and to grasp what he had known, he found the space of his thinking moving away and coming, and each of his experiences in the other as the other, able to be other than they. Xenis at last found vertigo once again, and he sat in a chair near the bathroom entrance. Now, everything seemed gathering again, came linear, and he focused upon one of the paintings on the wall, gave himself reference and arose in an effort to find again the seat and the sitting that comforted him not so long ago. He stepped forth and that step made move, and thus he comforted himself, but found he had not moved at all. He sat again in the seat near the washroom and again attempted to direct his thinking to where it might bring him home. He perceived concernedness before him and there was as well a blue and grey color.

"Blue and grey concernedness?" he asked himself.

No, it was not a "ness" that confronted him. That particularity was different from the particular and the same. Suddenly, his sight changed, he again perceived the care and the blue, but caring and blue what was the question. This mass extended over him and he heard a sound, not muffled but inaudible, that was nothing in particular, except that the sounds made into something that music which was voice. It arranged itself in a way familiar and yet Xenis heard nothing he was supposed to hear. He needed more than the mere vibration that entered his head, and then he heard letters, then words and gathered together these meant something, were not mere words and sounds but came language and spoke.

"Are you alright?"

Xenis recognized that a nod was proper at this time. He did not know that nodding was the shaking or the bobbing of the head, all these released from him. He understood that he felt again that bliss he had sought, this time more potent. The moment of liberation, or a version of it, came upon his beckoning. It was his and what he was differed from what he was when it also remained. Xenis was annoyed and frightened at once when the blue and grey mass again made noise.

"Xenis? Are you ok?"

He concentrated, though he wished to remain in that state, and he slowly brought back the he to himself, and the sadness

– mad depression – that came toward him heavily threw him back to linearity. The chair was again the chair and he recognized the washroom and that blue-grey and concerned noisy that was before him came again to make for him a comforting and decent man.

"Are you alright?" Dean repeated.

"Dean."

"Xenis."

"It's good to see you again."

"I'm glad you're alright."

"Where are we?"

"We're at the theater, headed back to our seats."

As Dean gently and in kindness brought up Xenis, the voice was not sound, nor noise and the blue was not only hue, nor was the grey and the kindness not only the reasssuring voice, but these, this matter, once again gathered together to make bus-station friend. They walked and again came clearer what Xenis needed in order to navigate once more. His clouded head made certain the tips of the things around him. He noted complete things and he thanked his friend who had found and taken him, returned to the aisle where he began. His wits wound round him, he found his seat with Brazil. They watched and the grand locution and beauty of the theater came deeper and more potent for him than ever it had before. "There's so much that is hidden," he thought. These supposed appearances folded into one another unfolded, un-straightened. A glimpse that Xenis decided he needed. Yet, he straightened and guided what was needed inside the track, and what-is came clearer still, now more limited and thus defined. He was able to make simple enough to see the folded what about him. The performance done, he acted as always, but looked around him. He had come again was his thought and all came to him once more as it had when first he came about, first-born. He had been away for only minutes.

"Are you alright? You seem dazed," she asked.

"'Not' has escaped."

As the pair emerged from the auditorium, they walked slowly, discussing the performance. The count singer had been particularly good, but Marico lacked something. They walked out and onto the sidewalk where a figure in blue and grey awaited and greeted. Xenis smiled as he pressed his hand into Dean's

"How are you?" he asked.

"I'm well enough," said Dean. "I ought to ask you."

Brazil cleared her thoat.

"Oh, yes. This is Brazil."

"Nice to meet you."

"I didn't know you were a fan of opera."

"I'm not, not so much, but a friend gave me a ticket. Excuse me a moment. I need to find someone."

Dean looked around the sidewalk and street, seeming confused and more than a bit concerned. He disappeared into the lobby and after a brief time emerged directing an old man. They moved slowly, but one was able to see clearly the animation in John's eyes. His effort to move himself was successful, though he looked as if he were sore from exertion. The two-pair of Xenis Dean Brazil John proceeded down upper Wacker.

"We can't take the train," Dean said. "We need to be dropped off near our door."

Xenis offered a taxi to accompany them with old John and Dean, sharing the expense; a comfortable van ride carried them north, the four finding themselves at John's home.

"Come in and have a nightcap," said Dean.

The Verdunkeln home was decorated in a Spartan manner. Plain, but aesthetic, flat beige covered many walls, but several paintings and colorful graphic art resided there as well – a lot of mahogany. There were not so many pieces of art to clutter the space, yet enough to cover most areas. Photographs, shelves with keepsakes and figurines, even a quilt adorned the walls. No dust coated the walls or floor, and the television-room, the dining room, kitchen and one of the bedrooms shined immaculate, everything seeming in proper place. Brazil and Xenis were deposited in the living room, awaited tea and wine. Old John remained with them while Dean collected potables.

"I had the most incredible experience," Xenis began.

Old John nodded and waited for the story.

"I was listening in the auditorium when everything around me went mad."

"Oh?" said John.

"It was the strangest thing."

"What was it like?" Brazil asked as Dean entered.

"It was as if the seats and the sounds and the persons around me...changed suddenly. But it wasn't a change, really."

"What's this?" asked Dean as he sat.

"You remember, when you helped me up."

"Oh, yeah. But I didn't help you up."

"You didn't?"

"No. You were wandering around."

"I was walking?"

"Yes."

"That's even more odd."

"How's that?" Dean asked as he passed round yellow colored liquid, each to each.

"I had no sensation of walking, only...I don't know. I distinctly felt that I was not moving."

"You were definitely moving."

"The whole experience was surreal and distressing, and at the same time I felt...it sounds trite but...elation."

John sipped his beer and winked at Brazil playfully.

"Everything...broke down. It was as if I couldn't tell...what belonged to what."

"That sounds frightening," Brazil said.

"It wasn't frightening, but it was distressing." Xenis laughed.

"I think I want to experience it again."

"Sounds strange to me," said John.

"Oh?"

Dean glanced at John and fidgeted with his hands, wriggled about in his seat. One or two more times the eyes of the men met. John confidently began.

"Are you a religious man?"

Brazil and Xenis exchanged glances similar to John's and Dean's. Xenis broke the silence.

"Well, it wasn't something that..."

"You're not a religious man?"

"Um. No. It wasn't anything like that."

"Very strange. It sounds like a religious experience."

"Why does that have to be?"

John turned down his head rolled up his pupils, maintaining eye contact with Xenis.

"What would it be?"

"A non-out-of-body experience?"

"You may not want to joke," John warned.

Dean shifted in his seat and cleared his throat sonorously.

"Whatever this was, it wasn't a religious experience. I...encountered what was there."

Brazil glanced again at Xenis. John sipped from his drink, and as he did so, he winked once more at Brazil who frowned thinly.

"What a performance!" said Xenis.

"It was beautiful," Brazil gladly agreed.

"I'm always amazed at how someone can sing with such projection. Just that much is an incredible feat."

Dean agreed.

"I tried to sing like that when I was younger, but my voice is simply not strong enough. I even took singing lessons at one point," said Brazil.

"Really? I never knew that." Xenis shifted in his seat and leaned away from Brazil. "I can't imagine it."

"You couldn't?"

"Well, maybe."

"I'm perfectly musical."

Dean laughed and taking cue Xenis smiled and attempted to join him. Dean asked if anyone wanted more drink.

"My boy, I don't know where you been. Those strange spells of yours don't sound so good," John said abruptly.

There was then the brazen outburst of a deadening silence. The two-pair suffered the discomposure for a brief time, talking opera and plans to hear more. Xenis asked how Dean and John knew one another. Dean related his fall from Bane Accounting and his satisfaction with assisting John.

"It seems you've risen," said Xenis.

"I like to think so," said Dean.

John winked at Brazil once again from the corner of his chair.

"Well, it's late and I think it's time we go." Xenis met his eyes with Brazil briefly.

"Thank you for your hospitality, Mr. Verdunkeln, and you Dean. Thanks for your help earlier."

"You're quite welcome. Any time," Dean said.

Brazil and Xenis gathered their belongings and bowed slightly as they shook hands with John and Dean. A strained quiet moved them along the hallway.

"Where did you meet that guy?" asked John.

"At a bus stop, I think."

NICHTS

They were in some ways the same, possessing no difference other than not. Yet, they possessed similarity – not similar not different. They drove away what is there, no matter what it was, banishing even absolute not. Having driven away themselves they beget, yet nothing comes from nothing. They were that part of what that is responsible for being other than itself, perhaps bringing about not or driving away nothing. They had a way of opening what-is, not merely opening what, but they opened something to becoming other. And what-is broke down and out of what it is. They in this case – also whats – make what-is not what it is at all in various ways. They deceive others with one kind of character to one, and another kind to another, species of not. Fully in the what, making possible, they are-were-will-be capable of directing someone here and there, into one thought and at once another. One may apprehend one manner of them now and later not. One may see something, what-is, that simply does not appear. Their not-ness was the appearance of appearance, no longer really not. Plays of heat and light were life-granting desert water; fruits were ovaries; bovines were steaks; cat-fights were baby-screams; knowledge was power; glass was sand; plants were rubber, and an impoverished aristocrat was an ontological baron.

NOT OTHER AS "NOT" OF WHAT-IT-IS

Alone the next, clear and hopeful weekday morning, John Verdunkeln pulled the plastic bin from under the Altima, and began to run his hands along its exterior. It needed some attention, but remained in sound condition. He was careful to retain as much of the black, viscous fluid as possible. Already dirty, he wanted no stains on his clothes; washing off oil annoyed him. The pan was cumbersome with the black in it and he loathed spilling the disgustingly dingy and viscous fluid, but John found a more permanent container with a cap, another petro house for spent lubricant. He de-stooped himself, straightening his back and wiping his hands after he stood.

"The old girl has life in," he murmured to no-one.

Ordinarily, he would not have thought twice about someone else changing the oil, but he felt motivated – had exercised his limbs, and moved his thoughts about, around and within what breathed into him. Nothing impeded him – at least nothing that had not impeded him when he was a fifty-year-old man. Dean did not assist, and John wanted none of the younger man's help. He opened the car door and put the key inside.

His fille started like any other day, this time fresh with thick mucilaginous blood. John backed out from the dark, detached enclosure, then made trek around and about blocks merely observed five years now. He maneuvered hastily, nervous occasionally, but with diligence and some determination he navigated five miles of streets – not yet braving highway travel. He even dared to meander into Nick's parking lot, overtop a section of curb-lawn.

"You alone?" Nick asked.

John beamed. The men rode around block about block, bought snacks, beer with spirit. When John reentered the dark and waiting enclosure, the afternoon had shrunk and a cracked tail-light and three fresh dings accompanied the Altima into the garage. Old John found himself in his seat. He awoke much later, still sitting in the chair where he had fallen. Nine hours had passed when he heard kindness coming – footsteps and a hovering over him.

"Are you alright?"

John was able to move his limbs only slowly as he arose. His back ached and when he ambled to his room, the only objective in his mind was bed. He resided there for a day, the next day able to move about his living-space but unable to perform most ordinary tasks. Dean tended to him, scheduled an examination with his doctor.

"I don't need it."

Dean insisted and John slowly recovered over the next days, at the time of the examination seemed to have returned to his able self.

"You have to act your age," doctor Drutter said. "You

can't just one day exert yourself like that. A gradual increase in activity is best."

John scoffed.

Dean opened the door of the Altima and John entered with effort. The walk to the car had taken some time, though Dean had offered to wheel the old man. John found his steps into the car exhausted and prepared again to make his way into that blissful and spirited, queen-sized cradle. When he was again risen and ambulatory, he had words in his head.

"He's wrong."

"He knows what he's doing," Dean said.

Once again alone on a weekday and lacking the kindly Dean, John walked toward the kitchen. He moved himself slowly into the living room, kneeling in front of the window where all the light arrived into his living-space. He packed a few sandwiches into a paper bag and walked down the stairs of his condominium as quickly as he was able, started the Altima once inside. Found himself at Nick's place.

"What's this?" Nick pointed to a long, fresh and narrow dent in John's Altima, resident with four somewhat older dings.

"What's what?"

Nick pointed once more to the dent.

"Oh. Dean. Must be."

"Oh. Where to?"

"Same as before."

They drove north and then southwest and came west-direct for a considerable time, not curious over direction. John grew annoyed at the road-bumps he encountered every so often – the city was obsessed with regulation he thought – but he beamed satisfaction and contentment came quick; his ability-undiminished navigated again his surroundings. Now John was no longer inside limited, feeling able to haul iron or fell the trees that blocked his way. Some shade that had fallen over John in his old age slipped away, not gradually not suddenly but as a cotton cloth slips from atop a statue, clean and smooth. He moved now, turned himself where he was going, inspired his friend to do the same. John pushed away that blackening, the darkening of his life toward another part of him – not wanting to say or think over what he had changed, though he recognized it as always a part of his experience. What John pushed he relocated, did not remove. It was something terrible and inevitable, a constant kept creeping upon him, and that odd, olive-hued friend of Dean reminded him of it. John certainly did not like that one at all. Something he had, some possession...no not a possession but some part of his constitution, made John wince, he needed to push that one as far from him as possible.

John did not recognize what street he occupied, nor to what street he ought to return. Nick and he asked for directions twice, purchased a map over which they argued; several hours passed before the men arrived at John's home. Still curious about the scrape, a patch of leaves a branch he found jutting out of his Altima when he returned home, John thought a moment. "Need to speak to Dean about the car" he wrote on a notepad. He turned on the television and watched for a moment, falling fast into another nine-hour convalescence. Again, Dean coaxed John from his chair and into his bed where he remained. He asked Dean to fetch his meals in his room, and refused a shower. Comfortable, he needed to do very little or nothing, knew his needs would be tended. Dean continued to clean his room cook food pay bills. John felt present and new, though tired.

"Have you been driving my car?" he asked Dean.

"No...not really. I use it to buy groceries, but that's all."

"Hmm. I see."

"I'm careful, Mr. Verdunkeln. Don't worry."

"I don't want anything happening to you."

Dean laughed.

"You laugh, but you need to be careful."

"I can take care of myself."

"That guy, Xenis is his name?"

"Yeah?"

"You need to stay away from him."

"Just rest for now," said Dean.

The next day John attempted to raise himself from bed, but found himself again unable to move. Always, he fell back into a drowsiness that pulled him into the sheets and pressed his head on the pillow.

Jumping about, a thought familiar and yet one whose presence was not always apparent plagued Xenis playfully. It poked him in the way an enigma does, catching interest and keeping one near, lightly mocking. This one sang, teasing, refusing to leave. He had never witnessed such a thing as he had at the Opera house. He had never found himself so confused as when he wandered into a recognizable space that abruptly became somewhere else. That theater had always been a beloved and familiar place.

"Everything was broken."

The resulting residual confusion broke his senses, shattered his momentum into a plethora of different, similar, directions. Xenis did not think badly, not illogically, but rather his mind moved with that April grace of a comfortable, new spring day. The glad mood that arose at the same time exhilarated him; not only was each moment cheerful and his chores the best thing doing, but his will had a desire for his own endeavor. It broke out upon the world in intense interest. Yet, Xenis knew not what to do. Though there was a fresh contentment in him, a fear enveloped him that pieces of matter and means, every every-thing, may become something else, as if disruption and scattering come pattering in an unpredictable, multi-levered seesaw. Now the fear tore at him and made him shrink and now his drive prodded him to leap into the unknown. Only some portion of his prior ground had remained, and the loss of certainty woefully distressed him. Still, that moment had given Xenis a path – somehow made more, though he did not realize it.

"Broadening in the havoc" came into his head.

Xenis flattened himself over his bed for a time, staring at the ceiling. Not willing to move, he wanted instead his thought to rouse him. He loved it, hoped for its continuance, yet was again fearful of what it was and what it meant. He arose finally from his flat piece of foam on the floor and formed it into a roll. He folded his sheets with his thin pillow and placed them on top of the roll, as he had done each morning for some time. The thought remained, bid him get moving. After he had eaten and dressed in tennis shoes and saggy coverings, Xenis walked out into the Saturday-morning air. The thought circled the space around him, a faithful purple. He had slept for a good long while and such slumber was not an ordinary occurrence. Rested and relaxing, he was at once vitalized with the energy of the morning. Eyes not wide, he did not play-act nor toy with games – he had rarely done that even in childhood. He felt the spring and step of energy, that working inside that had become familiar in recent years. No matter what he should learn about the day, he would be content until he slept. He began shifting his legs one in front of the other until a calm trot generated him. The cool air hit his face just right as the first comfort of jog arrived, that cool yet warm comfort of pin tapping locomotion without perspiration. His jog carried him around and about, locating him here and then an added here, and he again came upon the sight of his neighborhood. Not many places of real import to the city or anywhere else existed in his locality, except that said places simply were. His run took him along Clark street through a Hispanic section and south to Devon where he turned up toward eastern food and grocers. When he came to Damen avenue he turned left and followed the trains-path again south. The cement walkway pounded at his feet and so he crossed into the soft grass on the west side of the street, running against traffic. After a brief time he decided to climb the fence on his left in order to jog along the gravel and grass of train-tracks. The fence-climb demanded more effort than he expected, but presented no insurmountable problem, and when he landed, he stopped. Something ceased him, posited him there. There, beside the fence and growing into it, stood an ordinary tree slumped fairly, but pressing out into the space that it made, gave it room, its leaves and smaller branches swaying, acquiescing to the occasional push of tearing wind. Xenis gathered up the refuse left behind around the trunk, the paper-crumple plastic bag unbecoming the worthy Ash. He stared at it a moment and the great plant took hold of him, upholding and continually making the what of tree. Some moments witnessed Xenis and the tree regarding one another, but then things changed, or seemed to change. No longer a plant stood at hand with him. No, greater than that. Its stem came center and elongated, tree-ness alongside. This stalk arose as from a gathering of geometric shapes, a circle a cylinder a shaft presiding. Again it changed, an alteration faster that was no difference. Now it came to be the circle that made it and then the centerpoint that centered the circle, which in turn propped the stem that presented the tree. It remained this point for some time and then quite suddenly it was a line that circled the center, cycling the circle. The motion that made the whole great-plant-tree-ness arrived and at-once once-more tree appeared tree.

"What's this?"

Xenis stepped backward half-step and again regarded the sturdy Ironwood, and in all the time the great plant did not change at all, speaking silently as trees do. Now leaves came, no whole of tree at hand, the organs of the great plant turning light to vitality. The leaf was then green and green-ness; light within his eye; frequency-appendage-rain-gatherer.

"These are not tree."

When that thought emerged, Xenis realized its lack of truth while tree was suddenly tree again, yet there was a non-straightness to it. The frequency of green was not a leaf, nor was the green an appendage. Some kind of something surely was here and Xenis suspected a mischievous limitation held him. Some inherent part of each piece, green light appendage, was making each not the other and defining each piece by its very not-ness, the lack and the limit friends and conspirators.

"Not tree, not leaf, not light, not photosynthesis." All the same, "Leaf."

Xenis was amazed at this plain and everyday thought because of its lack of every day. Yet, his main concern was that this playful and dangerous whatever-it-was was bothering his person just as his thought pestered his mind. There existed, so to speak, something lacking in the buildings and wooden benches nearby, in the rocks beneath the tree. They were the air and his feeling of oddness as well as his worldview. Yet, they did not reveal themselves. No, these arose in whats, or presence of things. Xenis could not explain it, except to say that they are there and...not. He thought he recognized the tree and the grass the tracks the gravel. He did, yes. Yet, something other resided there with these things as what they were, unseen and un-hiding. No direct perception of them was at hand, but he was able to sense their presence, such as it is. Somehow he knew it through the acts around him. Not here but there was the leaf, not leaf but green was the chloroform, not green but rain-gatherer was the leaf. It was an experience similar to the on at Lyric, but he could probe more deeply.

"Wait a minute. The leaf is green."

All of these things were themselves their own kind, whats, yet each was something else. Xenis stood and thought about this simple, apparent fact.

"How did such a thing come to be?" he asked the tree.

The tree did not know, apparently. He knew that some of these things that were the leaf and not were themselves secondary. Green is not primary to leaf.

"No. I've seen yellow leaves."

Still, green was there. This leaf and this green were not separated, and Xenis sensed that the greenness was greenness and had a what all its own, except this greenness was this leaf - a chemical composition. So, the greenness was not diminished because it was not primary to leafness. It was this leaf. Yet, another realization arose and came to bother him. Something was perhaps toying with him. Not maliciously, no. It seemed as if it wished to make him perceive..., as if broken into perception that what what was seen, wreaking havoc with his morning. It, or they, teased him as his thought had done, singing-hiding and then revealing themselves momentarily, or so he thought.

"Nothing can do such things."

These were not multiple, nor were they lone, and they were not number nor singular, not multiple.

"Not quantity."

They laughed at him, showing angry faces.

"You cannot be rid of us," he heard.

Xenis knew that he had not heard a sound, and still he nodded.

"Remember the wood."

    "It's a violin."

"Or door, or paddle, or bed, or desk."

Xenis knew that he had conversed with no-one, no animal, nothing. He looked again towards the tree and again came not a change, but a difference that was same – the shapes and circle the light the green of leaf and now gray of trunk. Still, within this moment he concentrated and when the circle arrived, he latched onto it, made it what was there. Surprising him, the circle remained, stayed present. When he let go, the circle then left him – no farewell. The center-circle, one painfully necessary midpoint of what-it-is a tree, came next and again Xenis was able to keep it there – concentrating on that one event and thus pressing out all other. He perceived nothing else. The dot was fine and needed, but plain, and Xenis let him go after a more brief stay. He next brought the green of tree and the grey of bark the light, then the light made energy. Each in turn stayed as he filtered what else was there, always more available beneath-near-within-around and all other. When Xenis let go all of these things in order to return to his ordinary state, his annoyers again ran rampant; how many he lost count. Up came down and tree rounded circle and circle shone light, and these falsities that were whats revealed to Xenis how he had seen so narrowly, perceived tree simply. The only real presence was that appearance had made any what seem primary.

"There's a universe there," he thought. "Am I going mad?"

NICHTS

They moved aging men into greater age and grew animals from infancy. They opened what-is to what-it-is-not, and they did these things by breaking them out and sundering what they were. They made not what is; they lacked nothing as they enacted existing things, and so they were. That they were not really not came as no shock; they thought-nothing felt-nothing did-nothing. They or it did the nothing of what something, what-is, comes to be – what it is. Their whats did not fully exist, if we think of whats as not – no full being to being, but rather what one calls being really exists on the extremities of nothing. Not needing any place they hid somewhere between the being-not what anything is and being what it is not, emerging from what-is being. Not only a part of the particularity of what, they produced the not-what emerging as a not-yet-other. What-is then were not what they were; were what they were; were what-comes-prior as other-than what-is will be. All what-is need nothing. Having hid inside of things, they were what lies concealed, which is of course another way of saying what-is, and because becoming becomes being it is being – the being of becoming – and because becoming exits as its own what-is it is not what it is; it lacks. Nothing kept the all from being what-is and what-comes-prior and what-will-be in acts of becoming and what-is moved away from and into not. Our friends acted in no way if they did not transform what-is into what-is-not and what-is-not into what-is, where trees met men met what-is-not gravel and lost their senses as well as their minds.

ENDS AS ILLUSION

Xenis wanted to be rid of this moment; he pushed himself back into the space where he fussed no longer. He bid adieu the tree with a slight nod, thanked it for its time. The great plant gave nothing to him as he departed, but there waited impassive and heavy of patience. Xenis jogged along the train-tracks and pressed this notion into the back of his mind once more. The gravel was gravel and the metal was metal, but more was it track and what grass resided beneath his feet was grass, and he was grateful that they apparently remained what they were. These simple and straightforward integrities he treasured; they granted passage to him navigating a world that fed him one piece at a time. He trotted up to an enclosure made of glass with steel beams along its sides and a long, thick piece of wood centered in it. The wood was durable and heavy and the enclosure was fastened to cement as was the frame. Gladly, Xenis recognized this piece of what in front of him, and he sat within its confines for a moment – the train-track before him.

"It's nice to have a rest," he more felt than thought.

The enclosure presented itself first to him as a waiting space for persons for trains, but no such thing. It arose a shelter, then a glass cave – came a place to die and be born – then a cage for those in the social structure, a piece of the place where men-women pay their vitality for the price of mere subsistence. It gave-became an element of a transportation system and a godsend to those possessing no means of travel, a space where an older woman gained shelter and that place where ran a young boy cornered. Not certain what to think, Xenis thought he perceived in the corner of the roof a fragment of oblivion creep up in hiding. It was not dark not light, but rather it was a strange sensation to perceive this piece of...it was impossible to say. It had no substance and no light and could not be touched, yet it was there, in a manner of speaking. He exited the enclosure and noticed that the fragment was not evident, just a mass of material. He heard no sound and saw no sight that he had not already seen, yet somehow he knew, or felt, that some deception plagued him. These things measured true, it seemed to him: the shelter, the godsend, waiting space.

"So simple."

Something had deceived him, leading him to think that anything around him was really any one thing at all."

"Whoever they are, they're deceivers."

Xenis had need of removing himself from disguisers like these, so he climbed the fence behind the glass tomb and trotted onto the street safe and familiar: houses autos homotheria. His maneuver payed him in certainty and a made-glad Xenis cherished diminished vision that allowed him comfort. The cars were cars, but became economic prisons and spewers of life-lethal gas. They were comforters and conveniences and for some necessities, but also nets that entangled their lives doing service to others whose power permeated the food and the drink, the sleep and the homes, the movements and the joys of each persons who used them. The disguisers changed houses into shelter and conglomerates of wood, made them prisons for mothers and chains for fathers, wombs for children and heat from gas. Then, they had the nerve to make the houses homes where the same occupants enjoy company and find amusement. The propane they disguised as a giver of heat and a preparer of food, and made it liquid at moments and an odorless gas at others. They made comforters dog-towels and they regularly turned plastic bags and scraps of animal flesh into garbage. They turned wood that might have been violins into fuel, sometimes into desks and beds. They made quarrels into boundaries and touch they turned to intercourse, sex-pleasure pain. Animal flesh and coating became cloth while cloth became clothes for women who cherish their animals. Compassion became religion while religion opened to dogma.

"Compassion is dogma."

They turned hardness to inflexibility and liquids were solids and when they centered the cosmos around every point in space, Xenis realized that these were no plague. They told him the lie that was all and they did so with playfulness, true. He stood on the street and opened himself to them. Yet, his acceptance unneeded because Xenis, too, was one of them.

"I can't be."

He changed to water and calcium-carbon, pleasure and conflict, love and decision. He was at once weight and proportion, reason and hemoglobin. He was electron, what-is wave and particle at once; he was the balance and the stationary state of the tiniest bits of matter. Xenis found within not merely a wide world, but greater mass and more than his flesh did tolerate. He fell to the ground in a faint that brought a good man running. At home in his room near Brazil he rested.

"He has been having these…spells," she said.

She again thanked the officer who delivered her friend, unrolled his thin mat.

"You're such a pain in the ass."

Xenis awoke later that day, an afternoon of similar comfort. He ought to have thought the day destroyed, his senses befuddled and his mind shattered, but no. Somehow they had made themselves present, and he wanted again to experience the exhilarating fright of resulting disorientation. So, he invited them to come again, and they did not delay, everywhere in everything. His money was a conception, not real at all, his thought of possession just as insubstantial.

Xenis again thought how one may know another, what limits of familiarity.

"Dean is your friend. He cares for you," one explained.

He felt giddy dizziness, and he applied these substantial disappearances to all of what surrounded him. He was unable to think of something that did not distinguish itself from something else, yet remain the different to itself.

"Their game is a treacherous one."

The giddiness that had entered him refused to depart, and he again took up his thin bit of cushion and rolled it tight, sought out the door departed. He opened his wallet removed an address sought a taxi. When he arrived, he rang and after a time a voice emerged from the worn and well-used speaker.

"What do you want?"

"I'm looking for Dean."

"Isn't here."

"Do you know when he'll return?"

"No idea."

"Mr. Verdunkeln?"

"Yes?" the voice said after a pause.

"May I come in? I need to see Dean as soon as possible."

After a hesitation, the hum of the door signaled entrance for Xenis and he trotted up two flights of stairs to the mahogany door, recalling the place. He knocked and a longer time than usual passed before a spirited old John opened.

"Thank you so much, Mr. Verdunkeln."

"There's a chair."

John pointed to one of the recliners in the front room, the one closest to the front of the building. Xenis dutifully sat.

"Dean'll be here in about an hour. You can wait if you want."

"Oh. Fine. Thank you."

John slowly ambled toward the outer-most rear section of his unit, far and away. Xenis sat in the chair as forty-five minutes passed, but grew restless and anxious that they would come before he had a chance to talk; he made his way to the back of the condominium and found chair-bound a sleeping old John. Deciding to refrain from disturbing the old man, he settled at the dining room table where a few books awaited. He picked up a novel about a scuba-diving adolescent and leafed. Immersed in the thought of reading, Xenis heard no old John in the kitchen. When the old man slowly emerged into the dining room, his look of contented mild confusion turned to Xenis.

"You're here now."

"Pardon? Oh. Yes, I wandered back here. You were asleep."

John abruptly turned away and crept into the kitchen. He removed a snack from the refrigerator and disappeared, still there. Xenis read on. Packages in hand, Dean rushed through the opened door – delayed by traffic, errands and the purchase of pretzels, soda.

"Oh hello."

"Dean."

"It's good to see you. Been here long?"

"Not really."

Having set down the food and other sundry in the kitchen, Dean put himself next to Xenis who had no time to waste.

"I've been having these spells," he said.

"Oh," Dean paused. "Like the one at the Lyric?"

"Yes."

"I see."

"I'm not sure what they are. Maybe nothing."

"Mm Hmmm."

"I thought..."

"Yes?"

"I'm not even sure what I thought."

A layer of embarrassment enveloped Xenis as he pondered explaining his experience. He knew almost nothing about it.

"I... I guess I'm not sure what to do," he said finally.

"I don't think I've ever had that kind of experience. It must be disorienting."

"Yes!..yes." Xenis put his head in his hands.

The preacher Marvin Jackdaw emerged on-screen at that moment from what appeared to be a stage, but later seemed to be an pulpit and still later an altar, lights bright-chalice flickering. Marvin was a salesman, an advertiser, a man of god, an empire-builder.

"Hold on a moment," Dean said as he peered into the back room where Marvin stood. He gathered some discarded cups and a plate, took them into the kitchen. Xenis scratched his head and shifted in his seat.

"Are you ok?" Dean asked. Xenis nodded, looking around at chairs the table books, on his
clothing.

"Did you hear that?" Xenis asked.

"What? No."

"It was a giggle. I think."

Xenis stood up and turned his head back and forth, as if to survey the room. Something ran around, or was everything. He stared blankly into Dean's face, thinking that movement existed where he saw many...ends. He thought he felt the floor shake and the ground tumble beneath the condominium. No-one else sensed it; he ought to say nothing. He thought he felt a tap on his knee, several discernible pats along his midrif. He lost perception somehow suddenly and could feel and see and sense no thing at all. Then, all was normal again. He felt no different and perceived no more clearly, nor more poorly.

"Excuse me a moment," Dean said. "I'll be back in just a moment."

Xenis nodded slightly and looked out the dining-room windows, robust mahogany with bright yellow metal clips. He observed the craftsmanship and the cleanliness. Yet, in the wood he saw something grow. It was not an insect or bird, not a squirrel who might live in and around the building. He looked toward the lines of vitality amidst brown swirls and took in that absorption of moisture from ground, stretching overtop but within earth first and then reaching verdant hands out. They drew in light and made it their own, bending their limbs into the soil, slowly drawing nourishment from the form of dead things. Now they, of Sol-given light and green synthesis, grew. At times they starved and grew thankful when the wet arrived, seeming from nowhere, felt again the heat that sprang them up into themselves. This state they held for the longest time and though no contentment came to them – not possible for trees – they lived and grew, threw seeds onto the earth who dug their feet into the soil as they had done. The trees moved not at all and came subject to fortune, but chance favored them; strength made them mighty when winds came, throwing off water-filled palms that clasped warmth and gave strength. They turned rings around themselves and grew yearly out into... what, they knew not, knowing not theirs. They came to be thick and potent and the lives that made tree not tree but home lived with and on them, the flying things and the tiny ones who bit. These diminutive lives came and passed very quickly for the trees and then on a sudden the flying things vanished, the tiny bites remained. For the first time the limbs that stretched to the warmth felt a larger bite near the earth, and one single time did the trees feel the pull of one object for another, fell not in pain nor yet death but came dying. They sensed the warmth, but their feet had vanished; they stretched not high but around somehow. Then their hands were gone very quickly and no water no moisture came. When they sensed that the warmth no longer arrived then they felt no more. Now cut and ossified they shaped sideways rectangles and bent with brick of building, no longer living but smeared with hardening liquid and polished to see their innards. That what was there Xenis perceived not as immediate as others did, but there was not something that was there.

Xenis stepped away from the window, and focused. Again the wood came to window as prior had been. He shook his head and wondered at how he walked from one end of the room to another. He was now several feet distant from the glass and wood.

"Sorry about that," said Dean "John needed something."

"Um, no problem."

Xenis wondered why he had come, putting his face in his hand and sighing. When he looked to the floor, he perceived again not the whole living-space he had entered but rather bits of pieces of some kind of something moving in a strange manner gathering and, crushed by the force of one object for another, pressed together into a larger mass. This substance remained the same, unchanged, for so long no sentient creature can live, then felt the tug of a pull and fell into a chasm within the earth where the mass of pieces melted from extreme heat, forming a different kind of mass, one black and dense. There the mass-black remained for as long as it had before, now much colder and hard, when a slight warmth came touching upon its surface, not from below as before but atop, from where the pull of gravity did not come. Its enormous mass and heavy grace lifted from embrace of earth, it came down heavy on a bed of pliable metal, then found itself moved along a line and large parts came off made into squares polished and set a mere six decades on the floor where some of the frailest of fleshy creatures walked spilled and sat...Xenis shook his head. He came to himself again, perceiving Dean observing him.

"You were saying?"

"I'm not sure what I was saying. I..."

"Maybe you need something to drink."

"I suppose."

Dean again left the room in search of Xenis' need.

"These things aren't happening," Xenis thought.

He sat beside the dining-table and attempted to assess his senses. These events were, they were present, and.... They were past, that's sure, but something else was there that made them, as if what he were seeing was only a piece of what was immediate. Each part of everything he saw was not what he perceived, whats awaited. He was certain. He perceived some complete falsity; there was so much more present, so many more involved in some single what, like what of microscopic bits of iron that were radically different from the skyscraper, and the movement of protons and electrons that were nothing like that iron. Wood for violin, gas for a star, thought for a homotherion. These were not the same at all, and the perception that they were one single thing was not only mere appearance, it was...impossible.

"There's a bit of nothing there."

"We don't have anything but orange juice or black tea."

"But that's not nothing."

"Pardon?"

Dean sat near Xenis, unsure what to do or say, waiting for the right thing. Xenis again looked around the room, suspecting some new manifestation might return, and suddenly the universe would make no sense. Nothing happened, no change came and as the difference refrained from coming, he became more comfortable, but no relief. Xenis thought what was happening must be unreal.

"They're not after all," he murmured.

"I'm sorry?"

Suddenly, Xenis saw a strange man enter the dining-room, sporting recently short-cropped lively brown hair. Familiar, he was brisk in his step and one witnessed easily the leisure that enabled him. A well-tossed ball, it lived in his limbs and threw him around the room. His eyes were light, their brown invading the room with an old curiosity. His arms and legs were not muscular, but cut well, as though he exercised regularly, but not in a gym. He had the walk of a man who breathed the clean air of physical exertion regularly, one able to do so with resource at his command. He carried a chocolate-colored bag and wore a white t-shirt and like-white shorts, all hugging his form enough to display his vitality, not ostentatiously. One expected him to run his feet along the walls, one hand on the floor propping him.

"I need a bag from the top of the refrigerator," he said to Dean.

"Which one?"

"The twists."

Dean walked with the man around the corner. Xenis watched as Dean fumbled through three or four residents on top of the refrigerator. The young man moved not one bit. When he received the pretzels, he trotted toward back to his seat, active as any youth.

"Who's that?" Xenis asked.

"What do you mean?"

"Who is that man?"

Dean knitted brows and tried to refrain from looking perplexed.

"Ahm, that's John," he said.

Now this situation perplexed Xenis. Here something or someone was toying with him again, making not where there was. Yet, the John he perceived was active, trying to do impossible things.

"Yeah, of course. I must be tired," he said.

He stood up and looked around.

"Maybe I need to go."

"Stay a while. You just got here."

Xenis walked to the back room where John sat.

"I think I must be going. Thank you for your hospitality."

And the young man in white with vibrant brown hair waved, vigorously concentrating on the food and preaching before him.

"He's the same," Xenis thought. "That's not the John I know."

"Really, you should stay. At least for a while," said Dean

Xenis was unable to understand it.

"What kind of man was John?"

"What do you mean?"

"Was he...did he used to be an active person?"

"As far as I know, he was quite active, as a young man."

"That makes sense."

"It does?"

"What does he do now? I mean, is he active now?"

Dean took Xenis toward the front of the condominium, out of ear's range.

"He tries to be active, but he tires himself quickly. It worries me sometimes."

"So, he isn't active, but he wants to be."

"I'd say that's about right. How'd you know?"

"I'm not sure."

Xenis did not know how to ask his next question.

"This may sound strange, but do you mind if we sit with John?"

"We can ask. He may want to be left alone."

John received the two younger men well, though he asked that they be quiet while they watched Marvin. The vigorous John sat in his same chair, did the same things that the elder John did, yet his movements were quick, his ability to sustain continued movement still better. The old John wore long sleeves and baggy corduroy mostly. This John sported shorts and running shoes, thick fur vigorous-brown hugged his legs. His foot tapped the floor continuously and at a rate fabulous for an old man.

"This isn't an old man," said Xenis softly.

"What?" John asked.

Xenis made no reply. The televised-internet preacher Marvin, dressed in a breathtaking tan suit with black lapels, spoke to a theater of believers who howled and hooted in exultation. Preacher Marvin said that god gives us the earth to tend as we see fit, animals have no souls. He paced the stage before the pulpit and circled round behind it. He banged his fist on the sturdy, gilded wood, claiming no other creature possessed a soul like man. Marvin gradually walked out into the audience and touched the hand of an elderly woman, front row. She rose and hugged him. John's feet tapped higher and faster as Marvin talked and Xenis witnessed John's hair grow darker, his color come more red, blood putting in him more hue. Young John winked at him. Xenis saw a strong person with such vitality as anyone might desire, and no harm came from mere energy. Still, Xenis' irritation grew when he looked at or thought about him. The man whom he saw was not the man who sat before him. His vitality and potency teased Xenis.

"You think you're young and strong," he said.

"What?"

"You think you're young and vigorous, but it's a not."

"What are you talking about?"

"You ought to know. Stop running about. Stop doing so much. It's death."

John glared at Dean.

"Maybe we should get some fresh air," Dean said.

"There's no fresh air here. He's nothing An enormous, destructive nothing, and he'll die soon, unless he stops."

Xenis understood why Dean requested that he leave, but he

insisted.

"He has much more life in him as long as he slows down. Tell him. Tell him!", Xenis said as the front door to the condominium closed.

NICHTS

Varicolored homotheria perceive pieces of what they see, creatures discerning what is there. Properly some portion was seen, taken as whole and possessing only part, a whole not at all whole in perception. Pieces by themselves became, not being another piece. Easily hidden and continually present they did and acted and produced, but not as themselves. A shout precluded an iron gate, or a thought, pieces of cloth were clothing to the exclusion of all else but raiment and covering, There were others: cloth protection cotton elements shape size, and these were different. As to what-comes-prior, Nichts made nothing become. They produced in everything something else with no primal thing – or fundamentally invisible being – visible, and ensured the non-existence of no essence except that they are always a part of anything that is. Not-ness to everything. Not-ness incomplete reality of what-is, not it at all. Nichts opened what was there into the possibility of not, non-being or being-not-other or being-other-and-so-not or becoming what it is not or what it is not-yet. Being lay under being-what, or what-is, and the homotheria filtered out the other what-is in order to find the door or to see a rabbit's fur; they remained unable to encompass the non-being of aging, moving, altering, sensation narrowing. The homotheria filtered the what, what-is, and not being, but there were others who were groing that ability.

MEDITATION
OF CHANGE

Xenis had not words to explain, but he pushed an expression onto his face, his mind a bright lucent breath. He remained uncertain of precisely what was happening, yet he knew that to continue what he was doing, certain of only that much. A peace enveloped his jumble of difference that he called living, and he recalled experiencing a similar sensation.

"I miss the Xolos."

He was glad at the moving of metal and the cleaning of debris and the hauling of garbage, and he needed no grand conversation with intellectual giants nor time spent writing his thoughts for nuns to enjoy.

"Nuns to enjoy?"

He desired no sex no drugs no nicotine – not necessary – and he wondered where his desires had gone. He lifted himself onto the balls of his feet as he walked and shook his limbs, tapping the back of his head. The sensation that possessed him made simple this new stranger, Xenis. He neither wanted nor needed virtual culture, not phone nor video, and he left behind not merely objects and trappings, what his culture pressed upon him. When the perceptions departed and when thought no longer came, no longer came the same desire. Material and politics sensation and perspective were distractions that carried him away, if he permitted, and he had used them as distractions, but now the desire for them had nearly disappeared. He and Brazil repeated their mornings and Friday evenings, listening to music and discussing her art. She had forgotten the purging incident, or so it seemed. Yet, now within all of these things – warm and kind – Xenis needed that release. He removed himself, or at least attempted. No objects. No depth. No navigation in and among the world of things. No sounds, not music. No space. No method of doubt. The nothing came rolling, thoughts arrived thinking.

"Music is meaningless."
"God is nothing."
"Ears have no depth of sound."
"Decency can never be tactile."
"Empathy is a kind of violence."
"All men are human."
"All women are human."
"All women are men."

Thoughts rearranged as he proceeded, each perception differing in same. Xenis practiced such thoughts regularly, but he possessed other means to achieve the same goal. He delighted in the repeated investigation of same. Prior to beginning his regimen each evening he read once again the same text or narrative. He looked again into its meaning and attempted to extract from the same subject a difference, a delicious manifest disparity. On each effort he found something new with which to play, and when he did see a seeming bit of nothing – a kind of realness inapplicable to what lay before him – he found again an indirect characteristic. There was some thing, or not really some thing, that opened him and yet kept him from opening – a "no" to current Xenis.

"I don't understand," he thought. "I still can't quite see."

Again Xenis looked toward the difference, that realness inapplicable. Again he found what he sought, and yet no. A strange sensation lacking sense pressed upon him. He suspected his enemies again teasing him, but a thought came.

"Did I imagine these things?"

What he found was there, present in some manner at least, and so it was not nothing. It had to be. When he argued or contended with others, he again found what he sought. Even as he accepted others and passively listened he found that what was sought came always. As he grumbled and obsessed through intense anger over his present state – an aggravation that nearly overcame him and one that at necessity emerged – he once more discovered what he sought. He again met Carol, that found girl in the park some while ago. Not the kind of woman with whom he coupled ordinarily, cherubic of face and thick of figure. Here again.

"This is strange."

Brazil suggested that he use his education to find better employment, and Xenis was not averse to material comforts.

"I have no identity. I can use my skills, but not my credentials."

"Not good for employment," she said.

"No."

Xenis was neither certain that he liked that idea, nor sure that it bothered him. He enjoyed the position that he occupied, the labor that he performed, yet he agreed that he needed more command of resource. He required food and clothing, though he would have been glad to relieve himself of them. He needed a certain level of comfort within which to function, and he was curious as to what kind of labor would make a comfortable living. He possessed the skill of reading ancient Greek and had obtained a good education, yet he did not relish the idea of laboring in an office; work as an accountant or a business agent carried with it every manifestation of vacuity. He occupied himself as a tutor of college-age students, reinforcing various subjects. The work was much less physically demanding, and he enjoyed using his education. Xenis labored carefully for his students' benefit, yet some what seemed to accompany him. An absent presence, again; it was familiar in its affects, but elusive. He was unable to determine a specific time when it emerged, nor was he able to determine precisely what it was, but the same thing was part of his old labor, his friendship with Brazil, even his love. He continued to find it in tending to his animals, in friendship. It was present at dinner with the Davis family, yet he found it as he wrangled occasionally with Brazil, and it was there when his frustrations with his new circumstances made him curt with others and when neighbors aggravated him with their noise and quarrels. He had understood it to be there when he jogged that strange morning and it was present when he first rode a bicycle into Brazil's neighborhood.

When he met Carol, he felt still and again what he sought. It remained present when they were unhappy with one another and when they disagreed. It was present when they had physical contact and when they were apart. No kind or quantity of encounter lacked what he sought. When he talked to men who sold drugs to children, he found it. When he chatted with addicts, he found it. When he saw a man being beaten by another on the front lawn of his building, he rushed down in order to break up the altercation. After he had done so, he realized that what he sought had been there as well. A generous plate of steamed brown rice and salted boiled potatoes with flax oil and black sesame seeds offered it to him as did his morning emotion and the German conception of justice as well as his morning thought. When he made jokes and laughter with Dean and sometimes John; when he felt sadness over the absence of his Xolos and Dora; when he encountered men who hated others for their skin-color and culture; when persons he met claimed no allegiance to genuine sentiment or apathy he again found it. He found it in newsreels about lynchings and Jim Crow laws. He treid to eliminate it. He sensed its presence when friends of Brazil did almost nothing, except eat and drink, sleep. He found it in anger directed intensely at an enemy. It even presented itself in those who never learned no matter their efforts and in those who thought that success resides only in the acquisition of property. He found it in carriages and fans. Curiosity and empathy offered it to him. On one night there was no such thing as god and on another god was everything and always emerging. One day god had set the universe going like a clock and on another the creator was the universe and on still another the cosmos arose from nothing and into nothing once again it fell. It had no center and needed no creator. He began again to employ the changing of thought, and again what he sought was there.

"Not is not."
    "Something else is this something."
"Not other is 'not' of what-it-is."
    "Train-guides serve no purpose."
"A strange stash holds my pocket."

Now Xenis wondered what it was. Its affects were more and more familiar; he thought he might be able to investigate more thoroughly.

"What would that entail?"

He was convinced he was unable to reduce himself to nothing, to doubt enough that he became no thing. So, Xenis relieved himself of his everyday thought and later his perceptions and then when his mind had cleared to its own absence, he assembled himself from that mass of broken thought resulting from his relief. He did not deny himself; he did not tell himself that he was no longer Xenis, nor did he doubt who he was. Xenis found some part of him that was other than a bipedal, thinking, social animal. He thought himself into not the olive-skinned creature with the opposeable thumbs, but fluid and feral, a leopard, a giraffe – perhaps a dolphin. In these episodes, he had no need for names; possessed no property; foraged for food; fought for life. He returned to no domicile where comfort and regular sleep resided, resting when able and keen to remain aware of surroundings. He no longer held regard for possessions, nor did merely beautiful things capture his attention, unless eaten or useful. Xenis remained these creatures for a time. Later he became a porpoise and a frog, then a raccoon and a crab. When the time arrived for him to make a still more fundamental change, he stood himself down into the ground and remained still, swaying gracefully, absorbing sun, drinking carbon. Still later he tightened his body into fetal position, hugging ever more closely his knees to his legs. He sat impassive and granite on earth. No need of sustenance pressed him, no longer his own volition moving, the great strength of land hugged him, subject to the whim of creature-passersby. He sat in this manner longer than he had placed himself in the position of a tree, and then steadier he remained, no longer human, no creature – only matter. Minuscule motion, fluid replete with elements. Art and music passed him as he transitioned, no longer tending to harmony or melody nor noise nor sound.

The attention to wealth or poverty had left him even as he became first lion, later snake. The care for and order departed when plant then mineral and Xenis merged, and as he thought himself into the state of inanimateness, so did his frame of thought depart, foundation of thinking-being that occupies sentience. What departed then gave great relief to Xenis; the need to place a thought into setting and thus make-thought-possible no longer a necessity. He perceived not from here or there, not from within an already-given thinking, something presented to him by culture, but rather there stood a felicity when he simply was, and gave to the whats around him no manner of understanding. No movement necessary, he sat on the ground, but did not seat himself. He waited and remained until another came along to change him. When wind blew upon him, he felt no difference, no cold affected him significantly, neither feeling nor sympathy – not lacking in the regular need for food or fluid. He was immensely satisfied with his stone being, perhaps no satisfaction possible. When last he thought himself into new whats, his mind was gone and his reference-frame almost nil.

Still, he was unable to shatter thoughts and perceptions into small enough pieces so that he might become more fundamental still, really. When he broke down, he felt again the sensation he sought and when he assembled further he, again-stronger, felt the same sensation. He felt at least a relief, but at times a euphoria that encompassed him. All around was-not.

"Am I really already these things?"

At times, his thoughts and experiences troubled him, and he desired to visit Dean once again, but then they took him up as if without his will and placed him in another Xenis. Dissatisfied with something though he knew not what, he ceased tutoring and began again to work only with the old man, moving the heavy metal frames. He did not know why precisely, but he was drawn to this labor, sometimes refusing compensation. He moved the metal back and forth and the constant in the repetition gave him solace, as did the gentle words and relieving thoughts of the old man.

NICHTS

The hammock was hammock, shape, not material, nor wood. Hammock was different things, difference, that is the same. The same was the what that comes from the difference, the hammock. That hammock was hammock and not other than, nor parts of, hammock was first; appearance as difference become primary. One of what-is was perceived, the remaining filtered out. The diety of dieties would not see a hammock, but a gathering infinite. The difference was the not what-it-is, this difference an aspect of being and not being. Appearance is both: that difference also the same. That hammock was not an aspect of what-it-is that is hammock was the result of "not" or a nothing; the not that was being is that which separates and "makes other than" something else. Th e hammock was not insubstantial really; it was real. It was a negativity that the nothing-part-of-everything ceases hammock here and provides its structure, prevents one what from being another. There was a difference that is the same, the contrast of what makes up what-it-is.

UBIQUITOUS REVELATION OF NOTHING

At home on a wall in Brazil's unit, a pretty, adolescent girl hung in nineteenth-century impressionistic fashion, appearing a brief time ago. Xenis was unable to keep himself from watching her as he sat at the kitchen table. The girl wore a formal dress that flared into a wide skirt, covering all parts of her body except for the hands and head. The pale yellow hue of her garb complemented the medium-grey of the hound, and the outlines of the two subjects roughly demarcated what they were. Carefully observing, Xenis noticed something about the dog and the girl. Some part of the art-piece seemed odd. The contours of the dog did not clearly demonstrate dogness, but Xenis knew that there was a dog. The dog was grey and not black, nor white; he possessed a specific structure that placed him on the ground quadrupedal; his skeleton and muscle-structure made dogness of what comprised the dog, insofar as a painting of a dog is a dog. Yet, something remarkable and common at once occurred. He arose from the table and looked again closely. He thought perhaps it was that the dog was a painting of a dog that moved him, but he wondered at the limitations of dog. These demarcations ended where the dog was, but performed another task. The dog was represented as three feet in length and furry, seemed to possess a good disposition. The artist must have realized the limitations of the animal in order to depict it, so there was some limit of dogness that made dog dog. That the dog was absent here and lacking in characteristic there was present. Where he was and was-not was the result of something not present so much as absent.

Xenis quick-stepped away from the painting, and sat again down at the table. They were not making little nothings, nor were they truncating things as they had before done. Now somehow they were hiding in a different place. Xenis supposed that what he had seen was the result of the manner of painting, that the ends of the things were confused, but as he looked at Brazil's playing cards on the table, they presented to him the same end that began, witnessed in the painting. Rectangular and not circular, circularity was-not there. Pliant and bendable, stiffness and hardness were-not. The colors on the cards were white and red and yellow and black and so blue and orange were-not. What made them what they were was what made them not. They hid from him as the others had done, but in continuance. Not precisely like what not swept over John. Brazil's tawny wooden storage box refused the presence of triangle or plastic or thought. Thoughts and triangles and plastic simply were not and could not be there. These things were around and about him, and they seemed to be present. That is, Brazil's box seemed only to be, and was never not. Yet, they were somehow there, in some manner present.

"And, of course, not," he thought.

The shape and size of the card, its color, its flexibility, the ink used to create them – all these things – were they in disguise, limiting and truncating in order to bring present; objects in the world with Xenis. He picked up a card and felt it, bent it back and forth and then put it down. He encountered not some thing participating in cardness of card, but one of them that made is what-is. Xenis observed the contours of the table-cloth and ran his palms along the hard surface of the wooden table beneath, and they were there as well. He touched his own hands and the children of nothing made plain what was there to see.

"The same as whats?", Xenis asked absent-mindedly.

"What?" Brazil asked.

The table, the wooden box, the cards opened up to him, not-other, no other than themselves.

"They make each thing."

They disguised themselves as things in the world. He had seen them do it; disguise a part of everything. These things, these whats, were complicit in the deception; they were possible for who knew what, and what put them forth was not that they were there so much as that they are-not, size and shape, color and density, mass and duration or any other aspect that made them what they were. The Nichts opened to everyone a presence one sees as is when it is and not.

"I am finally understanding more clearly," he muttered.

"What?"

Xenis thought he ought to put aside these thoughts; they were nothing and he believed that perhaps he imagined them. He talked with Brazil about her bronze adonis and rested in her hammock, setting aside the fact that the hammock was not an egg. He fell asleep and found seeming infinite rest, a deathlike state. When he awoke, his thoughts rested on them again.

They were most probably in his head and nowhere else. He walked into his bedroom and sat in his reading chair. Beside it was a basket filled with clothing, all of which were folded neatly, ready for wear. He began stacking them in his closet on the upper shelves and the floor when he noticed that they were not his clothes. Their durable, canvass-like material – mostly blue – stood out to him as if to beg attention. The wide waistlines and the cotton softness of shirts, blouses, unfolded their character. Xenis pulled all of the clothing down from where he had stacked it and felt the material; he turned some of the articles inside out and observed the stitching along the seams. An odd sensation came over him, but one that was no longer novel nor completely foreign.

"Not nothing," he mumbled.

"What?" came from another room.

Xenis observed the quality and size, shape and color of each article; each aspect of these things, these whats, presented him with something, as an actress on a stage who presents substance not her own - with her the audience the lines the author the time of day the character of the character the setting the time of day *et alia* acting and being acted.

"The actor and the acted are not separate," he thought.

He concentrated on the blue of a pair of jeans that he held. The faded yet appealing hue brought him no anger, nor did it rouse him. This color was not red-like in its affect, but blue. It was not color at all but the affect of light upon the material reflected to him. It made blue in contrast to other reflection and other color; it was acted by the light and acted to the viewer. The material of the article comforted its owner with a delicate wear, a pliancy wrapped around the skin. This delicateness was not a thick protective and discomforting rubber, nor any other material that offered protection without the pleasant wrap of well-liked clothing. It was only comfortable because of the wearer, and the the one who donned the clothes made the color and the softness.

"Now, that's odd."

Something in the clothing itself misdirected him and at once presented to him what was there. Certainly, Xenis knew that he was able to misperceive. He had gotten it wrong. The clothes were not his. The articles that one wore remained folded in them as he had placed them on the shelves and floor. When he unfolded them, after noting an unfamiliarity, he found more of what they were.

"That must be it."

Xenis knew that should he unfold more, dismantle what he had, he would find still more things that they are, things that were never apparent to him even upon the closest observation; they acted as the color and texture and durability, and these characteristics acted them into existence, neer one act.

"I see nothing," he said.

"What?"

Yet something was there. He carried the pair of jeans with him into the kitchen and sat staring at them, whatever was there refusing to release him.

"What are you doing now?", Brazil said with a frown.

Xenis remained silent as he ran his thumb along the material.

"Those aren't yours."

Xenis faced Brazil and peered into her eyes without seeing her.

"No. They're not mine."

What he stared at hit him suddenly, then fled immediately, as if a thought had again come and then disappeared without being noticed. Brazil snatched her pants away from him just as he began looking around. All of the objects in the room had this...whatever...to them. It was part of what made them what they were, but it was not quality, not quantity, no kind of characteristic. The blue was blue and remained blue as blueness does, but it precluded the presence of other colors. The shape of the table in front of Xenis came about in the same way. It was a table and not a chair, brown and not blue, wood and not metal. These things acted and were acted at once, whole and part, a bit of nothing inside of them. It was an absence that he felt, but could not perceive. This time they were much cleverer. They were not now visible momentarily, no not at all. They were not completely nothing.

"They are not pure."

No, they were part of any present thing, and a part of things around Xenis and his world. That the blue was blue and not thought nor red or a politician nor an education was the is-not of the is. They were not only nearby and waiting to reveal a difference between and within things; they were there making things what they are.

"You're ubiquitious."

"What?"

Though Brazil encouraged him to another kind and quality of livelihood, Xenis continued to work with the old man. He wondered at what drew him to that sort of labor, why he needed little else. There were many opportunities for accident or inattentiveness, and most of his fellow workers cared little for how they performed their tasks, yet the old man was quite conscientious and careful each moment, it seemed. Xenis again moved the metal scaffolding from one place to another, stacking and balancing. He thought as he stacked and pondered as he balanced, and Xenis found that they refrained from bothering him, yet he knew they were there.

"If they are inside of anything that exists, then no-one is be able to avoid them."

His co-workers Bill and Mike assisted the old man just as Xenis did, and occasionally the three took lunch together. Xenis avoided them usually, though not out of dislike. Their coarse, simple humor refused his amusement, and Xenis had enough of jokes involving a woman's breasts, flatulence or flatulence and a woman's sexual organs. Today they sat while Xenis listened to a joke about a man and a hammer, another about a promiscuous woman and a third about a Pole before his attention turned. He sat nearby still, but his attention came to the things around him, his gaze latching onto one thing with a stare and then another. Once in a while he noticed something he had seen on the roof of the kiosk and lost his ease when they emerged, indiscernibles arriving in packages of angry and malicious lackings. It was a maddening experience that Xenis was unable to avoid.

When he turned his eyes onto a wooden box filled with tools – similar to Brazil's box in many ways – he noticed something odd about it. The shape of the box seemed distorted, as if a not-so-master craftsman had created a badly-formed container, not quite what it ought to be. Then the shape of the wood changed for no apparent reason, and the box was perfectly formed, the very kind of cube used ideally to house heavy tools – sturdy and useful. Xenis listened again to Mike, but soon decided the box was more interesting. It changed in no way again for another five minutes, and then it seemed to have formed itself into an oval. He laughed at what appeared to be a designer toolbox, made from wood and scuffed as containers of this sort are, yet ovularly stylish. Xenis only glanced at Bill and Mike before he watched once more the toolbox. It now seemed to conform to the shape of a circle more than an oval.

Then the box abruptly changed form again into a square, this time forcefully. A surprised Xenis walked over to the altering container, a meter square, and watched. Bill and Mike observed Xenis observing. The box then abruptly changed not into an oval, but a full circle and again the designer toolbox. Laughing, Xenis was unable to find a good reason for the change, and he remained unaffected by the apparent struggle. The only object to suffer was the container itself. Every so often Xenis caught a glimpse of a fold. No fold in any one thing, but rather what seemed to be a fold in the box itself. The material of the container changed in no significant manner, but the shape kept reconfiguring, and now and again one was unable to determine what shape the container was, yet the wood that comprised the box accepted any one of these shapes readily.

Leaning over the open end of the container, Xenis watched for a change, wanting to observe the very moment of alteration. When the next shape came, his shoe and foot were caught in whatever was happening. They became bloated and circular, though he felt no pain. When he stood away from the vicinity of the container, they shifted back, foot-shaped. He massaged them in order to be certain of no permanent damage or change. The container shook vehemently, shaping itself circle- or square-shape, only the two. Xenis could see the folds that had once more enveloped his foot. They were with him again; suddenly the container returned its former, ordinary shape. Xenis pondered the moment for some time while he worked. He feared explaining what had happened.

As he moved the metal framework again and again, Xenis occasionally looked back at the box and observed the other objects in order to witness another incident. He ate and went straightaway to bed that evening, and a strange thought awoke him.

"They were fighting?"

5:45am stared him down. Xenis ordinarily slept one hour more, yet his thought had driven him into too much wakefulness. He rolled about in bed for what seemed like ten minutes, and when he peered at his clock he saw that an hour had passed. Weary and fatigued by the early kindling of interest, he reluctantly washed, made active still more by the now-steady conflagration of sentience. He poured out the oatmeal and milk that would become his breakfast; ate and dressed in his ordinary work-clothes. He walked Brazil's dog, as he sometimes did, and when he returned he found that seven-thirty had arrived.

"What happened?"

Xenis rushed through the gathering of his coat and keys, hurried again onto his bicycle and out toward the warehouse where metal frames awaited. He moved sluggishly as the day began and the transfer of seventy frames of scaffolding wore upon him, into a truck and then from the truck and onto a construction site. Ordinarily, the moving of the metal took him quickly through the day, and time contracted before him. Nine and then ten o'clock would come and Xenis was unaware of time's passage. Yet, on this morning each moment of the transfer lasted ages, or at least seemed as much. Xenis felt as if each moment dragged him back into a former Xenis, time spreading out before him; an eternity he must endure before even nine o'clock. Normally, the transfer to one site took merely an hour, perhaps a bit more. On this day, time not only refused to move quickly, but slowed even as Xenis moved with concerted haste. When they returned to the warehouse, the customary amount of time had passed.

"That's odd," Xenis thought.

The duration of the transfer felt long as he worked it, and yet when they returned a quick hour and one-half had passed, time slow and quick. Xenis thought not so much over the passage of the morning, glad that it disappeared quickly. He wanted only to find home and rest in order to remove the thickness from his mind. During the movement of the frames from one end of the warehouse to another, the moments bunched themselves together in plodding torture; some refused to move while others tread terrain in imperceptible steps, yet when Xenis looked at the day's hour, he found these pedestrians had abruptly departed. Rigid stress of discontent departing, he took lunch, watched again the toolbox; nothing came. Whatever wrangled with that container struggled – no longer vying – its ordinary shape returned and abiding. Lunch passed, and he again came to the moving and the driving of the frames from one place-point to another. More confident of an ordinary workday, Xenis witnessed the minutes then hours pass quickly as he and the old man again-once-more dispersed materials, cleaned and disposed of building refuse. They took in frames and material from four sites and brought to the warehouse several piles of metal steps. Ordinarily, four such excursions consumed the afternoon.

"Only three would do it," he thought.

Yet, when they returned to the warehouse, merely one and one-half hour had passed.

"Good time," said the old man.

The sluggish forenoon pushed him and his fellow-workers rapidly through its early hours, and yet when time quickened his pace a drowsy-stepping Xenis found that seconds-hours compressed in tight lines, movement nearly still. Xenis and his older companion yet moved frames and materials within, around and toward three more sites, and a momentarily idle Xenis found merely one more hour passed.

"It's two-thirty?!" he said. "What?"

Again, the pair went out preparing three more sites, and when they came again to the warehouse only one-half hour had passed.

"Don't you think we've done a lot in one day?" he asked the old man.

"Morning go quickly, I see as well."

"Isn't it odd?"

"Strange thing, yes, but as you say nothing.'"

"Of course."

"What this?"

"It's nothing."

Xenis' week proceeded in much the same manner, time slowly making haste and quickly sagging. Yet, on the last day of the work-week everything suddenly moved as expected, sluggishly when slow and hastily when quick.

"They are pestering me," he boldly said to Brazil before he set out to work.

"What?"

"They are here...with us. Actually...I think they're everywhere."

"What do you mean?"

"I'm not sure how it works."

"*What* are pestering you?"

"Nichts."

Brazil stared.

"They're just mischievous, I think. They seem to be messing around."

"Oh Yeah?"

"They affect everything."

"You're sure of this?"

Xenis paused.

"Really, no."

"I'm glad to hear that."

Xenis laughed quietly.

"I don't know what to do."

"It'll pass."

Xenis tried to kep himself busy, walking dogs and working, reading and listening to music, but he was unable to refrain from thinking about them. Certainly, they would not have a positive affect, but what would they do, he wondered. That was Wednesday. A thought came on Thursday.

"Wouldn't they negate things?"

As Saturday approached, Thursday's thoughts did not settle. Perhaps they break things down; that makes sense. They would then eliminate things, and things were eliminated, certainly.

"No, no. Wait a minute! It isn't just a negation."

They were breaking things down, it seemed, but they were building at the same time.

"Yes, yes. One thing is completely other than what it is. They are every thing," he thought. "They act the loss of prodding time."

On Tuesday Xenis' thoughts from Thursday and Saturday seemed odd. Friday seemed to welcome his thoughts from Thursday, Saturday and Tuesday, and he remained attentive to the appearance of these things while he labored at work and housebound-chatted with Brazil. He watched for one beside the toaster or in his thought of knowledge or another on the neighbor's barbecue, but he discovered no crafty nothing anywhere. He thought better than to inform everyone of his concern, he and they partners and adversaries. When Xenis observed things, he saw in them not what seemed to be, but what not made them. The table in Brazil's kitchen was not a chair; he removed the plates, vase and cloth and observed it, an inexpensive piece, crafted from metal and plastic – useful, not strong. White, its color blended with kitchen-whats: toasters refrigerator stove. Flexible, its legs folded into the flat top for transport. The metal of the legs and the frame of the table gave it what durability it possessed. Whats made culinary that flat surface, not work- nor meeting-table. The metal held strength not exceeding in rigidity, a durable usefulness, yet not the gorgeous dark blonde of a banquet table. Another wood possessed certain robustness rivaling the metal, but not the harsh directness of the steel. These whats of the table seemed simply to be, not-made as well.

"Particulars," thought Xenis. "But they do not discriminate. None of them would refuse existence to one thing and leave another alone."

Material objects were not the only not-made whats. The thought he had on any given morning directed him and was directed in a specific way, not toward hate or jealousy, but a simple need to understand. The fear that possessed him, one that suspected Brazil might arrive and shout, was not a thought, not a material thing beyond electric impulses, but a sort of tone for his mind. It resided in the same place that emotions did.

"An emotion is like a musical sound, a tone of thought with no thinking," he thought.

He turned the table upside down; many of its parts were not needed for a wooden table. Each aspect of the table was not-something capable of performing its task as a table-piece. The screws, the black plastic caps for the legs, the rough, white-lined, angry-plaid-of-dark-gray plastic square that made up the top – all these – put themselves forth for him, not-being-other. Such mundane things were present and tangible, provable pieces of existence cutting off possibility for other pieces, different whats; at the same time they presented a variety of prospects for being other things completely different from themselves: not-potential. They made possible what was capable from things that were not altogether not. Xenis buried himself under them for day upon days. He talked less frequently with Dean not at all to John. He ceased going to poetry readings with Brazil. He observed boxes at work, and he returned to the bus stop and the street where they had visited him, but he saw or perceived none.

"I never really met them," he mused.

This thought reassured him. Xenis observed and sought more confidently the not of love, the not of Justice, the not of matter, even the seemingly less-significant the not of screwdriver and the not of tree. They appeared to recognize his desire to perceive them, yet remained distant, with Xenis convinced they were there, everywhere.

Brazil's neighbor loved his wife, genuinely tending to her needs. This affection drove off violence and anger; it made certain kinds of affection manifest and possible in future, thus driving away distance and indifference. It brought worry and weariness when she was ill, and most-times drove away carelessness and certainly apathy. Xenis watched Harold, met him in the dog-park when able.

"Do you and your dog sleep in the same bed?"

"Oh, yes."

"How old is he?"

"She's about four. We don't know."

"Does she have any medical conditions?"

"She had a thyroid problem, but it's under control."

"Is she your dog or your wife's dog?"

"My wife's." The man laughed.

Xenis had thought that they deliberately did certain things, that they wandered about – nothings on their own. Yet, they were compelled to manifest in certain directions. The not of this man's love for his wife and animal drove away cruelty. Yet, they were not, and by definition they were unable to have natures.

"They cannot be seen, or heard."

The ends of presence, they were neither particular, nor were they universal. At the dog-park, Xenis observed more affection and care, all that the love made to drive away and come to be. One woman led a great Dane who protected her. Another cared for a massive mongrel. Xenis looked at everything that arose around him, and saw parameters. He watched the emotional turns of Brazil and movements of bits of light up high.

"They aren't active in themselves."

"They cannot be anything or do anything without something that is."

He suspected that they were not only little nothings, but they must become. If they come to be in things, they cannot be elsewhere, though they must be themselves nowhere.

"No, they are part of whats."

If they are part of what comes to be, they must have some function. If entirely negation, they would do nothing at all.

"They simply end the activity of things?"

Xenis had fallen into the habit of retrieving mail for him and Brazil. Able to determine easily what mail was disposable, and what not, he discarded the disposable and retained the needed . Ordinarily, he placed mail that meant something on the kitchen table in the corner where Brazil found it. She opened and then further discarded. When Xenis found a correspondence from their landlord, an unexpected commotion crept into his eyes. He placed the envelope on the table, waited nervously. Brazil arrived late and in no good mood, ignoring the Xenis-stacked pile of words. When at last she read them, that same unexpected commotion arrived in the form of wide eyes and a quick pace; the apartment complex would change soon into condominiums.

"I wouldn't be disturbed, except that my contract ends in a month," she said.

"Tenants have until the end of their contracts?"

"Yeah."

"It's not the worst of news."

"It's an unwelcome change."

A grumpy Brazil and a wondering Xenis prepared. Xenis suggested rather strongly that they obtain a unit on the top floor of a building in order to avoid the stomp and drop of shoes and other heavies, and with the lifting of boxes and the discarding of pieces of nothing the pair began. The new space offered them a wide expanse of wood and a higher ceiling; a front bay window brought in the day's light, offering specs of reflection emitted from the white and yellows – bright pieces – of passersby. The surrounding motions of persons – hands, feet, eyes – leaped not quick, nor aggressively, but glanced over the tops of buildings and the peaks of trees, tapping sidewalks grasping necessities and candy.

"I ought to have moved earlier," Brazil thought.

The clothes and the belongings of the pair suddenly appeared to them as a mountain of tasks the likes of which only an ancient divinity was able to master. Xenis' few bits of clothing and stack of books fit quietly and effortlessly into a temporary corrugated home, but Xenis felt something odd as he placed belonging and book in the medium-brown hard-paper container. He thought of it as a slight touch of a minuscule finger on the back of his hand. He discerned no bite, nor did any tiny wanderer scurry away after a random encounter.

"We don't have bugs in this place," he thought.

He smoothed three fingers over the back of his hand, afterward opening the box and scanning its contents. He felt again the same sensation, this time along the side of his neck. He recognized now that this sensation was not really that of a touch, as he had thought. He was unable to place what the sensation was.

Brazil's apartment teemed with art and pieces of bits that surrounded her life and made her vital; their relocation would be painful, and the task of removing them entailed categorizing them after un-burying them from the stack of one another that lined her space. No piece of anything resided in a proper place, no system or plan seemed to emerge from the stack-piles of bronze figurines and watercolor musings. Not knowing where to begin, the pair of friends started in Brazil's bedroom closet where clothes combined with old computers and yellow-dirt-stained dog-toys. Some things were destined for a landfill, others donations. Xenis reached into her closet and moved a jacket so that he was able to reach several glass mugs on the topmost closet shelf. He felt again the same sensation, or lack of it, as he did so. This time, the sensation ran along his arm and down a part of his thigh, and no light touch pressed upon his limbs. The sensation now was needle-like, and yet not painful. He was unable to suppress a laugh. As he relocated object after object, many of these minuscule sensations rustled along his arms and sometimes up the side of his head. He laughed again. When the laugh subsided, his body tensed.

"What was that?"

"What?"

Xenis had no way of describing his sensation, but he suspected that they were again pestering him.

"Have you felt anything strange since we began packing?"

"No. Why?"

Xenis rested for some twenty minutes or so before he again removed and stacked and categorized for later removal. Brazil moved her glass jugs and a box of recordings onto the middle of the room. He located the small boxes, untouched since the last move, from the highest of shelves. As he lowered them, he felt again one light touch, this one running along his arm and back through shoulder-blades and out onto his other arm, disappearing at the tip of his other hand. Again, he looked at the floor and on his person, in the closet, and he found no insect, nor anything tangible. Xenis sat down in order to rest, and as he remained quiet and relatively motionless he felt no longer these odd sensations.

Brazil darted about, placing bronze figurines in white boxes and small paintings in large, thin brown cardboard. When she had finished stuffing the bronze into the boxes, she sat next to a Xenis who had not moved.

"Aren't you doing anything?" she asked testily.
"I'm resting for a moment."

Brazil paused a moment and then resumed her quick-stepped pace un-burying other belongings and frantically resting them one place and then another. She rested only momentarily, and when seemingly satisfied that glass jugs sufficiently filled a box correctly lining the space inside, she again brought out the jugs and placed them into another waiting box. She did so with the figurines, the glass jugs and the watercolor paint. As a result three boxes filled with belongings housed three different kinds of things at three different times.

"Are you sure you have the figurines in the right box?"

"They ought to go in another one? Do you think they're protected enough?"

Brazil hastily removed the figurines and the glass jugs, placing them in boxes that once housed them earlier.

"I think maybe they were better the other way."

Brazil quickly removed all of the objects and began placing them in the original boxes. As each piece traveled from box to box, a slight, thin, indescribable event emerged. They were not disturbances in the color and texture of the boxes as well as the paintings, jugs and watercolors. No. They did not change anything themselves, and no-one would be able to call them events, really. They seemed to jump from one object to another as each moved. When a jug fell to the floor and cracked, Xenis sensed them and when something rolled from one place to another, he perceived them. He rolled two jugs along the floor and watched, moved scarves dangling from a hanger back and forth, observing. Brazil watched as he tapped forks on the kitchen table and swirled water inside of a pot. They uttered not a sound and made no noise, but if someone should ask him to describe what he heard, he would say it fell somewhere between a tiny laugh and a distant squeal. They had no color in themselves, but made more or less vivid the color of things that Brazil moved. They moved nothing in themselves, but a shimmer of each object brightened or became dull with each shift of box or with every displacement. Xenis noticed more of them now that he had begun seeing, or hearing, or whatever he was doing, he was not sure; no perception was primary. The more Brazil moved objects, the more they seemed to swarm about what she initiated. And when she moved with the greatest of haste, flocks of them seemed to move with her and the objects she shifted. Xenis even thought he perceived one of these...things...leap from one box to another, but he perceived as well that the objects did the leaping. He ought to have been disturbed by the jumping and the curiousness that he sensed as they emerged. They sat atop Brazil's head, one on her shoulder. Oddly, Xenis was not able to discern their number, but he thought he sensed many, perhaps only one. He felt heavily an inability to perceive. At times, they swelled Brazil's color and distended her words and the sounds that came from her. They were there in her drink when she sat resting at kitchen table, swarmed in her breakfast eggs – were perhaps dangerous – yet he sensed no hostility. He sensed no grief or suffering or happiness at all. In fact, he sensed nothing that made the sensation. He felt an incredible urge to corner and capture one of these events, or motions, or disturbances or whatever they were. He waited for something to happen, one indication that one of these things would happen or emerge. He thought better than to look for one near Brazil, so he went into his room in order to hunt. He waited for a time, expecting nothing. They came when something moved, or as a sound emerged, or when someone perhaps tasted something. Xenis had witnessed one when Brazil ate that morning.

Xenis looked around and sensed one near his window when his drape blew into the room. It was too far from him to grasp. Again, he sensed another when he closed the door, but it disappeared too quickly. He stood quiet, waiting, but nothing came. He moved the drape again and saw one, but again something fled. As he walked across the room, his shoes tapped the floor, and he heard them somehow in the shoe-sounds. He tapped on the naked wood floor with his shoes, and each tap produced the desired effect; he grasped at each one as his shoe produced it. No tangible grasp of any one of them was possible.

"Maybe I can find them elsewhere."

Xenis moved into the kitchen where Brazil was heating water, moving in and out and storing objects of lesser use for future travel. He grasped at the fire heating the water, where he saw many of these things emerge, but ceased quickly. That was too dangerous. He moved a dish on the kitchen table and was unable to capture that one. He tapped a plate with a knife with one hand and clutched at insubstantiality with the other, on each occasion one emerging. He held nothing in his hand, but he thought certainly he captured...something, ceasing his efforts each time Brazil came into the kitchen. Xenis thought his best opportunity to grab one of these things was tapping his shoe on the floor. Those were large enough to capture, seemingly, and he was able to produce one whenever he pleased, but the floor tap was unsuccessful because he had to stoop down, so Xenis removed his shoe. Tapping the kitchen table first, he perceived many of these..things...but he caught nothing; tapping the wall second he perceived many stamping in herds as if in migration, but his hunt came upon nothing. The refrigerator and the counter were just as impossible places to grasp them. Xenis thought that the closer these things were, the more successful the hunt might be. His shoe was best at bringing them out, so he tapped his chest. Again and again they arrived.

"Pat-Pat-pat-Pat-pat."

He was not able to catch one.

"Pat-Pat-pat-Pat-pat."

He tapped more quickly.

"Pat-Pat-pat-Pat-pat."

Still nothing.

"Pat-Pat-pat-Pat-pat."

He tapped more forcefully.

"Pat-Pat-pat-Pat-pat."

"What are you doing?"

Xenis ceased his fruitless efforts and looked at Brazil, a wild and hopeless prospect upon him. He hesitated in order to bring up some words that would explain, but they refused to come. He hoped that she would grow tired quickly and return to her efforts, but Brazil moved nowhere. Explaining that he was smashing insects or some kind of bug would alarm her; she would not be able to sleep. Telling her that he was playing a game would anger her, but perhaps that was the best course. Trying to tell her the truth was the most hazardous course, given the position of his shoe and the act in which he was caught; he wanted only that the embarrassment and the need to explain depart as if it had never come – erased from all of existence. Surely, they would help him on this occasion. No, of course not. Xenis thought for a moment that a distraction might keep her attention fixed on another topic long enough to forget the situation, just so much time as it might take to go on to other things and let this issue die. He sighed and put his shoe back onto his foot.

"I'm not sure," he said.

"Not sure."

"Yeah."

"How's that?"

"I'm...hunting naughts," he said. "I think."

"You think?"

"I'm not sure what they are."

"What what are?"

"They're...disturbances? I don't know."

"Jesus. I don't have time for this. Figure it out and start packing again."

Even as Brazil unexpectedly delivered Xenis he immediately began again to move jugs and lamps as well as books and small paintings into boxes. The most important elements of Brazil slowly fell from the walls, the beds and the tables of her old life. The...things...Xenis had attempted to catch continued to tease him as he packed silverware and plates into corrugated cardboard and wrote **FRAGILE** on box-sides. Removal of paintings and bronze objects, including masses of tin-copper destined to be art, made them come alive, if one was able to assign living to them. They were not wide or fat or large, though at times they seemed so; more or less colorful Xenis was unable to determine, though they were comprised of what appeared to be color. When he touched one of them, briefly, he felt no smoothness nor rough nor bumpy nor any other surface. No quality could describe what Xenis perceived...if perception was even taking place..., but he knew they were there. One of them appeared to lunge at him, but he later thought that it was simply one of the most potent of them...if even potent was an applicable word.

"It's odd that one could be more potent than another if they have no qualities."

This strongest of them yet manifest emerged when Xenis placed one of Brazil's bronze pieces in a crate and took it to storage where it waited. Other moments made them emerge similarly, like when most of their books and clothing had been placed in boxes. Xenis was unable and quite unwilling to tell Brazil when he saw one coming, when disappearing; she seemed oblivious anyway. He almost tried to catch one when he saw it on her blouse and when she moved a bronze Dionysus.

These things had been around and within most everything they packed over a three-day course. Xenis continued to observe them, occasionally attempted to capture, saying nothing to Brazil about his efforts and frustration. The pair finally came to rest when they had boxed up almost every one of their belongings and waited to move. Only the bare essentials were available: some silverware and plates not already packed, toiletries and clothes enough to wear for a few days. They started packing all of the boxes into a truck on a Friday afternoon. The larger parts of Brazil's identity disappeared into the moving-truck first – bronze after bronze – each time one of these strange things appearing. Xenis alone noticed. He was amazed that the movers recognized nothing at all as they stuffed Brazil's very identity into a steel box. When the moving came faster and many boxes were taken at once or moved quickly, a virtual swarm of...*them* – larger than any of the earlier herds – popped up and out of boxes and rattled about each object and relocation. Some of them looked like spiders to Xenis, but then he realized that they did not run, nor did they have legs. They simply appeared, and never actually moved, but gave the impression of movement when they appeared. As the movers gathered everything together, they swarmed around boxes as before, but with every move. As Brazil's eyes teared up for her last look at her apartment, four or five came out of her head. Xenis could feel them as he thought that he liked this place. They sat about and around his thoughts as he determined what his thoughts were.

He tried to discern what shape they were, but he had great difficulty. They looked like spindly circles, which is why he thought perhaps they were spiders, but then they were square or angular, misshapen, shapeless even.

"How can they have shape and be discernible?"

They shifted their form regularly, or perhaps they were unable to come to shape.

"They certainly don't remain still."

Occasionally, he tapped at one or two of them when they appeared on a wall. One trembled and ran, he thought, but he was unable to say certainly. Another seemed to reside on Brazil's words as she asked him to watch the truck while she re-entered her old abode. He heard it, he thought. Alarmingly, the sound it made was much like Brazil's voice, as if the not came from whatever was. Xenis thought about it while he listened to Brazil talk about something – what it was he had no idea – and he realized that each time he sensed one of these things he had not sensed nothing, no. They were much like the thing around which or in which he sensed them. Once in a while he was able to touch one or two of them, and the sensation was again needle-like, yet pleasant. Still, he could not pinpoint what was the sensation he felt, though it was much like whatever resided there, and indescribable.

He touched one that continued the truck door and one of them on a word that a mover uttered. Every so often, he lost the sense of anyone watching him, and frequently he stopped what he was doing in order to perceive more clearly. Brazil stopped him on the stairs.

"Are you alright?" she said.

"Yeah, yeah. Why do you ask?"

Brazil went on her way, too busy to continue the conversation. Xenis walked out into the parking lot where the truck was now unloading boxes and the furniture crawled with them. Looking up for relief, he noticed a disturbance in the sky,...but it was not in the sky. Minuscule...whatevers...dusted the air with the same odd...presence. Xenis thought that these things had no substance, yet he touched them. He knew they had no color, yet he saw them. Curious, he reached up into the air, almost as if he were touching a piece of sky, and after a time of reaching he caught hold of what turned out to be the whole of blue and an expanse of nirvana. He held it only a moment as if he could bring down the celestial ceiling, and while he did he felt no sensation in his hand, nothing. No pain came, but it was almost as if his hand no longer existed.

"What are you doing now?" startled Xenis.

"Oh. I'm just resting a moment," he said, speedily lowering his arm. "We're almost there."

He nodded up the stairs.

"Yeah. What a pain." Brazil looked at the truck and up the two flights of stairs to her new high-height abode.

"Soon. Soon, my friend," he said.

Xenis now knew he was able to touch one of these things. He found that the ones in the sky he was able to tag once in a great while, but the hunt demanded effort. As he looked up into the sun's light, he thought a thought that touched upon another of these...entities.

"No, that's not the right word."

He found in his thought that the words and images combined with sounds in his head touched...something. He had touched one in this way before, but now it was not a blankness that fit into his mind, but some other thinking than he had thought but now was thinking him. It stretched him in the mindful way and made length of his words and brought everything together for him while leaving much out. He was unable to place what he experienced, but his engagement was not tactile, nor noetic. Something plagued him again, and now it was inside of his mind...or not. It incorporated itself into all what he was able to think, and what all else he might see he was unable to grasp. He no longer stood in the parking lot, nor Brazil's old home, not in his apartment nor his old condominium. He was unable to determine where he was, unable to understand that it was actually a place. His mind continued to expand in ways that he thought unimaginable, thinking-seeing, hearing-thinking, feeling-seeing and bringing his mind-sense into contact with more and still more and greater and larger. He yet withstood what ought to have been painful, but perception here failed and kindly pain refused to visit. All objects resided with him in beginnings as well as the connection between the things of any kind that made him understand. He did not recognize these connections initially, but they became first the similarities of language and then the calculation, pure, of mathematics.

"That's the most significant thing," he said to an overhearing Brazil.

Xenis stood near the rear of the parked truck when he thought his thinking. Motionless, he moved his mind into a nowhere that pervaded everything about him, even the things billions of light-years distant. Though he was unable to process all that this minuscule...thing...bared to him, he somehow understood that a bit of everything resided in the thought that now occupied him. It was not that every piece of every fact – of moment – resided with him, but rather there was something of all. An endless unsealing of every what was not only impossible to process, but it was entirely too much for his frame of mind. One moment in the parking lot of a city neighborhood, one minuscule mind-sense of the insubstantiality that entered his thinking-being, was enough to consume the gas giants of our system and then to as easily evoke and devour the super-massive black holes that center galaxies. Xenis cried out to his long-dead mother, but in the sable dampening field no-one heard. No sound, nor sight, nor matter nor presence was part of this present. He was reminded of his stay inside of an eternal library, that terrible duration

 "Are you alright?" Brazil shook him.

"Oh my," he said.

 "You are a real problem today."

"I was out of it." He touched his forehead with the tips of his fingers.

Xenis felt cold and a shiver slipped out of his head.

NICHTS

It covered the head of the stranger and drew in heat that warmed him. Cropped close and practically all of the same length, it betrayed here and there with grey strands the beginnings of age, an age that had changed the sable features of a once-savage male. Powerful and wealthy, the guest-stranger came to be more able and impoverished. These were changes whose origins demanded revelation, a coming-to-light that cannot take place, not because the causes of change were unknown, but because that change was possible came to be from nothing already the raven-headed youth – home-born stranger. Strange whats have strange ways, obfuscating what lies in plain sight, until someone unearths them, and then, when they have come to light, we find that they were not nothing nor completely something, but in part a shadow that kept away the light. The very thing that makes connection is what a what keeps from perception, though it lies clear as light on a plain day. They have hidden nothing and all that is has hidden what within a knotted not. Nichts perform this duty and all that is good.

RIDDANCE OF NAUGHT

X enis lowered the heat beneath the round screaming metal, brought it outside with lemons and honey, green tea-leaves. Into the light and under shade they went. Brazil ignored him beneath the diminished light while he sat, poured and the stiff metal chair tough-hugged him. The lemon and honey mixture felt good in his mouth, but he preferred green tea, its flavor.

"Not bad," he thought.

He sat at a circular, mesh-metal table with like chairs. Covering him and a reclining Brazil the black-white-checker courtyard umbrella diminished the light that meant to drive off their pleasure. Sol could be cruel. Brazil read an art-supply magazine as Xenis poured.

"It's an odd sensation," she said.

"What?"

"Being served by you."

"I guess that makes sense," he said after a pause.

"You used to be waited-on hand and foot."

"True."

A dollop of sadness sat atop his words as Xenis consumed tea, poured again.

"I...didn't mean to remind you..."

"No problem. I'm glad it's gone...in some ways."

"Still, it was nice."

"It *was* nice."

Brazil placed his comment in the rear of their conversation, yet it occupied her. She had been concerned about him when first they moved; he acted so strange that day. He had been so excitable after all the labor was done, just prior to situating themselves. Something pestered him as he tapped himself and stared into space. He calmed himself afterward, but his ordinary behavior did not return for several days. "Well, he's not normal." Normal or not, he had at least returned to predictability, a regular routine and perhaps even reliability again.

"I like this place," she said.

"It's comfortable. And not owning it means less worry."

"You *do* seem more relaxed."

"I do?"

"Yeah. I don't see you throwing my stuff away."

"Oh." He frowned.

"And you're not running around naked or something."

She laughed.

"But the day is young."

He nodded slowly. "You're hilarious."

She laughed again. "Seriously, you've calmed down."

He made no reply, but Brazil could tell that he recognized what she said.

"But you don't read so much anymore..., at least not like you used to."

Xenis was again silent.

"I've come to expect a book in your hands, or some odd thought expressed at dinner."

He looked away from her, as if to distract the conversation. He had nothing to read with him there on the patio. As far as Brazil knew, there was no essential difference between the Xenis of the old abode and the new, but some chance thing deflated him, took him from something. On the day of the move he had become so agitated when the last of their possessions were loaded into the apartment that she felt the need to sit him down, make him stop floundering. He sat, but continued to tap himself, sometimes with his shoe, and stare into the air, every so often raising his hand, needling his fingers together, but there was nothing in his hand. They had reassembled her bed and rolled out the wafer-thin mattress that he used, but he refused sleep entirely, it seemed to her.

"I wonder what was going on."

When her exhausted body had finally made rest in the new venue, she heard him rustling about in the kitchen, which was now comfortably distant from her sleeping quarters.

"He's putting things away."

Then sleep crept somnolent blackness upon her. Having arisen and walking to the kitchen, she observed that nothing had been removed from the boxes, nothing she could see. What he had been doing remained a secret, and she wanted to know nothing about it. Well, perhaps a bit.

"It's all so strange sometimes, so annoyingly strange."

His door closed, he had emerged only after several more hours to assist her with de-packing. He was helpful, but unusually quiet. He remained more sedate during that day, taciturn.

"I don't want to know."

Xenis wished only to rest. He had no idea how to control or confront such a...he knew not what. A powerful, swarming, imperceptible perception, a visage, of what he was unable to comprehend overran his thoughts; he felt more than thought the "image" away, but it held him there in Brazil's front room moments and moments. He wanted to do nothing, really. He worked each day, dutifully arising, laboring with the old man again sometimes, sometimes tutoring again. He surrendered daily needs to Brazil in order to make himself worthy, exchange his time and labor for respect. Her contentment gratified him; he wanted her to respect him. Still, he arose each morning with a feeling of impossibility and robust, oaken sadness. That heap of lukewarm, deadening emotion remained with him until the very end of each day, his ordinary interests and joys not delivering him as usual. A drug-like calm enveloped him, as if he were in the third-to-last stage of recovering from an illness. He watched online television briefly on Brazil's computer in order to distract himself, but a strong revulsion drove his thoughts away.

"Let's go to the lake," he suggested.

"The lake? Really?"

"Don't you want to go?"

"Well, sure. I go every so often, as you know," she said. "But I never thought you'd suggest it."

"Why?"

"Why? What do you mean 'why?'? You don't like that kind of thing."

"Let's try it."

And when they readied and walked they never found themselves near water. Several stores that they were compelled to pass dragged Xenis into them, Brazil compelled to accompany him. He found some pleasure looking through used clothing in a second-hand shop, and the scattered pieces of tired and spent lives that lay gathered on shelves – numbered stickers attached – amused him.

"Look at this," he said, holding up an ancient board-game, Password.

"Um. Yeah."

A pawn shop also interested him, some of its jewelry actually comely and appealing. When the pair came near the sand-colored water, they found a small, temporary amusement park obstructing their path.

"You're kidding," Brazil said when he suggested they explore it.

"No. Why not?"

"Are you feeling alright?"

"Yeah. I'm fine."

"You'd rather die...." She said in exasperation. "And it's so trite."

"That's the charm."

Brazil felt a sunken glance thrown upon her, one what spoke fear, frustration, weariness. He walked to the front booth of dirty yellow and orange stripes, purchased two tickets, handed one to her.

"Let's go."

They found themselves on a Ferris wheel and a roller coaster, both rickety and old.

"This is about as unsafe as it comes," she said.

Xenis nodded solemnly. She had expected him to laugh, what had been his old way. He made light of each moment that they played in the park, amused seemingly at the silliness and absurdity of the pair there who belonged quite elsewhere. The target practice that won them nothing and the cheese-smeared pretzel they purchased amusements in themselves. "This is so ridiculous." Xenis smiled, content in an amusement he found contemptible, drawing near a serious laugh. The following Monday that robust, oaken sadness became him again, but on this occasion less so. Brazil invited some friends to their place, a house-warming. Deter and his wife Elissa reminded Xenis of a couple with whom he once had acquaintance, many couples actually. They were visiting the city and wanted to see Brazil after some years. Deter worked as an office manager of a financial exchange firm.

"Financial exchange?" Xenis asked.

"Yeah. We assist corporate interchange of monetary necessities."

"I see. Or...rather I don't see."

Deter laughed.

The two pairs of friends prepared drinks and dealt cards, a game Deter called Egyptian Ratscrew. Tom Collins served a mild inebriation. Xenis' difficulty avoiding drink came strong, felt potent. Egyptian Ratscrew involved the distribution of a whole deck of cards to all players, four being the ideal. Players threw cards onto a table and slapped when doubles arose.

"Four chances to beat an Ace, three to beat a King, two for a queen and one chance to beat a Jack," Deter explained.

"How does one beat another card?"

"With another face-card."

"So, a Jack beats an Ace."

"Yeah."

Brazil won only a few slaps at first, but became more adept as evening passed. Deter and his wife rivaled one another in ability and speed, and they prevailed in the beginning. Xenis' quick attentiveness gained him some ascendancy, but he became no master. Still, the game soothed him, that oaken sadness burning away.

"This time of year is perfect for sailing," Deter said. "You sail?"

"At one time," Xenis answered.

"We should all go out on the lake when we have time."

Elissa groaned. "Time is the problem."

"Well, we make the time, yes?" Deter smiled. "We must make time for leisure."

"You own a boat?

"A small one, yes. Nothing special, but comfortable."

"We'll have to accompany you some time." Xenis glanced at Brazil.

The Egyptian Ratscrew ended as usual with Deter the sole proprietor of cards.

"He always wins this game," Elissa said.

The remainder of the evening saw five more guests and like Egyptian Ratscrew. The boat excursion and the changing of season; the annoyance with public transportation and the temperature of Brazil's apartment exchanged the thoughts of guest-friends. Each new set of guests gave Xenis and Brazil the opportunity-obligation to paraphrase themselves, and then again, again returning to the same subject once more. Xenis did not tap himself or reach his hand into the sky and a tipsy fever never lured him to drink that evening.

"I'll take what I can get" was Brazil's thought.

Brazil's dog kept Deter and Michael, a fellow artist, entertained with his insistence on reclining in their laps. One or the other were obliged.

"Just shoo him away if he bothers you," Brazil said.

"He's no bother."

The gathering lasted well into the early morning hours, Xenis un-realizing how late the hour had gone.

"You can stay a bit longer," he said to Deter and his wife.

"One more game."

"We really have to get home," Elissa said. "The sitter's waiting."

Xenis attempted to retain the three other guests who remained, but his efforts merely hastened their departure, and when all were gone a tired Brazil dressed for and climbed into bed as soon as she was able. Xenis sat in the front room when all were gone, peering under the chairs and into the artificial fireplace. Tired and weary to the point of exhaustion, he refused to enter his room, sat in Brazil's recliner until he dozed off, and only as he roused briefly did he drag his what to bed. When he stood, away from his bed, Xenis thought to talk with

Brazil.

"Let's invite your friends over again."

"Are you serious?"

"Yeah, why?"

"Really?"

Deter and Elissa arrived Friday-next evening and Egyptian Ratscrew was first on Xenis' mind. They were able to visit one more time before they returned home.

"Can we do something else?" Brazil asked.

"Let's watch a film and play a few rounds," Deter suggested.

The four two-pair reclined as *The French Connection* offered something easy to discuss, and they lost themselves in light-pondered recreation. After a few drinks, Brazil was willing to attempt Egyptian Ratscrew. Again Deter prevailed, this time crushing his opponents.

"You weren't trying the other day," Brazil said playfully.

Elissa nodded slowly as Deter grinned. The citadel of distraction towered deep into the very early Saturday morning when Elissa-Deter expressed interest in leaving.

"You can stay here, if you like," Xenis said. Brazil threw rolling eyes at him.

"No, no. We need to get to it."

"No, really. We can chat a bit longer and there's no need to stir until morning, when you're both fresh."

"Maybe we can," Elissa said.

"Good, then. You'll stay and we can play another round."

The one round became six as stygian-evening turned morning-light. When the couple departed early-day, Xenis and Brazil rested for a brief span.

"Let's find another film to watch tonight," Xenis said.

Xenis awoke early in order to prepare for work each day, and when he came home he almost always carried a new idea for a movie stream. Many were dramas, some crime adventures and comedies. Each night a film emerged from Xenis' box of suggestions: documentaries on natural events, foreign political dramas, occasional stand-up comedy. Xenis insisted that they both watch, but after uncounted weeks even Brazil's thorough tolerance drifted into weary dissatisfaction. On weekends the pair would watch movies in the park.

"It's just the same thing," Brazil said. "More film."

The ubiquitous movies in no manner bothered a Xenis who gladly immersed himself, arose at six am, arrived home six pm – screen-submerged in evening. Commonly, film ending his waking hours, Xenis never ceased until a quiet heavy sopor slipped unbidden-non-realized into him now drained of wakefulness.

"Let's have more people over," he suggested.

NICHTS

Whats are not in the past; the past does not exist. It is now past. Yet, the past reaches into the present; a what has a past that makes it what it is, and the whats as other-than have a priority that made them what they are. The past reaches into the present by being present as a what that has acted, yet the past does not exist, except as a what that acts now. The what, as it is now, is a part of the past that does not exist. It does have a not as part of its what. This part is part and whole of the whole; part is whole of part and part of whole. This part is then not itself and it is itself by being in the past. Them hopping from one what to another, cards changed places and slipped from hand to hand. The pictures moved and the hertz vibrated concept and tone from ear to ear, producing space and residing in place. Jack of spades kept time in place by not being queen of hearts, refusing her face from his and making black of color and not red. What transpired was sun rising and tea served; charging phones and showering – and all else mundane and fantastic that became permanently a what of the past.

NICHTS ALWAYS
THERE

Nearly every weekend, some friend or group visited Brazil in order to be entertained. Xenis taught several new acquaintances the simple rules of Egyptian Ratscrew; he sometimes won, never mastering. Most other times, the boat excursion and the changing of season; the annoyance with public transportation and the temperature of Brazil's apartment were topics of future-pleasure exchange. Each new set of guests gave the pair of others opportunity and obligation to paraphrase themselves, and later again, again returning to the same topic ever more. Brazil delighted in this turn of events, and friends whom she had not seen in years became regular attendees in a seemingly unbroken line of film-seeking movie-critics.

"None here."

Xenis had always been someone whose presence came difficult to others and now comfort placed gentle hands upon her, but Brazil also wished the return of old Xenis, a stranger whose difficulties produced insufferable moments.

"Maybe not."

Still, aware of her weariness, she was folding clothes or perhaps vacuuming her bedroom when a thought emerged.

"It's like it was the last time."

A need to ask him brought her out.

"You're looking for someone again, aren't you?", she asked.

"What do you mean?"

"You used to look for someone, a friend or something."

Xenis shook his head.

"Yes, you did. When you had the penthouse."

"Oh yes. Yes, I did, but no. I'm not doing that now."

"Are you sure?"

"Quite certain."

Brazil was amazed that she would need to take away from recreation and amusement a man who used to take pleasure in draining merriment from all what was around him.

"I'm kind of tired of having people over," she said.

"Oh?"

"It's fun. Don't get me wrong. It's just that...we've been at it for months."

"Months?"

"Yeah, it's been that long."

"Months?"

"Well, maybe not that long."

The friends walked downtown on Saturdays. "Just in order to see what's there," she said. They found a French restaurant ensconced inside of a building, regularly asked for a place on the patio. They sat and ate and discussed the last excursion with Michael or other comic interlude.

"None here."

Drinking orange juice and pomegranate extract, Brazil looked at the stream of pedestrians walking along the sidewalk only fifty meters below – faces, clothes and gait.

"Let's count hats," she suggested.

"Hats?"

"How many hats are passing by?"

Xenis looked over the sidewalk, hat-counting being surprisingly difficult so dense was the crowd.

"I count five, no six."

"I see at least seven."

That day concentrated on hats and ugly pants, counting and arguing over the aesthetics of trousers, and Brazil became immersed in the vacuity, yet was cautious. Should they continue to count things – chairs ugly-dogs screaming-babies bewildered-expressions and leaves on trees – she would become as annoyed with her own suggestion as she had been with the parade of friends and acquaintances that Xenis detained as long as possible. Thus, the observation of the habits and antics of one particular ant in an ant colony was interrupted by a visit from a Michael who burst into their presence lanky-armed and bone-legged, a small portable pot-belly complementing his person.

"None here."
"I have an especial aversion to work and dirt," he said. "Same thing."

Sporting a yellow and white striped shirt and rust-orange jean-like trousers with red high-tops, Michael took up a pencil from the dining-room table where he sat, scribbled as he talked. He made a habit of bobbing limbs and lifting fingers up and down. He tapped his foot onto Xenis' who shifted his legs in order to grant the trespassers room. Michael again tapped, giggled. Xenis arose and located himself at another part of the table where "footy" was unplayable. Michael pouted.

"You guys are no fun," he began. "Jeanie couldn't come to Meat-Fest last weekend," he said. "Something about not having enough money."

He rolled his eyes and tore off a sheet of paper from Brazil's notepad.

"You having people over this weekend?"

Michael folded the paper in half, unfolded it.

"I have some guests from out of town who want to meet 'urbanites.'" He put four fingers to the air, animating the quotation marks. Once his fingers had fallen, he bent half of one side of paper over and then the other side, making a point.

"Do you have any gum?"

He folded the right corner of the right side of the point up, forming a paper needle. He did the same on the left side, and without waiting for an answer,

"How long can you go without blinking?"

Michael then folded his original point back into the mass of paper, his two needles jutting out in front.

"You guys don't seem at all lively."

Xenis said nothing, rather observed – Brazil opening the cupboard door.

"None here."

Michael folded the mass of paper in half once more, bent the wings in the middle, and let glide a squat but sporty creation.

"That's called a hawkeye," he said as the plane flew gracefully around the three and spun twice before it hit the floor.

"Not bad," Xenis said.

"I can show you how to make one. Several, in fact."

"Really?"

"I have the designs stored here," he pointed to his head. "In my computer."

Xenis had been cruel to Brazil occasionally, teasing her to the tip of madness; she knew he would be difficult no matter what happened, but he had become not exceedingly intolerable. In fact, he worked; he paid his share of expenses; he even listened when she complained – ceased some of his more strange habits and their diversions filled her with mirth. He treated others with his presence these days, and she found one of those smiles and a grin inside her, letting them out, but as he and Michael made planes, she realized that something was not right. She enjoyed the excursions into the city, the counting, the guests coming to her home, but something.... After a tolerable amount of time, she compelled Michael to leave, Xenis and him explaining that the time was not right to abandon the construction of the fleet. Eleven pm had come and gone when Michael departed, and Brazil feared his speedy return.

"Let's rent a film," she said next night.

The pastimes continued to amass with Xenis and Brazil during long-another month's time, Brazil carefully managing to avoid the trap of constant movies by occasionally tumbling into Micheal visits or other almost unwelcome visitations. The pair played chess and learned to knit. They rode the commuter train around the inner section of the city. "A poor man's tour," Xenis called it.

"None here."

His unsuccessful attempt at learning origami entertained her, but what was somehow at last the most annoying of exercises was Xenis' solitary habit of playing with a blue thumb-tack. He removed containers, dishes and the cloth from the kitchen table and twisted and turned the tack with his fingers, flipped it and attempted to spin it like a top. The blue cyclone rolled onto its side, sometimes meandering around the floor and beneath the table where Xenis searched for that specific tack.

"Found it."

"Why do you need that particular tack?"

"It's the one I'm accustomed to."

"Accustom yourself to another one."

"It's not so simple."

"It isn't?"

"You don't understand."

"No, I don't."

The grocer around the corner was glad to see Xenis regularly, Xenis developing a habit of purchasing two eggs wrapped in plastic each day. Possessed of penny-filled pockets, he came to the counter, pulled out a handful of stray copper Lincolns and counted them by sliding two at a time across the counter.

"None here."

"I can see that happening once, maybe twice. Maybe. But you do it every day," Brazil commented.

Xenis ran his palm along his forehead, massaging.

"You do that purposely."

"Do what?"

"Go into the grocery with a pocket full of pennies. Daily. No-one has that many loose pennies."

Xenis held his fist against his mouth and bobbed up and down, a percolated laugh leaking up and out of him.

"Oh my gosh! You do! You slide the pennies to that poor cashier every day...purposely!"

Again, Xenis laughed.

"Why would anyone do that kind of thing?"

"I don't know," he said and shrugged.

A laugh seeped out from Brazil's teeth. The following two months were moved in pairs from Xenis' pocket: Michael arriving willy-nilly, friends visiting on Friday nights, counting leaves on trees and greeting individual insects in the courtyard by name: Constance, Beauregard, Anthony. He pressed Brazil with details. Constance was prissy and loved Beauregard, but Anthony was the more proper suitor who was flawed because of a gambling habit.

"None here."

Xenis folded his thin foam pad on its edge and rolled it up, then into a corner it went. He walked into the bathroom and disrobed, entered the shower-stall. While he cleaned himself, he began a thought as sudden as it was unpredicted. The absurdity of showering only to kick up dirt with brooms and sweat the moving of heavy machinery struck him, as if a sudden turn. Why he was cleaning himself for a dirt-filled day he was unable to fathom. Work-days came ordinary enough, yet he wondered – as he had before – at the meaningfulness of his labor. He cleaned after those who built edifices with such low quality materials that the same building would need to be razed in thirty years. Most of the money that circulated during his efforts found its way into the hands of those who already possessed too much, needed no more, and yet these same persons continued to long for yet ever more. They spent it on themselves and at the same time they took everything possible, and wished to be congratulated for being not captains of industry, but generals. During that day Xenis thought about the day laborers who believed what others wanted them to believe. They faulted those who tried to better their position, manipulated emotionally. They voted into power the adjutants of those who own too much, and they were in turn manipulated into detesting those among them who recognized an imbalance and who wanted to create a more just economy.

"I want to be neither a day-laborer nor a businessman."

Xenis came home on his bicycle, as usual, locking it to one of the racks affixed to the cement floor of the basement in his complex. He stood away and wondered at the need to affix his property to something so that no-one would take it as their own.

"'Only a thought."

He and Brazil had planned to watch a new series online, something acclaimed by critics. He was unable to recall its name.

"Not relevant" he heard more than thought.

Xenis contentedly cleaned himself once again, wondering again at the absurdity of cleaning after having already cleaned, and sat once more at his prepared place. Having watched fifteen minutes of *Silver Seed*, Xenis was unable to latch his interest onto the drunken detective protagonist.

"I need to walk," he said.

He grabbed his coat and departed, testing the neighborhood with his feet, watching the sky for naught and entering dollar shops, not wishing to eat, nor purchase baubles. When he arrived at the lake, he found that he did not intend to remain there as well. Climbing a tree and walking along the railroad tracks brought no solace, nor did it generate interest. The next day was similar. Similar thoughts in the shower that morning and like feelings in afternoon. The legitimacy of work, play, sleep, eat, work, eat, sleep, play again eluded him. When an unannounced Michael visited that evening, Xenis thought that the man would be a useful distraction and a bit of entertainment – as had become the long custom. Yet Michael's antics, middle-aged footy play and caddy-talk paper-folding, only deepened a sense of irritation. The weekend arrived after more similar days of consternation, Margaret and Eleanor arriving on Friday and expecting drinks and personal chitchat-gathering that occupied most Fridays. They stayed until twelve.

"Maybe we can have a visitor-less Friday next week," Xenis suggested.

And the next week was guestless, free from card-playing and internet television watching. As more weeks passed, Xenis relieved himself of the counting of hats, the naming of insects, association with Michael and films. He again arose from his thin mattress, rolled it up in ritual. He dressed as he wished because today was Saturday; he need not sweep or clean. He powered on Brazil's laptop, but was unwilling to jump from site to site. He considered showering, but denied that absurdity. He would clean later. He ate breakfast and found himself in the basement of the complex, fixing a bicycle he planned to give to Brazil. He had taken off the back wheel and was looking at a broken derailleur when he felt something tap and then enter the back of his head. Massaging his neck, he felt nothing – no blood, no bump. He looked behind him and saw only the concrete wall of a dingy apartment basement whose not terribly clean surface housed no pests. No-one had come down while he worked and no-one had been able to come up behind him. He scratched the back of his head and felt quite normal – lively even – though his interest in the derailleur had apparently vanished.

"No. Not again."

He abandoned the project and the four tools he possessed on the heavy-mass, gray floor and walked around the basement. He needed movement.

"I feel...wonderful."

He raised his hands and stretched wide his fingers, fanning them into fives. He hopped around near the laundry room and felt the need to jump and stand on his head, which he did somewhat awkwardly but not without grace. Abandoning the basement, he trotted up the stairs, enjoying the step-up stair-jump when his feet were not on the floor, as if he were in air. Each of these motions was a rich and heavy pleasure, though why suddenly again eluded him. He entered the flat not knowing to what he paid attention, but whatever it was it resided not in the kitchen, not the bathroom, not the bedroom, nor even the living room. Unable to sense what it was, he suspected an old experience.

"What's going on?"

He knew what it was, but did not want to perceive or think about it. It was there without seeking and it was too much, just as Michael, card-playing and movie-watchcing had become too much.

NICHTS

The what is a kind; it is a what. The what has a specific configuration of existing that allows particular whats to follow, yet the future has no being. The future is not-yet. The what of the present is then a now that reaches into a what and state that does not exist. Its being imitates itself by continuing into a state that is-not, and that future is a not; the present of the what reaches itself into what is not; its continuance residing in a similar state of non-being; the non-being is the when and where that the what is as it continues in the present, but the present is the not of the past; the not of the past reaches into the future; it reaches into the future not as the past as much as the present; the present is the past and the future and it is neither the future nor the past. The what resides between all of these as a what-can-be-other that continues to open through the not.

THE PAST
CONTINUES THE
FUTURE

Brazil's apartment was near the top of the complex, yet Xenis had some difficulty attaining the ceiling-door to the roof. A few locked doors and warning signs were there, but as a final threshold was thrown down, Xenis found himself on the roof of the building. Perhaps suddenly moments blinked into one another, a pleasant and familiar confusion. He had just arrived on the roof, was disrobing and sitting for hours, dehydrated already, feeling the sun-soaked black tar hot beneath his bare legs – wanting food. Only several seconds passed, but rapidly events dream-like came to him. A shout below from some angry large woman, or possibly a man named Christian; the words arose unrecognizable, identities unformed and foreign. He shook his head; he did not know these persons. Someone had barred the passage-door to the room, Xenis suspecting he himself had done it, but he was unable to determine if that were true. The moist air blew past him and scattered itself. Radios blared screechings of mostly males who seemed to be in pain – the noise disruptive – but it was followed by the hop of string from divertimento 563 in E. The variation lifted Xenis sadly off the roof, though his legs stretched still upon it. Here there was no understanding or knowledge as such, only some aspect of mere existence. Xenis wished that his present state never end, but seeing the men in badges and short sleeves lifting him down the ladder and onto the stairs then to the cell and back at home on his thin mattress happened. Why had all these things transpired he was unable to know. All happened once more at once in sequence.

"This again," Brazil. Studying him, she placed his clothing by his head as he rested on the thin mat.

Xenis twisted the mechanism up and let it drop down again. The derailleur seemed to be affixed to the cycle properly. Now he needed to test it. His ride along the dirt walkway near the lake pushed the hot air past him, reminding him of his effort. He locked the cycle to the rack once he had returned and walked up the stairs casually.

"This is very nice."

Brazil would not come home soon, so there was still time to sit. He read some of Nietzsche's *Twilight* as he rested. He had not been to work in several days, the old man calling every so often. He had enough money that rent and other expenses would present no problem for many months, but that was no concern. He had come to understand that there was no need. The moving of the scaffold and the cleaning of the cement floors carried no meaning, other than the end each had in and as themselves. They were not essential. The same had been true of the visits of friends and the making of paper planes. He wanted again to remove all of his clothing, but he had been told that one more episode would make him homeless.

"Do I need a home?"

He did. He required shelter, food and a place of rest, regularity as well.

"One doesn't really own anything."

Xenis was not a possessor any longer. He accepted that now. He needed material things in order to survive, but none of the things around him were he. He labored and played within a community, but the gathering of others was not specifically he. It grew within him and gave him the parameters that defined him, so it was and will be he in that manner, but Xenis belonged elsewhere, wanted out of even those parameters from which there was no escape. He walked out of the apartment and down the stairwell, out into the cool, clear sun-blue of day. He felt a pressure in his head, as if an emotion wished to emerge, but he was unable to recognize what it was. He wandered without aim for moments and moments and found himself in the building courtyard where he sat on an iron chair. A gradual slip of mind moved about inside his awareness, and he felt as if he would emit at any moment, but...no. It was not a physical driving or purging from his body. It was a different sensation he experienced, a palm soundly rap-tapping on the skin of a drum. Xenis would have thought that his sensation arose from within him, but it arose not inside as much as outside, yet "where" did not describe its place. He searched the courtyard, looking for what was affecting him in this manner, but he knew already what it was. Xenis wondered when his sensation began and recalled the moment when he thought something entered the back of his head in the basement. He felt a compulsion to hop and leap again, and walked where he did not know.

Brazil had been reassured by the recent turn of events, Xenis being Xenis. She liked that name, and wished that he continue to use it. She opened the hidden door on her circular table with a small key and lifted out a bottle of scotch, Heilmann's own. She poured a half-glass and shot a bit back along her throat, leaning over to peer into Xenis' bare, empty room, certain that she was alone. She drank only rarely, and not in front of Xenis, if at all possible. She needed no relief of that kind, but occasionally deadlines at work, artistic frustration of one kind or another and the agonizing management of her weight drove her to Heilmann's.

"This only makes things worse."

She thought of her weight. Still, at the moment she refused to concern herself with it, her self-delivered respite only temporary. Someone else might have been disturbed.

"I'm not sure why these things comfort me."

She thought that the reason may have been a familiarity. She recalled thinking about how an abused woman returns to her abuser.

"It's not that she wants to be abused."

It seemed to her that women return to abusers out of fear sometimes, sure, but also because they return to a kind of familiarity.

"They know how to manage an abusive male, but they don't know how to manage the necessary change."

Brazil was certain that she had found at least one cause.

"But Xenis isn't abusive."

He threw off his clothes and climbed trees naked; he ran about the neighborhood like a child and he slept on the hard floor. Yes, he did all these things, but he did not abuse her, refused even to tease her in the aggravating manner that earlier occupied him. Still, his rejection of the hat-counting and Michael's nonsense and the card-playing – even the social visits – relieved her.

"There was something un-Xenis about those things."

She laughed aloud.

"I got him to count hats!"

She thought about how a bronze top-hat would look on one of her morose busts, liked the contradiction. Brazil felt the slipping of her thoughts into a puddle of words and whirling images, that initial intoxication hitting her. She heard a key moving into the first lock on the front door, and panic grew. She swung her arm up and let flow the remaining scotch into her system, a significant amount of liquid, moving as quickly as possible into the kitchen where she washed the glass. She realized the need to stash the bottle in the cabinet and ran to the circular table, closing and locking the door just in time to pretend that she was not concealing her drink.

"Hey," she said, straightening out her words as much as possible.

"Hi." Xenis scrutinized her a moment. "Anything wrong?"

Brazil only shook her head, lifting her hand up and shaking it.

"No. Why?"

"You seem...distracted."

"Oh!" Brazil chuckled. "*I don't seem myself?*"

"You're intoxicated."

"I am not!" She sat down on the recliner and scratched her head.

"Yes, you are."

"No."

"Yes." He laughed. "It's alright, but thanks for the attempt."

Brazil merely looked around, a bit groggy. "*I'm* not myself?" she said.

"No."

"*You're* not *yourself.*" She pointed at him with unsteady finger, scotch words disjointed. Xenis sat on the chair beside a reclining Brazil.

"I'm not myself. I don't know how that can be," he said after a pause. "Seriously, I don't know."

"No?"

Xenis sat beside his old friend on the couch, looking away onto no particular spot.

"I'm not an artist."

"No."

"I'm not an academic."

"No."

"Not any of those things."

"No."

"I reject wealth. I flee poverty. I disdain fixed beliefs. No nationality occupies me. No one way of thinking, no method, predominates my reasoning. No particular way of perceiving fuels my reason. I want thoughts and I want to go without thinking. I'm dealing with pests."

" You make decisions. You have opinions," Brazil said, seemginly comforting him.

"I'm sorry. I'm just thinking a lot about what I'm doing. I didn't mean to unload."

"I am a pest?"

"Not you, of course. You're a good friend."

During the next week, Xenis' fidgeting came worse to him and he passed many hours on the lake, in the library, attending concerts and listening to poetry, but he was unable to contain what he found. He sought for weeks while Brazil worried over finances and complained, but Xenis did not occupy his time with money-earning or social gathering. His priority arose again for him. The child that had befriended Clara emerged through the rage of her death; his rejection at the hands of the students at Lumen Novum fueled brighter that anger; he recalled his Paulina and her indulgence; the intoxication of exceeding wealth and the arrogance of privilege continued to form his demeanor; the loss of the resource that had stretched his will upon many and that had made him eccentric and aloof occupied his future with its suffering and sadness. His time spent in the eternal library and the strange festival of the commoners in that community reminded him of the absurdity that confronted him. He thought these things but he continued through them as well, not alway aware that he was doing so. His futture fasted itself to these event and carried him forward, but that future seemed blank with the presence, or absence, of these pests. It was largely unknown, somewhat predictable. He continued his thoughts and distractions privately, passing fewer and fewer hours in the apartment.

"Where have you been?"

He explained little, and it was a strange thing to Brazil that Xenis was gone, giving no clear notice. She sat in her bedroom and awaited his return, expecting him soon, surprised to be without him for as long as she was. In her dresser she found a roll of one-hundred-dollar bills, enough to last until she found another roommate.

NICHTS

The what resides as present between future and past. it is not what the present is; it is not what the past is, yet it flourishes through the breaking open of what is there into its new what. Yet, these aspects of what do not truly exist. Nothing truly exists; nothing is the only eternal experience. it is form that all creatures encounter, a kind of material procession from one end to another, continually, but it is not real; one form resides within and gives work to another, no matter. There are a series of discernible forms and acts that seem static, and they give the illusion that one momment follows the next, but they merely act. All is act and nothing is eternal. Where one is is the moment of time, and that one is there directs the living through change and immediate purpose. It all, however, opens to one final occasion for being, and it is the form, sometimes mistaken for matter, that vanishes.

INTERMITTENT
ACCEPTANCE

Goodness was summer on that day. He had departed again, his face new. Marbled blue and white covered the air and they were there, with the configuration of shape, color and mass, that motion of bits of them that were not quite they – atom-play. The hydrogen and the oxygen put water to the sky, not quite heavy enough to fall, to become other again, and now remains the fine blotches in the sky-covered blue. That blue was there, demarcated by its own stretch of ray into the eyes of creatures about the earth-surface. Azul was the illusion because nothing – no barrier – held the earth in its grasp, just a reflection of the blue of light on an empty space that opened out into void and outer wanderers. That system put forward ellipse and movement of heavy-mass, titanic collections of similar atoms and particles. All of these stayed beautiful in their own without which they would not what their they, that they being what being came of them. On the dry, gray surface he pushed with ball of foot and propelled himself further, saw the blue and white and the contrast of brown-green from tree with the clear welcome-seeming expanse. The dark green of his shirt made itself as did the sky-blue and each atom-not-atom-particle-not-particle of his body labored as did the elements that comprised the mass of cloud and sky, gas on Jupiter, ice on forgotten Pluto. The awkward triangle that shaped the bicycle on which he rolled was there as well, making that part of bicycle in that place at that space that glided along the asphalt path. The circles of wheel came of themselves, forming the shape that provided the glide. The flesh that made skin, wrapping the muscle and calcium of frame in the man, made presence just as did the gray, cement-flesh of avenue and the atoms of Jupiter's storm, larger than planets. The thoughts that found essence of the man came present as well, just the same "there-ness" as each of these other objects framing the world and the larger order of things. He stopped in order to find drink at an enclosure of wood and metal, housing other like masses of hemoglobin and muscle-fiber. All of these were there, even the thoughts and concepts. The gas that these creatures breathed was there for them, though they took it granted. Unseen presences gave continued life, and these – crafted from the same kind of minuscule bits – were as there as the titanic mass of Saturn and the thought in Xenis' head. Nothing was able to be present, its own availability to itself and /for all around it. Nothing was able to be present with what called it as well. Something placed them, themselves, out and into – a there that was they no matter that they were sentience, concept, substance mass or what. That there was the commonality, sometimes the most tenuous of sympathies. Nothing was common to them, possibility of no crossing mutual paths.

The bicycle tire rubber stepped upon the gravel and sand while the laces in Xenis' shoes tightened the canvass around the top of his feet and the hungry cry of a gull meandered into ears between which sentience rolled over itself again and over. These makings of creatures and configurations of what-is all surrounded and comprised the that-they-are-there for them. Even those parts of what was there that were not were there, in some odd manner. The lack of fact in a man's assertion that he holds a degree and the missing presence of a ape-headed dog were there and had to make present in some manner. Otherwise, no lie might arise nor chimera exist. The bicycle bicycled and the long-haired dog dogged what dogs do as did everything. Still, sometimes the availability was unwilling, and then those things there clashed and relinquished the what-was-other out of them, came to be other. Many of these things did not know the other that resided within them, until the metamorphosis occurred. The words of Xenis came to be no meaning he had uttered; the mass of dead creatures came to be fossil fuel and barking of dogs became the genesis of strife. The drink became the man and the air fueled his emotions, coming to be he. The ride became a trek and later an epic and the soil slipped into the trees that grasped the sun and moved the same there into a greater height. Water glided within the gills of fish and propped up the boats that moved along its surface in order to make play ready for the inhabitants. Some lack kept moving these things along into other place, making other being, a from some what altering into another unknown. No solitary lack, Xenis knew, but rather it was many that was of a single being.

He had attempted to avoid them and that ought to have been simple; he had never seen them, but in some manner perceived them, and he wanted nothing of them. They were all of that presence and making of air into human and lake into water-beast. These were not the green of blue, and not the rectangle of circle, nor were they the physics of metaphysics, yet they made not into something through being. They presented themselves as any thing in the world, but Xenis knew now and accepted that they were indeed the not that made be. He was not fooled; they had brought about the color of the eyes in a woman with whom he talked later that day and they were the tones and hue of the music at the culture center. The what they crafted appeared – and only appeared - to be complete presence.

"Yes."

They were indeed part of anything thought or felt or perceived.

"No, no, no."

Anywhere a demarcation came about, any time a limit reached, he thought, they were there ceasing – the not that made the what of Xenis laugh at his recent homelessness. They had nothing, were themselves absolute naught. Thy were so well-disguised that they appeared to be some altogether anything that made itself present. And most homotheria knew nothing about them.

"That's not surprising."

They drove away from their space a place for another there, some being that might occupy that out and into.

"Strange."

These came to be were altogether. They were there, wrapped inside of the decrepit shelter bed on which he rested. No, wait, not wrapped inside, they were the bed and the Xenis that was there. He had no idea how they had made clear their reality to him.

"Not, but not altogether."

He laughed. The color of the brown blanket on top of him made a frequency that his eyes felt, and that measure denied everything else except what it was, so mammoth was the strength of them. The water that made the flesh of the man in the bunk beside him presently denied dry, but a cat's being as well. There was a not-other presence somehow involved in the dawn that arose on the morning that Xenis departed. They revealed to him why his belief was incorrect that water in his temporary room would never run colder and not drinkably lack its unthinkably brownish color.

"No end."

They made the holding of the sun in Xenis' palm impossible, though he attempted more than once. That impossibility made sol brilliant with lethal heat. They made the DNA of human leave him no taller than nine feet, they made the euphoric moment of triumph in music last only so long when Xenis listened, and Xenis was now calmly listening.

The bark of a tree felt graceless on his hand when he leaned against it. He had slept in the park near the lake, avoiding what persons possible. He was able to wash in the church across the thick street from the life-growing carpet of green, the inhabitants and administrators of which knew he and others stayed on the moistened grass. He tired of what had driven him from his comfortable home, yet no-one, no Xenis, had any means of escape. He felt not-thrown into his circumstances and toward obedience to what part of community had brought him to be.

"But that's there."

What Xenis felt was a creeping understanding. It was there in him, just below the surface like an insight that has not yet emerged into one's mind. It was not as if he were able to unearth it and put it to the world, like giving birth. This sensation that had no name and was unwilling to emerge from his head remained inside, though he attempted to push it out. He knew no-one was able to see it and no-one was able to touch it, or experiment on or experience it. It had remained in the open along with everything else that came to be, continually calling out to everyone. It had cried out in each and every particle of all of what is at each and every moment. Truly, it had been there with everything that became of everything because, it insisted, it was everything. Xenis heard this whatever-it-was talk to him as he turned the knob on the shower stall in room 238. The warm and then hot water rolled down his back and along his cheeks, down his legs. It explained to him how some did not like it, did not see or perceive it no mater what.

"They don't like me," it said.

Yet, it had given these tinkering thinkers what they wanted, granted to them each and everything that they touch and hear and all upon which they experiment.

"Everything I am they take, and I can do nothing," it said.

Xenis wondered at this thing in his head.

"Where are you?" he asked.

    "Don't know."

It then seemingly slid out of his mind. He perceived nothing there, but he recognized his lightness. It no longer spoke to him on that day, but he detected its presence in the silence of the room, feeling around the nodules of the carpet in order to grasp at nothing. No noise came from it. It was not as if this piece of all was mere demarcation; that would be too simple. Xenis felt that this new friend was a permanent companion. He still was unable to believe it, sometimes.

"It must be my imagination."

And when the clock's number changed, a new what occupied a place where the other had been. The number was there and lacked its own limitation, but it came about that it made itself present where it was. It made not of all around it, itself, and these were its there. The number was what was everything else. And then, this number, tyrant of being, opened the not of two upon the room, and spread upon the table the three that it was. That three was also two and one and neither of those two, but three alone. It was not even itself, a not of it inside-residing. When Xenis left the central room in order to splash water, wondering at his perception, he returned to the number three no longer, now four.

Xenis lay on the bed where he stared at the clock, some otherness within the number arising now opened before him. This one was not nearly as friendly as the three had been. Some part of it vibrated, seemed nervous to Xenis.

"Silly."

Still, he watched not this moment but the next, and some child of not remained there, within the number, not laughing but still disturbing. It would emerge soon, and that number was compelled to accept its moment. Xenis waited, a sweep of laughter swelling, and with a whimper and a cry the number was no longer. Xenis grinned. Xenis listened to each moment as they broke down what was, and every piece of thing in the room each moment, ought to have feared a breaking out and altering what would then simply become something else.

He ought to fear all of them because they were at least ubiquitous, if not omnipotent, but no. Xenis called the kitchen, ordered soup and grilled cheese. During his wait the mortality of everything in the room entertained him. Not now, not yet future, not present. There were no times when the whats were no longer moving, and time arose from the things that carried and were not, all whats gradually breaking down with nots that they were. Those that Xenis perceived made the others that resided in things and waited to burst anything into myriad other things that themselves were myriad others. They drove the movement that begat the time that made change, a maze of cruelty. And still they were not themselves responsible for these things.

Xenis placed the now-emptied tray at the door of his room, and walked back inside. He wanted to remain where he was. Still doubtful about what confronted him. He wanted to live with it, beside it, as long as it was not oblivion and began to fear its disappearance. He counted three-hundred dollars on the nightstand, most of his money having gone to Brazil. He called the front desk and asked that the television be removed from his room, and fifteen minutes later a confused man in an ugly red and white uniform unplugged and placed the set on a roll-cart.

"Take this too," Xenis said, handing him the remote.

The room came delightfully silent after the man departed, and Xenis watched the brilliant orange and red mix with the blue of sunset. The buildings near his window obscured and deadened some of the view, but this sight was spectacular nonetheless. He sat on the floor for what seemed like only a few moments, but what turned to three hours. Growing tired, he merged with his bed and slept how many hours he was unable to know. When he awoke, he felt deeply refreshed, death-like and deeply quiet his rest. He showered and as he did so, realized that his clean that day was of high caliber. The step that he made upon the light brown carpet dropped him place-to-place with great alacrity. He twisted on the ball of his foot instead of turning in a new direction. The thought that he walked differently, that his motions were more pleasant and moving made thought of him something else. He was the same person, remembered the same things, made the same sort of sounds. His body had not changed in a significant manner. His arose as better thought on that today.

Next morning nervous, he wound around the corner and observed the thick mass of hometheria bustling around him. He had no need to concern himself in the way that these others did, and so his stay downtown made pleasant feeling. All of these persons carried themselves in a similar manner, each distinctive. A bald man in a derby carried a seemingly permanent smile on his jaw, swaying as he walked. Xenis listened beside him as the man talked on his cell-phone, explaining to the world everything in mind. He had some means by the way he talked. "Myra, it isn't so dire," he said. "Give it to John. He'll have it done for you before the convocation. What would you do if there was a real problem?" After a moment's listening the man laughed. "Then don't let him," he said. Xenis kept up with him and entered the lobby of a large, sand-colored building where the man sat at a booth, ordered brunch and a drink. Three other men met him and each of them carried themselves similarly to the bald man who refused to remove his rust-orange derby. Xenis finished his soda and lemon. The rush outside had not yet merged with the lack of clear streets, so an anxiousness gripped him. He walked again along Michigan avenue, listening to a smaller man of almost the same height, again talking on his phone so that his fellow pedestrians might listen. His hair vanishing, this fellow wore a thin, dark blue tie and his jeans complemented a button-down blue and light shirt. Tennis shoes made his walk easy and comfortable, but seemed to displace the higher quality shirt. "Tear it down," he said. "We can't afford to take any risks right now. Put it back up later." Many of the things that this man did were similar to the last, yet he possessed a definitive character, one made crisp and clear to those observing. He ended where he began to give off a specific way of being, and Xenis stopped walking suddenly, a woman behind him nearly smacking into him.

That was it. They are at work.

Xenis watched other characters among the crowd, but became nervous once more. He sensed none of them near him as he did in his room, and the desire to return spread about his mind, like flame on paper. Suddenly, he quick-walked back to room 238 and when he opened the door he was relieved. Nothing greeted him.

NICHTS

The what that they all had been was the there that they had been, an act that produced work. That what was not itself, and it thus had no time; it possessed no space, not in any permanent manner, but the humans that perceived it counted time and space among its characteristics. What lay between the apparent place where the acting is always done and what it alread accomplished as well as what trajectory it headed was a continuous breaking. It opened to what was there from another there, though both theres were not. All was comprised of part and so illusion. None had substance in the way that the living expect it. Time, space, arrangement of presence, all of these, were not merely illusion. They were not. That is their desitination, but it is also their what.

NICHTS

Again, he sat on the wooden chair, looking out the window, no light arose from the tiny lights of buildings and the dark blues and black of night to him. Xenis compelled himself to eat, but his appetite had been scarce. He ordered from the kitchen and sat after his singular sandwich and water had come and gone, half-eaten. The stillness of the room lacked great comfort, but he desired yet more still, as if only cold comfort spread about his body, not the kind that warmed or moved him. The near-hot bath water surrounded his frame in a pliable embrace, which calmed him somewhat, and he drifted into semi-sleep. The potency of his need to remain in his room gripped him ever moreso the next morning. He wanted only to sit before the window in silence, but the day set within light pestered him with its intrusion. The night prior had been far more to his liking, and he had only an inkling why this was the case. Once more, he merged with Michigan avenue, this time a series of folk songs performed at the culture center. Xenis listened alone though he sat among a group that lacked largeness, the long solitude satisfying him. He feared association with others; his sensation of absence centered around a solo acoustic singer on the stage. Why he concentrated on this one person he did not quite understand. It was there.

Xenis saw the things before him as wood and guitar and flesh and thoughts moving about in the shape of words and the organism of water, calcium, hemoglobin, yet all that he was able to sense was that they lacked otherness. The stage offered a this and not a that to him, closer to his attention than, say, the curtain behind the performer. This word was not the woman's blouse before him there. The here of the man who shook Xenis' hand after having performed lacked itself into contrast with the there of the white and yellow-clad woman who noticed Xenis' oddness. When he ate a meal in a bistro near the culture-center with the performer and his wife, the suburbanite who noticed him looking closely at one thing then another, the words that came from him and the living ones that found themselves inside of him all made lack of what they did and how they moved, a kindly destruction. He was unable to concentrate fully on the pulsating opinions of the musician who charmed cello and viola. The corner of the bar took his attention as well, and Xenis could not keep himself from spreading his thoughts into everything surrounding his conversation: the tables, words emerging from a waiter, a man using his phone-toy. The lack of words made substance and the tables supported others around them with a ceasing that made it what. The musician's opinion over the quality of music and the need for more raw talent and less technology was itself one of these things. Even the gathering of friends to which the musician invited Xenis was left in the background of his awareness as mating ritual lacked charm of the man and political conversation lacked the concern for good statesmanship. His conversation with a woman about her dog shelter and her former husband lacked the substance of canines and marriage, yet how precisely lack and what were the same he was unable to articulate. The sound of a woman's voice needed the matter of her tongue and the experience of her marriage in order to finish her complaint, and so a conglomeration of Nichts brought together the things around and about him, each making function one another. They supported one another not as brothers or family-members, but gleefully conflicting, against one another, the table requiring gravity for purpose and the gathering of homotheria for construction. Even the anger Xenis sensed in the words of this woman had need of past nuptial arrangements and physical interactions long since done in order to perform its task, and her history had no direct connection to anger itself as an emotion.

"I notice your emotion has little to do with actual emotion," he found himself saying.

The woman paused. "Pardon me?"

"Emotion itself cannot exist, but it seems that way with everything."

Some imposingly other lack residing in her – somewhere near her head but also her matter – took his musing. She departed abruptly in some frustration that built upon anger, not quite resentment but some degree of annoyance. Xenis thought less of her reaction than perhaps he believed, but all this coming-to-be-what continued to distract him from her concerns. When he returned to his quiet and solitary unit, he mused over the desk and chair. He called the front desk and asked that they remove them. Some powers of convincing were needed before the management removed the items, but Xenis was glad that less occupied his living-space.

SEARCH FOR THE DEAD

Brazil shoved open the door and walked quickly down the cement stairs of her building, her brown bag and maple-covered envelope accompanying her. The car may refuse to start and the number that Elizabeth had given her may be incorrect. These were practically the only thoughts that occupied her as she hurried. The gallery was cool today, air conditioning repaired.

"Crap," she mumbled.

Glad of the comfort, she hated air-conditioning. The front desk would be comfortable for a time and then demand occasional shivers, and the air had been cleansed of any particle that gave it flavor, made it living. She rummaged through some spare articles in her back seat and found a cardigan that would have to pass. Long and gray and oversized even for her, it covered what she disliked. She had grown accustomed to the extra income Xenis brought with him, his annoying habits and occasional madness notwithstanding. Now, her need was to work more and create less, which carried the benefit of inspiration and desire to return to her projects more often.

"I have to admit."

Yet her concentration always fell away from what she intended to do. When at work, she thought about coming home; when at home she thought about creating; when doing all of these things a feeling of great anxiety emerged.

"What is he doing?"

She had learned where he was staying, and it made no sense. Away for three weeks, he would return.

"He's got nowhere to go."

They had lived at her place for three years after all, and

"He has almost no money."

She opened the envelope and signed the new rental contract, put it in the office mailbox and sat. She opened her schedule planner, a contemptible necessity, and looked at the number of the hotel. She had learned the room number and a moment's time was needed to call, but she refused. He had departed like he did, without saying anything at all. He possessed almost nothing, so she need not clean up after him, nor dispose of his belongings, and he did leave money enough to pay his share of rent for two months.

"It's the decency of the thing."

She closed the planner and opened her sketch-book. Thank goodness for Ethan and all his money. This job was easy, almost no work at all, and she met connections to the "art world" while thinking of new ideas. Still, two jobs were tiring, and she was able to visit practically none of her friends. Two more weeks passed thus. Her idea for a bronze crooked table accompanied by figures with distorted bodies came along fairly well. The already constructed table waited for the card players who would be picking up small metal cards after they had fallen from a steeply bent table. Their heads would be slightly larger that normal for the small bodies she planned to give them. Each day passed very quickly – was inspired. She enjoyed these times alone – fit and comfortable – yet as she worked on the card players, Xenis would not leave her.

"Maybe I can talk to what'shisname. That guy who Xenis liked. Not the old man, the other one."

When she was eating and reading about a new technique for welding,

"Dean. That's his name."

Dean packed the suitcase as John and Ellen waited in the "Air-Bus" van. The trip had been fulfilling, but tiring. He did not enjoy some of the conversations John had pushed him into, but he had fared well, the sun-provided vitamin D, the conversation granting him some set reprieve. He had made contacts who would, he hoped, be friends for years. His mother told him the trip might do him good, but his parents had not contacted him, seemed to be away from home.

"That's not good."

He called several times. They never refused to talk with him, not at any time. Even when his father was angry, they still talked. He rushed through re-settling John in his condominium, the clothes the chair John's sleep food prepared all done. He walked quickly to his car and drove to his parents' flat. He found his mother reading Phillipians.

All this I can do through Him who gives me strength.

He sat on the divan in their living room and mused over his great love for that very passage. She always read the things that most interested Dean gave comfort. She asked if he had a girlfriend. He had no prospects, too busy with John and other sundry. She told him to find a good woman and make a wife of her. Dean descended into the apparent blackness. He always had difficulty at this point, his father so careful to drive all light from the room. He smelled the dampness immediately, but that scent was a comfort to Dean in many ways. He was uncertain that breathing it in was healthy, but he had done so all of his childhood.

"Ah, yes."

He found the light in the room, lurking around the corner, waiting to assist. The old rocker and the player piano were now visible again. A wooden door directed him to the laundry room with the tubs where he and his father had cleaned, caught fish and the closet they constructed from thick drywall waited. Behind the opened door around and into the corner stood four bottles in a six-pack. The beer was cool, not cold – just the way father liked it. Dean snatched two bottles greedily and held them in one hand. He ascended once and then twice, glancing at his mother still reading on her recliner. She said he ought not leave before they talked again. The television room, converted to computer room, was surrounded by a thick layer of wood paneling – there for ages. Dust gathered in its crevices, and neither father nor mother cleaned after it now.

"That's alright."

The wood floor creaked as he entered, the light to the computer the only illumination. He handed a bottle to his father and sat on the metal chair, neither saying anything at first, twelve minutes remaining until the close of the show. The thirteenth brought the two men together. Dean's father asked if he had a girlfriend and he explained again. Had he talked to his mother already and when will they be able to meet his new friends were more questions. Soon, soon. His father brought him into their living room crowded with magazines, a kitchen table and two couches. Dean sat on the bench in front of the pile of magazines Ben Abrams finally converted. Dean's father made it official. It was hard to believe that Ben had come home, but Mat had done it. Dean was unable to repress a grin when they told him. Dean's father Matthew had accompanied him on many conventions and the two argued regularly on vacations, in restaurants, anywhere. Mat suggested the three go to Mary's. They always enjoyed the greasy spoon there, and he almost always met someone he knew. They entered, Mat greeted them personally, they came over to the Fromm family table. Mat Fromm and whoever it was drank a bit and later Mat found himself helping them move, or fixing plumbing. His police skills put to good use, he befriended good, reliable persons, most just as generous as he. On this occasion, however, Dean refused the offer of a meal. He needed sleep and John would be exhausted.

"I just wanted to be sure you're alright."

Fine just fine, they said.

Dean made certain they needed nothing. Their mere presence comforted him.

"I don't know what I'll do when they're gone."

He opened the door only slightly, peering inside. The queenly bed and its blanket appeared a bit rumpled, but vacant. He edged in carefully, as quiet as possible, the floor creaking as he moved. No movement in the bed.

"Where is he?"

Dean moved closer, coming near the edge of the bed where he saw a slight wisp of hair jutting out from under the dark brown blanket. The old man's frame did not have enough muscle and vigor on it to make a visible impression. It was as if John disappeared under the sheets. Dean leaned forward and held his breath. He heard only a slight noise, but the unmistakable sound of breathing emerged from the thick covers. He noticed then the temperature of the room, a heat-box, but John in no way sweated, stirred not at all, nor did his head shake. No movement of limbs. As he departed, Dean knocked a candle encased in glass onto the floor, a resounding thud the result. He froze for a moment, waiting for reaction, but none came. Again no movement under the blanket. Dean walked more confidently and noisily out of the room. The broom and dustpan made not enough noise to rouse the stillness, and John seemed oblivious. The unit clean and food prepared, Dean eased himself into a wooden, kitchen chair with a straight back. He moved the chair closer to the table, ensuring that his posture was straight and the table was a comfortable, useful height. The room was rather still and quiet, and he breathed easily, brought out his book and put it before him, its beautiful cover greeting him with the warm golden cross and the ridged cover. "Come to me, all you who are weary and burdened, and I will give you rest," it said. He needed no more that day. His gait freely pushed him toward a walk around the neighborhood and he talked with anyone who would listen. He wondered what happened to his new friend Xenis, and thought to contact him.

"He's odd, but entertaining."

Dean felt the ability to do almost anything, as if his youth returned and he sat on the lap of his mother, listening to father. Some slight sadness entered him. He sought its origin, then as he attempted to comprehend what the sadness was, it faded, like an idea not written down quickly enough. He set the clock in John's spare room and slid pajamas over his frame. A slumber much like John's came.

Brazil felt as if she were awash in a sea of information. She recalled the man's name and had an idea where he lived, but the street address and the exact unit she had no notion. The one search she performed online produced nineteen "Dean Fromm"s, seven located in Ohio, three in Kentucky. Nine lived near enough to be he. She printed a list, hoping to eliminate each one systematically.

"Where do I begin?"

She buzzed the door of the red brick condominium. No-one answered. The time was seven in the evening, so it made sense that he would be home. She waited twenty minutes and decided to return, try again. Eight-thirty was almost too late, but Brazil needed to determine if he was the one. She pressed the button and waited one or two minutes, looking up at what she supposed to be the correct window. She pressed again and no answer came. She turned to leave as she saw a large, overweight man near the building.

"Was he that size?"

The man walked to the door and opened it with his key.

"Excuse me," she said. "Do you know Dean Fromm?"

"I am Dean Fromm."

"Do you have a friend named Xenis?

"Never heard of him."

Finding him ought not present such difficulty. Brazil had met him more than once, but his face remained unfamiliar. She spoke to him briefly, almost a year ago. She took her list of Dean Fromms to work and looked over each one. Only two remained. She dialed the number of one of them, expecting no answer.

"Hello."

"Hello, yes. I'm looking for Dean Fromm, please."

"Who's calling?"

"I'm a friend of a friend."

The man laughed. "A friend of what friend?"

"Mr. Fromm? Do you know a man named Xenis?"

"I'm sorry. You have the wrong Fromm."

Brazil looked at the last address, a great deal of unnecessary information accompanying her internet search.
Name: Dean J. Fromm DOB: Dec. 4th, 1964
Occupation: CPA   Employer: Bane Accounting

Address 1: 3060 Maryland lane., unit 5E
Address 2: 2554 Josephine drive, unit 3C
Address 3: 6456 Larry avenue, unit 1E

Relatives:
Matthew Fromm, September 23rd, 1935 – December 11th, 1988. Father
Elsie Fromm, October 22nd, 1937 – August 8th, 1999. Mother

ONEIRISM

If she should be unable to locate the Dean Fromm she knew this time, Brazil would be at a loss. She called, but only an automated voice greeted her. No way to determine if he was the one.

"These Dean Fromms need to return their messages."

She pressed the button.

"I'm looking for Dean Fromm," she told the man.

"He's not here."

"Do you know where I can reach him?"

"He stays elsewhere. He takes care of an old man, I think."

"John Verdunkeln."

"That's his name, yeah," the man said with some surprise.

Suddenly, Brazil remembered the old letch. Him she was able

to find. Next day, she knocked on the door to his unit, recalling the night they had seen the opera.

"Oh, hi!," said Dean

"Dean? Dean Fromm?"

"Yes, and you're...Brazil, right?"

"That's right. May I?"

Brazil entered the well-kept unit and noted the hospitality of oil soap. The sofas, wooden chairs and paintings all shined and smelled of sleep and distended bellies. She recalled the ease of living she had taken from her visit.

"You know what's happened to Xenis, right?" she said before they sat.

"What's happened? No, I don't. No."

"He left."

"He left?"

"Yeah. He didn't say anything, or gather up his things. He just left."

"And...."

"He's living in a hotel, I think. I don't know why."

"I'm not sure..."

"I know you're maybe not so close a friend, but you are a friend, and he needs someone," Brazil paused involuntarily. "And...I don't want to do it alone."

Brazil's confusion made Dean nervous, but he was unable to refrain from helping.

"Have you talked with him?"

Brazil thought a moment.

"Well...no. I'm concerned about him more than anything," she said brows knitted. "...but no. Not really." She shook her head and frowned into the corner of the room.

"He's such a pain in the ass."

The two laughed.

"I don't know that there's anything we can do."

Brazil felt the moisture welling up in her eyes, but no. No tears for him. The pair agreed to search for Xenis, but Dean remained unsure. He liked the oddness of Xenis and he wondered if his father would approve of the stranger. Dean had no time to think about it now. He had much to do. John wanted a ride to Mary's and he had not prepared meals for this evening. Wanting to talk with his parents, he dropped off John and stopped by their place on the return. They were as they had always been, his mother reading in the front room. His father and Ben Abrams enjoyed the sun along the back stretch of patio behind the house. His mother always produced a calm within him, this time her sitting in the parlor did it. An intelligence mixed with a deeply-rooted compassion allowed her to warm the room, though not many knew it. Her husband often focused everyone on himself with his antics and charm; she paid no mind to attention, wanted little. "She's like a chimney fire on a bitter-cold winter night." She folded her long blue house-dress and drew mints from a tin cup, offered one to Dean and one for herself. She quoted a well-known verse: Greater love has no-one than this, that he lay down his life for his friends.

"I love that verse."

Dean thought of Brazil. Perhaps Xenis wished to be left alone. He wondered what was it his concern, wondered why she panicked like she did. Still, she cared for Xenis like Dean cared for others, for John.

"Something troubles me," Dean said aloud.

After hearing about Xenis, Elsie set her book alongside the red chaise lounge, and turned her eyes up toward the ceiling, looking inner nowhere. She quoted again, this time the old testament: Faith is confidence in what we hope for and assurance about what we do not see. He would know what to do when the time came; it would come to him. Ben Abrams had taken leave when Dean stepped onto the rock path of the back patio. Mat stood up as soon as he saw his son, reached out his hand. Dean took it and felt the strong grip of certainty. Dean's father demonstrated his talent again and again. He wondered how his father was able to walk with so many lives from so many different paths. The pair talked about the price of beer, the recent election of a new mayor, environmental issues, Dean's new job and the descent of the question in philosophical reasoning.

"Maybe that's why he's so good with people."

Their conversation lasted several hours, Mat leading mostly. Dean placed his key inside the door of his car when he remembered to ask his father about Xenis. He found him inside the computer room again, about to watch a crime series. Dean and Brazil were unable to do much legally unless there existed extenuating circumstances. They may, however, be able to do something. Mat suggested they try to convince Xenis that they are able to do something legally. He may come home and to his senses without them actually doing anything. Dean was unsure about that plan.

"He may be difficult to convince."

Brazil felt better, but only by small measures. Talking to Xenis' friend lightened her spirits, and when he visited the weight of her mood buoyed, but only a bit. He asked many questions, and Brazil believed he suspected something. She explained to him that Xenis was welcome to go and to live anywhere he pleased. She understood and sympathized with that, of course. Still, he had been running around the neighborhood like a cockeyed child – sitting naked on the roof – and a host of other odd behaviors had emerged. He slept on hard wood and owned practically nothing.

"This coming from a man whose wealth knew no bounds," she said.

Dean thought initially that Brazil was overreacting, but when he learned more about Xenis' strange behavior, he reconsidered.

"Perhaps he's dangerous to himself."

Xenis had not done anything wrong; he was guilty only of being somewhat eccentric.

"And there are many of those."

The two agreed that they would at least visit Xenis, confront him if necessary, but they simply possessed not enough information about his mental condition to make an informed judgment.

"My father thinks that there's little we can do, legally," he said.

Brazil leaned forward, placed her hand on her mouth and paused in meditation.

"It's not as bad as all that."

"No?"

"No."

"We need to work in an extra-legal way."

"What does that mean?" Brazil said in a nervous tone.

"Oh, no no," he said. "I don't mean anything except that we try to convince him to return."

"Oh."

"Yeah. What he does voluntarily is all legal, right?"

"Sure."

"So, we convince him."

"Yeah, right."

Her voice told Dean how problematic convincing would be. Conversation with Xenis was not difficult, but efforts at directing behavior twisted always into knots, and he would never do anything simply because someone suggested it.

"We need to be very careful."

"You got that right."

"What I mean is we need to act as though we're not attempting to retrieve him, or whatever."

"I understand."

"We may even need to visit him more than once, just pretend as though we miss him and want to visit."

"And delicately nudge him out the door."

"Well...yeah."

"He'll be onto us right away."

"We'll be circumspect. He'll be suspicious, but we'll visit two, maybe three times before we do anything."

"We need a united front."

"What do you mean?"

"We need to agree that we won't let him turn one of us against the other."

"He wouldn't do that," Dean was indignant.

"He would."

The hotel was located near a lake, gloriously manicured. On a clear, cool day one may walk around the rippling water or take one of the boats out for a relaxing bob along the fluid.

Park benches and fire-barrels scattered themselves around the grass near the lake; a stone walkway led back to the hotel, one hop two hop three stones the length of one's gait. Not many other buildings were located around the hotel, so long stretches of grassy earth made lawn-cutting a necessity. Ducks and geese lined the seam where the lake met the well-tended grass, slipped into the water when someone arrived. One took away the impression of affluence and a certain level of subservience from the many windows and wooded marble that greeted Brazil and Dean as they entered the building. The edifice sat near a street not more than three miles from Brazil's apartment.

"It's amazing this place is so close to mine. It's a different world."

The servants at the customer counter greeted the pair quickly and with many smiles, their uniforms not quite uniforms – attractive gray with dotted pinstripes.

"May I help you?"

"Yes. We're looking for one of your guests: Xenis Deinst."

"We cannot give information about guests."

"It's an emergency."

"I suggest you contact the authorities."

Brazil slipped a twenty dollar bill onto the counter.

"We need to see him for his own health."

The front desk sentinel clicked away at the keyboard. Brazil turned round and observed the lobby from his perspective.

The daylight brought in enough illumination to expend the already-expanding space. Many guests sat at the restaurant and the lounge, the hall a bustle of activity.

"Room 238."

"How did he manage to afford this place?"

Brazil shuffled the objects in her purse without realizing it. She looked heavily at the door, which opened quickly – apparently expecting someone. Unprepared for the entrance of friends, Xenis pulled back his head as surprised persons do, moving slightly back. Assertively taking Xenis' surprise as an invitation, Brazil entered. The glimpse of his space gave her concern. The lack of a television she expected – nothing new there. The clean space had no dressers, nor the customary desk. Again, nothing new. One felt the difference in humidity and temperature immediately; the window that looked out upon the lake was open. Xenis' space gave a sense of disorder, but somehow everything sat in its proper place, in some way like a small section of forest. Brazil looked at a painting that hung on the wall, one of a silhouetted man walking through tall grass. A slight change of color betrayed the former presence of a different wall-hanging.

"I remember this," Brazil said.

"It's from my old place."

"You had it up there for years."

Brazil sought a chair, but none welcomed her. She looked at the edge of the mattress, which rested on the floor of the room. She turned back and forth, seeking a welcome place to rest.

"Just sit anywhere."

Dean and Brazil squatted down on the floor atop the bedsheet that Xenis had spread over the carpeting.

"We wanted to see how you fare," Dean began.

"The hotel is nice, and well-kept."

"It looks expensive," Brazil commented.

Xenis continued his thought.

"I don't know why it feels good to be here, but it does."

Dean and Brazil exchanged a quizzical expression. There the conversation cut short, strained words clutching and holding. Dean made himself comfortable on the edge of the mattress. Xenis walked to the window, looking over the lake. He made no effort to continue the conversation, comfortable in the silence. Brazil wanted desperately to ask why he left, what was there in that hotel, but she remembered her agreement with Dean.

"We just wanted to know how you're doing," Dean repeated. Brazil glared at him briefly.

Xenis felt the urge to climb out of the window, walk down along the roof and descend until he met the lake. He had done so a few times already. The water in the lake was a bit too cool for him sometimes, but his best-loved moment was when he first entered the water and felt the liquid surround him – embrace of substance all round. He later suspected that the new surrounding, the literally new environs, were what comforted him. He had been changing everything around him, insisted on rearranging the furniture – eliminating much of it. At one point he asked for an additional bedsheet and no more visits from the cleaning crew. Some effort was required to convince the staff that he would clean his room, but they relented, thinking him strangely. He paid no mind; the cleaner they used on the carpet was filled with toxins, and he wanted no more poisons. Certainty made him ill. The insulation in the walls, a thick layer of concrete, kept many sounds from entering, and Xenis enjoyed the absence of vibration. Sometimes, he enjoyed focusing on one sound only, even the muted hum of a vacuum cleaner. He had listened to voices without comprehending the words and the clink of some machine at the end of the hall. He had not yet wondered enough what it was, simply liked its sound. He had been listening to the buzz of a light in the hall when Brazil and Dean arrived. The light, source of his moment, shined just outside his door and he heard footsteps that he thought may carry off the sound. Hoping to convince the caretaker to leave the light be, he had opened the door. Not a bad surprise, but not what he wanted.

"We came for a visit because we haven't heard from you," Brazil said, interrupting Xenis' oneirism.

Dean and Brazil exchanged glances again.

"You're doing alright, we hope."

"I'm better than I've been."

Xenis left the conversation there, not curious about the pair of friends in his room. He adored them still, and he appreciated their efforts, yet they disrupted something he needed, something that he still did not comprehend fully, a vague sensation both not quite a thought and not an emotion. He desired its return. The three talked about his accommodations, and Brazil asked if Xenis needed any of his books. He said he would meet her at her place in a few days. A week passed and no Xenis.

Brazil awoke with a start from her nap, a sudden realization or perhaps a memory pushed her into awareness. She needed to talk with Xenis, if only to know that he fared well. All of this nonsense needed to end; he had been gone long enough. Time to come home.

"Yes. It's time."

She ruminated as she walked Murphy. Having made her way to the hotel, she and Xenis' dog-pal arrived at the lobby and she was unable to continue. Some fear crept in, preventing her entrance into the elevator. At home what she needed to drive off the fear escaped her. There was no reason for her to feel this way. She had no anxiety over Xenis himself. She visited John Verdunkeln's building in order to chat with Dean, but no-one answered her call, nor did he return phone calls. Another few days passed and she felt a panic when no-one answered again at John's building. She checked her search on Dean Fromms. The only location she had not visited was that of Dean's parents. Astonishingly, she found their building readily and pushed the unit-buzzer.

"Hello."

"I'm looking for Dean Fromm..."

"There's no-one of that name here," the person said abruptly .

"Is this the Fromm residence?"

"No."

"This is not the residence of Elsie and Matthew Fromm?"

"No."

"Do you know, by chance, where to locate them?

The speaker came silent. Brazil looked again at the search, this time concentrating on the relatives section. The address was correct, but she noted something to which she had paid little mind. There were birth and death dates for Dean's parents on the search.

INDEFINITE FIX

The departure of Brazil and Dean made him glad; there was an opening to their absence and it was welcome, but Xenis felt an obligation at the same time. He had said he would pick up some of his belongings, and he had not done so. The matter was not the utmost importance, but Brazil seemed to want his visit. He owed her that much, so he removed his sleepclothes and turned on the water for a bath. He remembered that he had forgotten his wash-cloth near the bed, went to retrieve it. As he retrieved the dried, yellow towel from a bare, bedless floor, Xenis regarded the large window overlooking a section of grass and trees and opening out and into an outline of the city. He paused inside the appearance of the lake and well-trimmed lawn outside, arising in his mind. A moment later he glanced at the clock with the amber numbers. Three hours had somehow elapsed, and he had no idea what he had been doing. Xenis realized that he had been in the middle of something.

"What was it?"

He considered the issue inside a lost mind.

"Brazil!"

He was still able to visit her after work. He rushed into the bath and found himself looking into the dripping faucet, no real thought just a stare. He lifted his frame from the water and dressed. All ready. Except...staring out the window again he was unable to see the skyline or much of the city, noticed darkness thrown over everything outside.

"What?"

The time was eleven-thirty pm. Not understanding why, he understood that he was tired. He thought he needed sleep though he had only just awakened and tried to concentrate on removing clothing, unrolling the foam and resting. He noted then that he stood near the sink, water running. An instant later he glanced again at the clock: two-thirty am.

"No Brazil today."

He rushed to his bed and stretched his body down. The next moment was his waking, nothing out of ordinary in that. He often slept, awaking later with the sensation that no time had passed. He arose as usual, washing his face and then in the shower he spread his frame once more.

"What did I want to do?"

Xenis thought about the matter for a moment. Really, it was not thinking; his attention wandered onto his breakfast and then it was blank, lots of images of persons he had never met and scenes he had never seen suddenly presenting themselves to mind's eye.

"What was it?"

Blankness came for a time and then he found himself beside the mirror. Somewhat anxious, he forced his attention upon each moment, dressing-eating-walking. He passed three hours of his day in this fit of concentration; wandering downtown; a walk around the lake; visiting the animals at a shelter, deciding to volunteer. He forced himself to eat, a strong desire to refrain from food occupying him. He had needed to do such things for several days now; he knew not how many times.

"...no hours...wait, days...days...yeah days" he felt this way. "It doesn't matter."

Nervous more, Xenis vaguely recalled something.

"What was it?"

He thought he ought to change.

"Brazil! Oh no. I forgot again."

Then, another thought about a synthesis between Leon his friend and his first grade teacher entered his consciousness.

"Where did that come from?" He had no idea.

Reading always used to help, so he picked up "The Nature of Atoms", putting aside the remainder of his ordinary activities. Suddenly, he took up some favorite Borchert short, *The Kitchen-Clock*. He read four lines and thought, but no thinking came. He began again, but as his eyes passed over the letters he saw no words, and so no meaning penetrated. He sat up in the chair where he was and concentrated. The words came, but with some difficulty.

"This should not be happening. I've read this before."

He tried again to read and four paragraphs came quickly and easily to him. He drank some of his lemon-water and as he peered overtop Borchert, his eyes fixed on a section of the wall. He was unable to remove them from that place for some minutes, and when he returned to the book he felt as if he was waking from a dream. He began reading around one pm and when he at last came to his awareness the clock said five pm. It seemed no Brazil today either, given that he continued experiencing these spells.

"or whatever they are."

He needed to determine what was happening, or at least stop the apparent lapses.

Really, he knew what was happening. It was plain to him, anyway. They had begun to seep into his everyday life in an ever-growing capacity. They had been converging around him for some time, and now they – or was it "it"? – had grown closer. They were in everything, though they were unseen, and he was glad of it. He himself owed the very characteristics that comprised him to them, or it as the case may be. He tried to keep them away from his mind, or at least to keep them from making his mind a blank. But they apparently had other ideas.

"I guess they or it likes me."

He wanted to gather himself together at least enough that he gave the appearance of some kind of normality, but that goal seemed distant. He knew only one practical remedy. The next week saw Xenis making rigorous his schedule in an effort to bore his consciousness into and on himself and not lose to them what was Xenis. Awake at seven-thirty. Breakfast at nine. Afternoon walk. Reading in the evening. He visited Dean for moral support, but also because he knew somehow the man would gladly assist. Old John and Dean welcomed him. At first Xenis merely sat in a chair, observing Dean and talking with him about casual topics. He arrived in the afternoons and remained for two hours. The talks were some of the most soothing moments Xenis had felt in years. Dean was not merely generous, he was kind and thoughtful. He enjoyed talking.

"My mother is a saint," he said. "She has excellent insight into people and knows what to do in case of an emergency."

"It must be comforting to have good parents," Xenis said.

"It's one of my greatest comforts. What about yours?"

"My parents?"

"Yeah."

"Oh. Well, they don't really exist."

Dean's face turned down and interest lighted his eyes.

"I never knew my parents. I've only heard about them, and not much."

"Oh. I'm sorry."

"My mother apparently died when I was very little."

"Apparently?"

"She disappeared."

"Oh."

"My grandmother brought me up, so I guess she was my mother...and father."

"I'm sorry. I mean, I'm glad for your grandmother. I mean, I'm glad she was there for you."

Xenis smiled.

"She was a good parent, but yours seem as though they're ideal."

"They are. I'm so lucky. It must be hard, though. I mean, without parents or a family you must have had a difficult time."

"It wasn't so bad. I've lived in an extraordinary way. I rely on friends mostly,...as you know."

Dean smiled.

"Maybe one day I'll be able to meet your parents."

"Maybe."

"I can make friends with them."

"I'm sure that will happen easily."

"I need friends at the moment."

"You have them."

"I do. I do."

"Speaking of which, have you contacted Brazil lately?"

"I haven't."

"I know she's concerned about you."

"I need to talk with her, but I need to take care of some things before I do that. I need to solve a problem."

"Oh."

Xenis continued to visit John and Dean, each time working in the yard at one pm, washing the car on Tuesdays, odd jobs in early evening. He helped around the unit as much as he was able, fixing windows and realigning doors, things that Dean knew nothing about.

"You don't have to do this stuff for free," Dean said.

"It's helping in ways you can't imagine."

"I don't like not paying you."

"Just feed me every once in a while."

The work helped Xenis maintain a steady hold, keep his mind concentrated in himself and not be abducted into another bit of nothing. The labor reminded him of the moving of scaffolding from one place to another.

"It's the same thing in some ways."

Xenis sometimes accompanied the old man on various trips, but mostly John would not drive without Dean present, and so the three were packed into the Altima, leading to initial grudging accompaniment and later actual affection. Xenis was grateful for their patience and understanding, but when he returned home, always them. They were, of course, there when he did things with John and Dean, but for some reason their vanishing-affect diminished as he kept himself tending things. After a month of working with the old man and the good one Xenis began to think that he had mastered his dilemma. His victory overjoyed him, and his near mirth made him more active, more capable. His small room had become somewhat more tolerable as well. The lapses came fewer and fewer until at one point they seemed to vanish, and Xenis remained overjoyed but he knew he needed to continue seeing John and Dean He arrived regularly in the afternoons, attempting to ensure his welcome.

"Your mailbox door is coming unhinged. I can fix it."

"Knock yourself out," said old John.

Xenis repaired the door to the mailbox, unfroze one of the old wooden windows, patched holes with plaster and installed a new faucet. More to do he was unable to find. He said little about it, but he was anxious that he might be asked to return home. John seemed to tolerate Xenis' presence, but Dean kept him comfortable.

"I hope you don't mind that Xenis visits."

John mumbled something and opened his paper to read a paragraph about a dog recovered from the debris of an earthquake.

"But a...why not just tell him to buy a dog..., or a cat maybe."

Dean chuckled. "I think he may need human contact," he said.

"Maybe he could use a parakeet," John continued.

"Or what's's called? A...ah...begins with an 'M'."

"A Muskrat?"

"Yeah, that's it. Muskrat. Maybe he can buy himself a muskrat."

The two men laughed.

"But he can keep coming, right?"

"Yeah, yeah. I guess."

And after another moment of paper-reading and counter-wiping,

"Could still use a muskrat."

John thought a moment.

"If he was living with that woman, what's the name?"

"Brazil."

"Yeah. If he was living with her and he needs company, why's he not there?"

Xenis fixed the screen on the back door, patched more holes in the ceiling and walls of the living room, feathering the new paint into the old.

"You may want to paint the entire room soon," he commented to John.

John said nothing, but looked hard at the younger man.

"You ever own a pet?" he asked finally.

"Me? I used to care for animals."

"'Care for'? You didn't own 'em?"

"They were my property legally, yes."

John grunted. Xenis paused, then turned to Dean.

"I was hoping I wasn't becoming a pest."

"You're not a pest."

"No. I come too often."

In truth, Xenis wanted to be alone, very much so, but he also needed something from the regularity of his visits.

"There's something about them being there that isn't quite right."

When he returned home, he was able to keep the lapses from overtaking him. He was certain to wake at precisely the same time each day and go to sleep at the same time. He fought with the hotel staff when they wanted to move him to another room. Not only would he need to walk a different path each time he entered and left the hotel, but the new room would have a bed and dressers and other items that he would need to remove. He convinced the hotel to permit him to stay with desperate pleas, and they reluctantly relented. Xenis was able to maintain the same and the same path and the virtual same moments each day. His routine continued for the month he was visitng Dean and John with only minor incident or lapse, but he had not been able to visit Brazil, and now he was unable to detract from his ordinary regimen. She would interrupt his regularity. Xenis needed at least to be at the condominium around the time that he ordinarily visited; he stole keys long enough to make copies and when John and Dean were not home on a given day, Xenis visited nonetheless, performing tasks as usual. They found dishes cleaned and hallways swept when they returned home. Xenis was careful to do only so much that they would perhaps think they had done the work themselves, or that they had forgotten about it somehow. A concern about dwindling funds unnerved him. Still, he was unable to cease his efforts for fear of lapses that would surely come when he refrained from waking at seven-thirty; dressing before eight; lunch at two with Dean. Occasionally, Xenis visited John when Dean was absent. Xenis learned from Dean how to cook ribs for the old man.

On that most dreadful of days the men met in good spirits, nothing hard no lack of camaraderie or presence of ill-will. Xenis entered as he had always done and worked at another of the ancient wooden windows, that it would come loose and work as always it had done. He was making an effort at fixing all fifteen, which would take a long time. As he heaved at the window in order to see exactly what was needed to ensure its safe and smooth operation, he found he had arrived at John's place around nine am. He had memory of working at the window, but then realized he had only just come on that very morning. He grew restless immediately and directed his attention to the same activity, this time repeating what he had already done. He noted the time: nine am. He took up the tools again and heaved at the window in the same manner he had already done and found himself sweeping the kitchen floor a second time at two pm. He rushed to the back room where John watched preacher Marvin.

"Have I been here all this time?"

Xenis pulled back his head as surprised persons do, moving slightly back. Assertively taking Xenis' surprise as an invitation, Brazil entered. The glimpse of his space gave her concern.

FIX INDEFINITE

Xenis had performed each task according to its time and place with great precision; he had concentrated on the present thing and Xenis, deviating but negligibly. Yet, he stepped along the sidewalk and found himself upon his bed and instantaneously later motioned to the concierge. A growing anxiety of the perception of others kept him silent about his more fundamental dread. Xenis no longer awoke at seven-thirty-one or seven-thirty-three, but rather each morning without exception at seven-thirty. Up immediately. He dressed in the same clothing and placed the day's cloth on his body at precisely eight-fifteen; out the door at eight-thirty and on to reading at a cafe across from the hotel. The dash to John's place could be maddening because he needed to arrive at two pm precisely. At times he arrived only minutes before two and wandered around the building until precisely two.

"It's an ordeal."

Neighbors witnessed him arriving, coming near the front door and then wandering around John's building until he rushed at the door and demanded entry, knowing that he must ascend before thirty seconds had passed. On some occasions he brushed madly past a bewildered Dean into the unit only to calm and chat once the concerned at-home assistant arrived moments later. He took to sitting in the front room chair from two until two-twenty-three, at which time he abruptly departed his seat and tended to some chore or assisted in some manner, until three-thirty.

"He's always been a little strange," John commented.

Sometimes, the condominium was unoccupied when Xenis arrived at two pm; he needed to enter the building. Fortunately, he had a key, entering at precisely two and moving into his ordinary regimen. More than a few occasions saw Xenis barely avoid the men as they entered, Xenis having been already there for an hour or more. Cautious, he would wait some time and then knock as if chance had happened upon all of them. Yet, there were times when Xenis was detained by a flat bicycle tire or made to rush by cleaning personages in the hotel. Sometimes, he was compelled to cut short conversations once he realized he may be detained just long enough to ruin his efforts. He became enraged at a late train that disrupted his early arrival. The living Xenis grew more aware of the actual arrival of buses and the motions of pedestrians on street walkways. He wove into and around persons who simply moved too slow, or ones who detained him with the confusion of direction. Xenis obsessed over the shine of the mirror in the bathroom and the placement of towels on the thin metal bars in the lavatory.

"I'm threading a spindle with taught strands of infinitely fine and delicate thread."

Almost immediately, when he stepped upon the sidewalk and conitnued his path, he experienced one moment after another and not some moments suddenly differing, no longer changing his place-time without notice.

"Success."

Still, his anxiety upon arriving at two-thirty-one pm on a given weekday grew fatigue in his limbs. Xenis tightened his schedule and occasionally pushed others out of his way, if any chance of delay or deviation from his current path existed. He enjoyed the chats with Dean and John's ornery generosity often made Xenis smile. John sometimes talked about his younger days, offering the practical advice that comes with age and aggravation. Periodically, Xenis received messages from Brazil, asking him when he would visit.

"I'm just so busy right now," he said.

She would never understand, at least not completely, her habit being to judge quickly – wedding a good sturdy emotion to her thought – that regular anger mating with straw men. Once she had decided he was growing insane, he would have no luck convincing her otherwise. She would not understand why he kept away, but her exclusion managed his difficulties better than her presence accompanied by a supposition that he was out of his senses. Xenis tightened again the regimen: awake at seven am; breakfast consumed by seven-twenty; washed and dressed by seven-forty; out at eight; into the cafe no later than eight-fifteen; consume first sip of Earl Grey no later than eight-twenty-five. He wrote out each demand he placed upon himself and laminated the sheet so that the list would remain an eternal agenda. Mostly and incredibly, he was able to adhere to the strict regimen, but several nearly-regular encounters with cleaning persons and hotel staff were in order in order to maintain order. If Hose was cleaning the hall, Xenis would have no trouble because he was regular and reliable, but if Sharon was working, he would need to determine when and if she had arrived at the hotel, she being tardy and apathetic regularly. Sometimes, she hid in order to avoid exerting herself. Xenis watched for the delivery drivers as well, since late arrivals of certain resources would slow or quicken the pace of the staff. Such regularity of movement produced regularity of reaction that connected each moment to Xenis; he strove to continue without interruption a life without lapses.

And he delighted in the quiet.

Xenis found the task of freeing the windows assisted most, since he was able to give reason for his presence at John's home. All the other, much more needed, regularities came as a result of his excuse, and all just as well.

"Neither John nor Dean would understand."

He never explained. So comfortable had his efforts become that the tasks one after came to him without thought or effort.

He decided to take the risk of seeing his old friend, and gladly he prepared a very strict schedule for that particular day. As he arose on a Wednesday – prepared as usual and at precisely the correct time – he dressed properly and ate at the correct time and place. He wound round the corner of John's building and to the door. He pressed the button and demanded entry when then he found himself lifting one ancient window from a frame he had not yet touched. The sensation produced in him a dread and surprise mixed. He looked at the window and then nearby. Dean stood beside, addressing him.

"That one seemed to have given you a hard time."

"What one?"

"The window."

"Oh. Yeah."

Xenis had a bit of terror and some speck of surprise spread

across his face.

"Something wrong?"

"How long have I done this?"

"What do you mean?"

"How long have I been here?"

"You mean...at the condo?"

"Working at the window."

"An hour or so, I'd say. Why?"

Xenis replied only after a thought.

"Just...lost track of time."

"Have somewhere to go?"

"...no."

Xenis continued his shaving of the frame, yet he recalled nothing of anything he had done for at least two hours. He had no idea even what time it was, but the fear and the shock of another lacuna drove away belief. He shoved his concern into the back of him and continued his labor. Xenis found that this particular window needed only a few more adjustments. It would then freely move. He may be able to complete two today. He set the window in the frame and began sliding, up and then down stuck then down and up again. Just as he acted, as he moved, he noticed that the recliner needed a slight adjustment. He sat in the red-carpeted easy-chair of his hotel with Wolfdietrich Schnurre on his lap. He had fixed himself a lemon-water and was still moist from an evening's shower.

"What was it I was supposed to do?"

Xenis was unable to understand. There was something he had known or done or moved or something had come after he did something. Nothing came to mind. His first thought was to reach into his pocket in order to pull out his laminated schedule. It was the same as it had been, now being the time to rest a bit and read. He loved Schnurre now that they had discovered one another. A sip from the lemon-water relaxed him. He turned to another page where the Gibbon was attacked, afterward the father and son saving the animal and beginning his convalescence. Xenis turned to look at the window.

"I'm not supposed to be here."

He observed his hand that held the book with the Gibbon in it and tried to recall when he had made himself a lemon-water glass. He was unable to remember the precise moment that he had walked to the small refrigerator near the dresser. He opened its door and found several lemons, which had not been there. A fear arose inside when he recognized that his concentration had waned, if only a bit. He sat quickly down into the chair and took up the Schnurre again, certain to concentrate on the present task. He resumed reading as the injured primate began to show signs of recovery. Xenis focused his attention on the current activity, not wanting them to return, and just as he did he closed the door to the hotel room and rushed through the hall toward the cafe. He had only thirty seconds before he would be late for the Earl Grey. He recalled how a few days prior the cafe had a depleted supply. He had been in a panic and ran to a drug store beside the building, purchasing a box of Earl Grey and running back   to put the bag in the hot water obtained from the cafe. He had barely managed to assemble his task that time, and now he rushed toward the cafe again.

"Wait."

He stopped and stood for a moment, ignoring a front desk worker who asked him what he needed.

"I was just doing something."

He was unable to recall.

"What was it?"

Again, he was unable to think on it precisely, so he continued his rush to drink the tea. His task was well-timed and there were actually a few residual moments he had to slow himself. He sat at his expected table at precisely the correct time, relief. He sipped and recognized that something nibbled at the back of his head.

"Wait. Wasn't I reading something? I'm in the cafe?"

The night had only begun, immediately after his afternoon. He was barely able to recall that he needed to recall something, yet it remained in the back of his mind.

"Wait. What was it? I'm not supposed to be here."

It was clear to him that he had lost something, but what it was he did not know. He contemplated his customary seat in the cafe. He recalled the episode with the window clearly, but in pieces and then he was sitting at night in his room. Now, abruptly he was passing through his morning routine.

"What happened?"

They returned, but that made no sense. They had disappeared because of his routine. Now, in an even more well-directed and regimented scheme they had returned.

"And there's something else."

Xenis was not able to set his mind's eye on it initially, but now that he pressed his concentration well upon the issue he realized that there was some problem with his solution, though precisely what it was remained elusive. On this occasion Xenis' head began to shift back and forth, and he rocked in the chair near his bed in his hotel room. He looked around, confused, not knowing if he ought to be in this place or that. Setting aside his disorientation, he again took out his laminated schedule and noted that his evening shower ought to begin. He removed his clothing and reached for a washcloth, stepped into the shower-stall concentrating on his here and now, and

"What kind of window would you install?" he asked.

"I'm not that particular," said John.

Xenis looked at the old, wooden guard who had served the building so long. Its sun-cracked cherry betrayed long service. He had not enough skills to rebuild this window, but this one was the second-to-last on the list of broken and fading hosts of aperture in the unit.

"I don't know how to rebuild this window, but I recommend you do so."

"Yeah?"

"The other two can be repaired without reconstruction, so

replacing them all would be a great expense and a waste."

"Well I agree with that," said John, thankful that he had Xenis to perform the labor. "I can pay you."

"It's not necessary. The work performs a service," Xenis returned.

And he paused in that thought. Somehow it had happened again, though this time he recalled the time he spent between the evening shower and the discussion about the window. It had simply slipped past him.

"At least that time actually existed," he said aloud.

John stared at Dean

"Dean will get some money for you."

Xenis related none of his difficulties to Dean or to anyone else, though a strong desire to discuss these strange occurrences possessed him. It seemed to him that surrendering to the episodes would only bring about more episodes. The strict regimen had proven itself effective; there was no reason to believe that less structure would decrease his problem.

"I need to make the schedule that much more precise."

Xenis restructured his daily agenda, including general expectations at very specific times but excluding all chance and accident. He was unable to avoid random events and unexpected circumstances, but he was able to make his overall schedule more rigorous in general. Awake at seven-thirty; shower – no bath – commences at seven-thirty-five; dressed in same clothes by seven-fifty-five; out elevator at eight; recline in lobby until eight-twenty; Earl Grey in specific place and chair at cafe at eight-thirty.

"It's working."

The time lapses and memory deficits disappeared and each day returned a complete whole once more. Yet the strain was great, and keeping in the radically specific regimen Xenis began to sleep less comfortably; intermittent slumber begrudged him rest. He grew tired and weary of the absoluteness of his decision, and was unable to change the things that transpired as well; any random change or accident potentially altered his path. Still, another week passed and Xenis found few of his tormentors in his trip through each moment. Again satisfied that he had brought about a regular existence, he began to plan a strictly-guided visit to Brazil. Awake at seven-fifty-five; breakfast in because of possible random circumstance in the world; out by nine-fifteen; meet Brazil between ten-ten and ten-fifteen.

"You're finally coming to visit a single time," she commented.

"I needed to straighten out a few things."

Brazil thought it odd that Xenis' visit precluded a visit with others, and the timing was strange. Not the timing as in when it may occur, but the duration. Xenis had stressed that he would come to her apartment at ten-fifteen on a Wednesday and stay until twelve-thirty. He had to stay precisely that long, not leave earlier not later. Still, she was glad to hear from him. Xenis prepared by integrating that particular schedule into his already-existing regimen. He rode to Brazil's place between the cafe and John's condominium, waited there. It seemed to have worked. Perhaps he would be able to visit her regularly.

"And if I integrate different patterns into my activities, I may be able to do anything I choose, as long as I don't disrupt the overall pattern."

The idea again was to drive them off, and this kind of alteration of schedule would be inevitable, should he want to live in any even semi-normal manner. He was, he believed, able to keep them at bay, if he controlled each and every event he encountered. In fear of them arriving before his visit, Xenis again tightened his regimen, as if each piece of his activity inevitably led to precisely the same new activity in a series of tightly-clenched causes and effects. Awake at seven-thirty; shower – no bath – at seven-thirty-five. No trouble came, and Xenis thought even to contact Brazil and confirm, and then he opened the door to the shower stall and the window would not move.

"That one's particularly bad," said Dean.

"It gets most of the rain," John added from across the hall.

Xenis thought a moment as he read the Schnurre; the Gibbon returned to the zoo. It was a betrayal after all, but the father and son needed food for themselves. He drank some of his lemon-water and buzzed John's door for entry. He pressed his lips onto the hot cup of Earl Grey and looked at the morning light brightening the glossy wood and the dark floor of the cafe.

"I'm not sure we have one," said the attractive woman at the front desk as Xenis turned his hands together, lathering them with the ginger soap.

"No."

Xenis sat on his bed that night, whatever night it was, and

decompressed. Not only had the they returned, but they seemed to be activated by his actions.

"How can this be?"

PATH TO FINALITY

X enis shook as he poured water into the porcelain cup with the pool of yellow juice inside. The time was eleven-fourteen and he had only then awoken, his sleep sound and unexpectedly healthy. He had thought his anxiety would keep him vigilant the whole night, but somnolence came easily and early the night before. He rotated the hard, white matter in his palm. Unsatisfied, he grabbed a spoon, inserted it and thoroughly brought the keen yellow sting into the water.

"Much better."

Now there came a great, unexpected unwinding – released from his body and mind. It felt good. He waited on one of them to appear, largely because he lay on the couch, but also because he had not yet showered, not yet eaten more than leftover stir-fry. He had not dressed in the same freshly-cleaned clothes, not sat at the proper chair. He lifted again the lemon-water cup and noticed how it shifted back and forth in his shaking hand. He ought not vibrate as if someone had shot at him, but it happened in fact that he was unable to cease shaking. He had been able to endure harsh friends and survive a community of mimetics he had bathed in the sunlight of friendship and indulged himself dangerously, but he had now no more ideas how to contend with them. They did not return stronger than ever.

"No, not that."

They simply returned, at a kind of constant strength. They were now nerve-fraying experiences, and he waited. He looked again at his hand as it lifted itself back onto his lap, fingers shifting up and down regularly. He remained on the couch for another hour that seemed like fifteen minutes, though he was awake entirely and for the whole of the hour. A light shade and then darkness slid overtop of him. In his dream he met one of them and asked it what it was doing.

"Nothing," it replied.

He felt foolish for asking the question. They seemed to have no sense of humor, only answering him in very plain language and in a quite straightforward manner. Whatever happened, happened. They could not care less about the result of any action or the action itself.

"You have no morals," he said.

   "Of course I have no morals."

Xenis reached his hand toward them.

"Tinnndle-dang, Tinnndle-dang."
"Tinnndle-dang, Tinnndle-dang."

They were making noise. But that made no sense. They cannot make noise.

"Wait. They can't talk."

"Tinnndle-dang, Tinnndle-dang."

"What are you trying to say?" he asked.

"Tinnndle-dang, Tinnndle-dang."

He leaned overtop the diminutive nothing, trying to again grasp it with already-extended hand. As he did so the colors faded around him and a light-spot opened in his line of vision.

"Tinnndle-dang, Tinnndle-dang."

He opened the connection, but did not talk immediately. A male voice came from the phone.

"Xenis?"

"Dean," he said groggily.

"Sorry. I woke you."

"It's alright. What's going on?"

"It's afternoon..."

"Yeah?"

"You're not here. We got to worrying."

"Oh. That's nice. I mean,...it's considerate of you."

"Are you coming today?"

"What time is it?"

"Three-fifteen."

When Xenis arrived at John's home, he was surprised to see the two men meet him at the front of the condominium.

"Thought you broke a leg, or was arrested maybe," John said after a long pause.

"No. Thank you for the concern, but no."

Xenis thought to arrive at John's place more regularly than usual for the next few days. He ought not have no structure at all simply because too much structure had not produced the desired effect. He resumed regular activities with the exception of performing each task at the precise-most time. He slept, but his hands shook and his anxious mind wandered. He had no idea what to do, and he feared explaining himself. Still, he needed some kind of support, so after a few days of waiting he related to Dean his need for structure and the strict schedule and tight-fitted living.

"Suddenly I'm not in one place, but another. And time has passed that I haven't experienced."

He left them out.

"I see. Now I understand better," Dean said.

"We were wondering."

"I'm not sure what to do."

"Let me ask my folks," Dean said.

Dean was only too happy to assist, and he knew his parents were capable in these matters. He asked first his father, who thought that perhaps Dean's friend suffered from a breakdown of some sort. One ought to relieve him of stress, and the most important therapy for the young man now was visiting friends and normality. Dean's father emphasized that things be ordinary, that everyone act as though nothing was amiss. Dean was curious what Xenis ought to do directly. He had no experience with such things, and his first thought was to suggest Xenis visit a psychiatrist, but his father insisted he avoid such things. Psychiatrists are the very edge of mental institutions, he explained. Xenis may be institutionalized and if not lucky enough never find his way back into the mainstream of humanity. No, father insisted that Xenis remain working and contributing with all of his associates and friends. That would be the best therapy. Dean thought this advice terribly wise. Again, he admired his father's quick, yet in-depth, assessment and advice. Dean's mother thought her husband's thinking sound, yet she offered something different. She told her son that human reasoning and action was finite, that god's was infinite. That is what god is: transcendent. That is why healthy, faithful persons appear to have no contact with Him. She suggested that Dean tell Xenis about a bible verse:

I have told you these things so that in me you may
have peace.
In this world you will have trouble, but take heart. I
[3]
have overcome the world.

Dean was overcome with emotion when he heard these words. He had, of course, heard them on other occasions, but now they spoke as never before. They were such great comfort that he had an unquenchable urge to share them, but he knew better. He explained to his mother that Xenis simply was not a religious fellow. If he wanted to help his friend in any way, he ought not attempt a conversion, and his mother agreed, at least in part. She said that if Dean and Deans like him wanted to bring Others to the flock, they ought not proselytize.

Perhaps the best way to conversion was a lack of converting, and no-one likes religion stuck in their face when troubled. She again quoted:

Do to others what you would have them do to you.

So, Dean thought that his best way to demonstrate the reality of Christianity was to be Christian, not to preach or impose.

"That's done by so many people anyway."

Still, if he should leave conversion out of interactions with Xenis, what he would do remained nebulous. His mother said that he ought to keep Xenis close and act normally, as father had said, but also to comfort him in some way.

"How do I do that?"

His mother thought that perhaps some kind of relaxation therapy was in order. She said that there are several such things in the city, even online. Dean knew that Xenis would not want some kind of impersonal exercise. He looked into different techniques and he found one that showed promise: a sensory deprivation tank. The experience may relieve anxiety Xenis obviously felt, and the expense was not so great. Dean decided that he would purchase the first visit for him. His mother thought his purchase absolutely benevolent. Dean found a place in the city where visits were rented: Tank Sixty. He purchased two visits online and printed the receipt. His father and mother discussed with him the merits of his gift. In the least it would calm him and give him pause to think. At most it may change his way of perception. Dean proudly took his parents' idea with him to John's condominium. He would present the gift to Xenis as soon as possible.

Xenis cleaned and dressed casually, trying to keep

himself from thinking about the precise time and what must come next. The loosening of his attention felt good, but another anxiety arose. They seemed to congregate around him, as if they were capable of liking him.

"But that's impossible."

He had relaxed his schedule for many days now and they had not returned, and again just as he began to feel comfortable enough that any randomness would not summon one of them, he found himself drinking lemon-water in the shower while he opened one of John's windows.

"The Earl Grey is not so great today."

Perhaps he was simply going mad; maybe he needed psychiatric attention more than he needed to rid himself of bits of nothing that could not even be called bits. Perhaps he would be able to ignore them. He wanted to visit Brazil – had wanted very long – and now his schedule had freed itself from his expectation. He was able to visit at any time.

"Now is any time."

So, now it was as a more content Brazil permitted him entry into her building.

"I can't believe you're here."

    "Good to see you."

"I thought I'd never see you again, or only very rarely."

    "I've wanted to."

"Then why not just come?"

Xenis let the question dangle as they sat at her kitchen table, discussing Xenis' work, or lack of it, and various other sundry. He realized that he had not much to talk about; he had done very little, actually. He described the Schnurre he had been reading and how he had enjoyed his living-space. There was not much to say and so they ate and enjoyed a card game. When Xenis arose to leave, he said that he planned to visit John and Dean. Perhaps Brazil would like to come. Brazil agreed readily, a swell of tears in her eyes.

"Oh, I never meant to exclude you, Brazil," he said.

"No?"

That Sunday Xenis felt quite well when he walked to Brazil's apartment. He had slept and cleaned and eaten quite randomly and no lacunae arose. Amazed quite glad but still nervous, he entered Brazil's unit and the pair prepared, mostly Brazil readying herself. The pleasant and continuous walk to John's condominium left Xenis relieved as well. His mind drifted from that concern as they chatted about mostly nothing, or rather unimportant events and things. Brazil sat beside Xenis in the front room of John's condominium, happy to see these men after so long. Really, nothing had changed essentially. It was the comfort of their presence that she missed. Now there.

"I have an idea," said Dean. "You'll forgive my frankness, I hope."

"If you need frankness, I'm curious," Xenis said.

Brazil chuckled.

"Well, we noticed that you have been feeling anxious lately."

Xenis looked at John who seemed as surprised as he.

"We?"

"Oh, yeah. My parents and I discuss things like this."

"I want to meet these parents of yours,"

"Anyway, we thought you may benefit from a bit of thorough tension relief."

"Uh-huh."

"And so I...bought some time in a sensory deprivation tank."

"Oh my," said Xenis.

"It's only two visits, but it seems like something you would enjoy."

"I would enjoy it very much, I think," Xenis said, looking at Brazil. She nodded as John winked at her.

"We thought it might take your mind off of things, maybe relieve some anxiety."

The four drank first coffee and later beer and wine, Xenis partaking only of lemon-water. The long hours passed short, and Brazil smiled within. She felt the need to protect him, in a way. He had never been so vulnerable. Enduring more attention from John in the form of a few personal questions and nods, she ignored him properly, focused her attention on her Xenis. When evening fell, Brazil and Xenis walked back to her apartment.

"Dean is certainly generous."

"He is," she said with an unsteady voice.

"I wish I could be more like that."

"More generous? You're generous enough. Besides, you don't want to be like him."

Xenis passed to Brazil a quizzical look, then gestured a question with his hands.

"I've known you for a long while now, and it seems to me that no matter what happens, you want to know the truth."

"I'm not sure what you mean."

"You want to know facts and...truth...whatever that is," she paused. "I'm saying you're not deluded."

"So...Dean's deluded?"

Brazil stopped walking.

"When I was looking for you, after you left, I had to do some online research to find him again."

"And?"

"I paid for some public records."

"OK."

"His parents have not been alive for over twenty years."

STRANGER NO MORE

John patched the hole with the shiny-gray, threaded tape. It would suffice for a while at least. The summer warmth already kept the sticky fabric together, holding the hole. He was glad that Dean was not there; he was a good kid, but a kid nonetheless.

"He's so nervous."

He meandered about in the kitchen, looking for those pretzels.

"I don't give a damn about salt," he thought.

As he fidgeted, he changed the channel. Reverend Marvin talked again about faith and contribution, but a syndicated something would be better. Marvin always said the same things, only in different ways. John tapped the switch again and again as the light-spot in his back yard silently illuminated. The shout of a man outside lacked into vibration, voicing his angered sentiments over his Volvo - with the sounds around him themselves moving to drive others away in a symphony of not: the click-knock of a diesel engine, the low-vibration, slow-pitched scream of cicadas, the faint ululato of a speckled rock pigeon. The fan near John made limit by lack the breeze that met the old man and his favorite food ceased-by-not the salty-bread, sour taste of his childhood. The cherry wood around him lacked red into kind while a train making two miles distance no more than two drove off almost all sounds but the clack and click on track and a clear-resounding bell. John made not-sedentary by lean, slanting his body aback into his favorite-most chair and the arms drove off in themselves all but creaks. He enjoyed that sound, but at that moment kept it completely from his mind, because of its familiarity. Today was a good day, bright and coming-to-be-hot but pleasant. The air would soon enough cool, the humidity tolerable. John settled into an old-time movie, something he had seen as a child. He thought he heard something, but then he drifted into a conclusion that whatever it was, it was not a sound. It was as if his mind heard something, but that something did not actually exist. John disliked such occurrences intensely; he despised uncertainty. His eyelids began to droop, feeling more and more heavy as he attempted to force them open. He thought he needed to wash his car tomorrow, expected to be as pleasant as today.

"I can do it in the morning when I have the energy," he thought. "Wait, Dean will be here. Damn."

John continued to feel drowsy, not merely a lack of continued sentience but the lack that was sleep slipping him into a comfortable rest. Dean would not return until tomorrow morning.

"Good."

John watched George Bailey cross onto a bridge and he again heard another one of those sounds, like the rush of flowing water pulsing again and again; he looked around and there was nothing present that had fluid in it. No reason for the regular push, nothing that made it happen. The rush of the fluid suddenly ceased, and as quick there was a kind of silence that John had never perceived. He had the same experience; it seemed to have come from nowhere and continued as a kind of phantasm. John could sense it, but not because he perceived it was there. There was something surrounding this silence completely, but it was nothing, other than the silence itself. That same nothing seemed to be there, with him, though it made no sense. As he watched George wring his ear with his hand, John listened to the words he had heard so many times.

"Shoey flou lanky hep tannigan," George said. "Hep tannigan!"

John was confused, but he was able to sense that silence as well as the sound that was not a sound. Unphased, he took another pretzel and continued watching. He fixed tight his brows when a young woman in soft light said "Rip whas griftin quot." John became frightened and attempted to reach the phone nearby with his right hand, but his arm would not move, as if it were not there. He saw what seemed like a cloud of impossible black dots encircle his vision.

"Shput sit bramma hamb," he thought.

Again, John became frightened, but he had no idea what to do. He was in a room, he knew that, but he had no idea where. He was not certain, but he thought he was unable to swallow. Tiny pins and needles crept the entirety of his body, but he knew they were not there.

* * *

Xenis looked again at the printout Dean had given him. He would be able to soak for an hour twice, or two hours once. Certainly, he would be able to relax, and perhaps learn something. He distractedly wiped the counter in his room and looked again out the window. An unpaid bill from hotel management awaited him inside a dark white envelope. He wanted to see Brazil, but the fear of blackouts – visits from them – still kept him away most days. That Saturday's light-fall brought out green of grass through the window of his motel room, comforted him now as ever, but the final window of the series in John's unit would not budge.

"This one seems like it's regularly hit by rain," he explained to Dean, who stood beside him.

"Can we replace only one?" Dean asked.

Xenis did not respond but put his forehead in his right hand.

"Did it happen again?"

"What day is this?"

"Thursday afternoon."

"I was just at home."

A perplexed Dean knew he must say something, something-anything.

"What could be causing these spells?"

Xenis refrained from explaining, again. His finished his work on the window without incident, distressed. He had no credible explanation; now he simply wanted the episodes to cease. The lacunae departed three days long when he then found himself again in the cafe drinking Earl Grey and suddenly

"I'm not sure what that means," he said to a curious Brazil who sat at her kitchen table in her unit.

"What is it? You have a strange look on your face," she

said.

"I don't know. I just don't know what to do."

He asked Brazil where he was, what they had been doing. With quizzical look, she replied that they had been chatting, pleasantly she added, over the last hour. Apparently, he did nothing out of the ordinary – for him at least – during the time he was blank, and so his anxiety did not compel him to wonder about harming anyone, or stealing or anything like that.

"Still, they're disturbing. I don't want to suffer these...vacancies the rest of my life."

"There must be a way to leave off of them, drive them away."

But then another thought occurred.

"Maybe I ought not drive them away."

He spent time considering the matter alone, and as he was tightening the chain on his bicycle – completely distracted – another thought arrived.

"The tank. The tank."

He had no idea what consisted of an hour's worth of floating in a tank and decided that he needed to learn no more.

"Ignorance is better in this case."

He took himself downtown to one of the deprivation centers. The building was not terribly large, and he found himself down in its brightly-lit, mirror-filled bowels descending stairs and into what seemed to be a basement. The office smelled of salt fused with incense. A simply-dressed-sweater-hugged young woman made into pony tail and smile greeted him. She asked if he had ever floated. No. She summoned a young man who asked Xenis to chat for a moment and explained how new floaters sometimes had anxiety.

"And so you want to explain some of the experience?"

"That's right."

"Please don't."

"I'm sorry?"

"Please explain nothing. I want the experience to be as novel as possible."

"We have to ensure..."

Xenis interrupted.

"If you must explain these things to me, then I will leave. I don't want to know anything about the experience before it comes."

The man paused for a moment, excused himself. When he returned, he escorted Xenis to one of the chambers, of which there were three kinds. One was the traditional unit, looking something like a tank without treads or wheels welded to the floor. A metal casing surrounded clear fluid and a slanting door opened into a dark pit. Another chamber appeared to be a shower at first, though quite large and without heads. The young man led Xenis along a hallway and into another series of rooms where more tanks awaited. The door to this room was wooden and flimsy. Xenis had expected something a bit more secure, but the tanks themselves presented the appearance of certainty and steel-potent experience. They were more real than the things around them, or at least something in them was most real.

"I realize you want to know almost nothing about the experience before it begins..."

"But there are things that you must tell me."

"Exactly."

The man pointed to a shower in the corner of the room.

"Be sure to clean up before you enter. It's a matter of sanitation...and respect for other floaters."

"Sure. Sure."

"Use the wash and the conditioner too. That's best."

"OK."

"Some people refrain from using the earplugs."

He lifted a bag containing small, blue blobs.

"It's not a good idea. Use the earplugs."

"Is that it?"

"Do you have any cuts or abrasions? Maybe you shaved today?"

"No."

The chamber that the man finally opened for Xenis emitted the same certainty but was shaped of different contours. Egg-shaped, it sat on the floor of the room, as if waiting to birth a baby brontosaurus. The man lifted a latch on one end and opened the egg one third on top with the remaining on bottom – the cavity inside filled with the same clear liquid as in the other tanks.

"Here is the eye mask," the young man explained.

Then, he pointed to what looked like a life-preserver.

"This will help keep you afloat. The lights in the chamber will dim and then go out after thirty seconds. Be sure to turn off the lights outside the chamber. You can listen to music..."

"That's not necessary."

"Alright, but some people need something to latch on to."

"I want to latch onto nothing."

Xenis showered, carefully scrubbing each part of his body. He had two hours since he would be using both float sessions. He had clipped his hair to one-eighth of an inch and cleaned himself thoroughly, in expectation, but he again washed. He leaned forward, looking at the fluid in the chamber. The air-moisture rose to meet him, the liquid warmer than the temperature of the room. He put his hand into the fluid, expecting the consistency of water, but the aquant felt heavy in his hand, and viscous – not water at all. The whole of the chamber smelled of salt; some kind of saline had been dissolved in the fluid. He stepped into the egg after having turned out the room-light. He sat first in the center of the egg and looked around at the controls. There was a light switch and what looked like dials for a radio. He stood up and pulled the top of the egg down by a handle affixed to the lid as he again sat. Some kind of cockpit. He spread himself over the board that would help him float and turned out the light. One small bulb illuminated the chamber. He lifted his head and looked for the switch to extinguish the irritating light, but found none. Suddenly, it went dark and he had to adjust himself in the thick, slippery fluid before he was able to float comfortably. It was viscous and strangely oily. His eyes adjusted quickly, but he was unable to see very much.

"Good."

He floated and waited while he tapped occasionally against the inner shell. He heard nothing unusual and perceived only the ordinary lack of illumination when one first turns out the bedroom light before sleep. Each time he brushed against the inner shell, he grew more aware of himself and his thinking grew louder. His thoughts were everywhere. On his dilemma. On Brazil and her dog. An image of a woman he had never seen, never read about or met appeared in his mind. He envisioned grass from the perspective of a hedgehog. His mind raced; he attempted to slow them with a meditation on the blackness spread before and into him. Then, without any remark or warning, his session ended. The room-light came on and music played.

"Nothing."

Four times he returned on consecutive days and he experienced the same in his same egg. Thoughts rampant and darting back and forth in his mind. Images arriving suddenly and then fading into other images.

On the fifth attempt Xenis had grown accustomed to the practice of floating. He arrived as usual and the pony-tail greeted him as an old friend. He showered and prepared himself as usual. He entered the tank and began, and custom brought him a quiet before not begotten. This darkness drove into him an unforeseen calm not experienced in some time. He adjusted the eyepads on his face so that almost no light at all found its way into his eyes, but realized that no light emitted whether or not he wore the eyepads. There arose a few slaps and swishes of fluid against the walls of the egg, but otherwise no sound entered him, as before when the day's noise rushed through his mind. No. This time, each sense in turn sifted slowly, melting into the salt-solution around him until he was able to sense nothing. Even the sense of his bobbing frame dissipated into the salt and oily fluid. No anxiety arose as he floated and thus no images arose nor thinkings of whats; he was thankful for the welcomed bits of nothing that came to him in shreds and bits. After a time, he ceased driving words around his mind and let loose all images, at least all images possible. Shifting blue blobs meandered about in his vision, such as it was, but after a time he was unable to calculate they broke into smaller pieces and disappeared. He was able to see only the dark, and it seeped comfort into him. He had no idea how long he had floated in the tank this time and was grateful for his ignorance. Perhaps he had lost perspective as well. Still, the darkness did not bring the lack that he had felt, even when he was unaware of acting. He felt more as if he was rejecting present things rather than welcoming something that was not there.

"Hell," he muttered, as if sentience emerging abruptly.

After a time he felt less like himself as he gradually lifted his thoughts that dissipated into mist and his mind stopped. He tried to release his feeling, all of his sensation, but that seemed impossible. The blackness accompanied him like thought in his mind, but he encountered no nothing, nor did he feel any closer to nothing. In fact, his experience seemed to be one of being close around him as before he always had been, yet here-now more present and thicker came he, like the liquid where he floated. He had no idea or thought with which to determine how long he had been in the egg, been at all, and no awareness of when he ought to depart or that he had something from which to leave came to him. A thick molasses enveloped him. Xenis-rested lacked what lack he was able, and if this exercise failed, he would continue to attract them, though no continuation seemed possible or desirable. Much to his disappointment, a tap at the shell of his egg made him aware of something, rousing him from a semi-somnulant awareness.

"Already? I just started."

He remained where he was. He would force them to retrieve him.

Another tap he heard against the eggshell, but no sound from him. He then heard what seemed like the latch on the egg open, though no light entered. Xenis knew that the hatch had occurred and the shell was now open, but he heard no voice and saw no latch nor shell nor anything. Instead, a clank of metal upon plastic emerged and then the clear fluid surrounding him shifted, as if another body had entered the chamber. A sudden anxiety drove him from his relaxed state and he sought whatever accompanied him. He felt his way around the chamber, one side, pressing with hands to feel for something, whatever it was, truly anxious, when the chamber suddenly lit. He was able to see everything because of a light that came not from the controls inside the chamber but from a small ship metal and stern, strong and potent. It searched with the light all around the inner surface, as if assessing its surroundings, passing over the water and the controls, then light fixed upon Xenis, the ship suddenly ceasing movement – beams on Xenis as if the diminutive vessel came scared. Something that sounded like a voice in a loudspeaker blared at Xenis, but the vibration of the sound was so faint that he was unable to understand the words, if they had been in his tongue. Minuscule bipedal beings wandered around on the ship's deck and the sound of tiny metal cling and clangs came. He stared at it for a time, thinking someone was playing with him, and he did not hear the latch or see the eggshell open, but behind him on the water was standing a tree thick of trunk with roots set deeply into the water, soil and fluid one. Xenis was able to discern its orange and red leaves falling in a breeze that he felt, only slightly. A squirrel, chased by a dog, ran up the tree and disappeared into the tiniest of rodent slink-holes. A man walked around the tree with a push-mower before him, trimming the grass and picking up fallen apples. He noted Xenis' confusion and waved, stopped to remove his cap and wipe his forehead with a kerchief from his rear pocket. Xenis knew nothing about what to do, but he backed away from the ship and the tree with the man beside and his head struck a large, heavy spherical object that floated nearby. Enough light from the ship allowed him to see a sphere whose surface was smeared with much blue and white, green and brown beneath. Suspended in the air, it slowly rotated on its axis while at the same time orbiting the circumference of the eggshell. Xenis was distracted from the sphere by the light from the ship, falling upon something that seemed to vibrate, a nucleus of twelve pieces six-one and six-another, he was unable to see them clearly but he somehow recognized their number. Two bits of something circled the nucleus in an inner orbit and four in an outer. This thing seemed to vibrate with motion, moving itself into its own. Xenis knew that this thing was incredibly small, although he was able to see it clearly and in great detail. The whole of its nucleus and orbiting electrons moved with extreme rapidity and all around and about the chamber, somehow not striking globe, and not ship. The man now sat beside the tree and fixed his eyes upon the globe and then the atom, watching it vibrating and darting about the chamber. The shell of the egg opened once more and in emerged other ships and more atoms, now hydrogen, then helium and iron. More coming. Suddenly, a bright light illuminated the whole of the chamber much more radiant and hot than the ship's lamp, as if a distant source abruptly began. The light made the globe settle into an orbit about it, and Xenis now saw that the chamber of the chamber now had no end. He reached out his fingers into a spiral glob that he now saw in the distance. Its body felt warm and moved in his hand, like a frog who had been caught and wriggled free. He noticed a sable hole in its middle, wanted to know. So, he reached one finger into the black and was unable to pull his flesh out, so potent was its expanding grasp. He braced his legs against what ground he found, his feet touching something not the edge of his chamber. Still, he found some leverage and pulled out his finger in some pain before the hole was able to swallow more of his hand. A piece of his finger had been removed, it seemed, and his hand was now numb. He rubbed his flesh and moved away from the minuscule but threatening hole. All these things did not scare him, for some reason, yet he now wondered where to go. The liquid in the chamber became less viscous and more watery – now disappeared – and the footing he had grasped now left him, but he did not fall. He floated in the seeming black, the ship now hundreds of millions of kilometers distant, the planet orbiting a distant star. Xenis lost all sense of where and with the when lost him the time. His body extended out into each corner of the black that now encompassed him, painfully spreading rapturous pieces of Xenis across what had become of his chamber. And when he had spread around and over each piece of everything that came about in his sphere, he at last gained his objective.

RUNAROUND

Brazil tapped the counter with her short, unpainted nails. Fingers roll up, rolled the fingers down. She had plenty of time, and she had wanted so much free space-time to begin a new glass and lead project. She decided the color would be a robust, medium green, still the shape yet escaped her. She had remained in her unit for three days – not abnormal – but she felt slightly claustrophobic. At the moment she occupied a strange space, that interval between the inspiration of a new, seemingly good idea and her actual movement on it. She always felt not anxious about the beginning, but in some way sluggish. A phone call, an internet video, a message from a friend all take her away at this point. Once she had gotten started and immersed herself in creation, she would be thoroughly annoyed at any distraction.

"Speaking of distraction."

She thought of Xenis.

"Thank goodness he's gone."

She pouted as the feeling of abandonment recurred. Her phone rang from an unknown number.

"Yeah?"

"Hello, Brazil."

"Who is this?"

"Dean, Dean Fromm."

"Oh. Hi, Dean."

Dean wanted to know what happened to Xenis, but Brazil knew almost less than he. She talked to him for nearly an hour, reminiscing over the challenges of association with a maddening man. She ended the chat somewhat relieved, but painfully melancholy. She wanted him back.

"He can do all those strange things, if he likes."

Her thoughts ran over the many male figures who had entered and exited her life. Her mind and affection were tired and the desire to grow old with someone overcame her momentarily. There had been friendships before and after Xenis, but this one brought something to an end. She had only a slight idea what that was, and now there would be a blank where he had been. He had become nothing to her. She stared at the floor, as she sometimes did when in thought and pondering a discomfort. Then, as if startled into awareness, Brazil thought to prepare. She was expected to meet Gail and Steven in twenty minutes and wanted to clean up. Now, showering would not be possible. Suddenly, she arose and began to give herself a desultory wash, on the ears and neck over her face. The hair would wait. Brazil called Gail and asked her to come pick her up at her apartment, then found clothes and checked how much money she would allow herself to spend. She was in the midst of washing her face when "Brrrahht" came the door-buzz. She was unable to see, but she found the "open" button on her intercom. Gail was safe. Brazil reentered the bathroom and scrubbed her face, then ran the wash-towel over it again. Gail would be in the apartment by now. As she dried, she looked around her place. No Gail.

"Gail?"

No Gail again. Brazil walked back and forth in her unit, looking into each room and finding nothing, no-one. No-one in her place except Brazil and dog. She walked down the stair-flights in order to see if her friend was there, but no. No Gail. Brazil opened the front door and looked back and forth. No-one. As she was walking back up the stairs into her apartment, almost inside, her buzzer clanged again.

"Brrrahht."

"Hello," she spoke into her intercom microphone. No Gail. No answer.

"Stupid fucking kids."

Gail arrived fifteen minutes later.

"I'm late. Sorry."

    "Were you here before?"

"Before now?"

    "Yeah."

"No. Just here now."

Gail and Steven entertained Brazil, but her mind kept her distracted. She kept thinking of Dean Fromm and their conversation. She hesitated contacting him over the next few weeks, but he possessed some element of Xenis that contented her somehow. She contacted him again and invited him to her place, hoping he would not think she was interested in him.

"That's always a problem."

She was happy to have again a piece of Xenis.

"I'm glad you had time to come," she said.

"Me too."

They both laughed.

"I'm sorry about...John." Brazil was barely able to recall the name.

"I miss him, but I have a way of coping."

"Yeah?"

"I talk to my parents."

Brazil had forgotten. Dean was so comfortable and comforting. He was kind and considerate, and he always seemed capable in practical matters. In fact, almost every aspect of him seemed well placed. He was capable of tolerating suffering, and he had discipline that others lacked in a very serious way. His physical heath seemed excellent; he ate well. Everything in his life was so well-adjusted, with some rather ordinary exceptions.

"My parents are a big influence and help."

"You're pretty close to them, aren't you?"

"I am. They give great advice."

"I can imagine."

"My mom says that even atheists say there is wisdom in the New Testament."

"She reads that book a lot, it seems." Brazil was curious.

"Constantly."

"And you read with her."

"I do," Dean said. "When we're able" came out almost as an afterthought.

"But you see her often. I thought so, anyway."

"Oh, I see both my parents all the time. We do a lot together."

"What do you do?"

"We talk and watch shows. They attend the same parish I attend."

"So, you see them in church on Sundays."

"Every week."

"You visit them at their place, I suppose."

"That's right."

"I wish I had that kind of thing. You seem to care for one another. My parents are not the best."

"No?"

"They're religious...in a bad way."

"That happens sometimes."

"But your parents are a great comfort."

"They are."

Weeks later Brazil received a letter from The Vincent Hotel. It looked official, perhaps a bill. Xenis' roll-up foam bed and the occasion when he climbed to the roof of her apartment complex ran through her mind. She tried again to contact him by phone. The number rang and his voicemail picked up, but no message prompted him to return the sentiment. She sat heavily on the earth-brown divan in her rear room and tapped the dog's hindquarters. A wag proved the feeling returned. She read about a man and his efforts to ride a bicycle up a mountain, just for amusement. It was a stupid article that held little interest for her, but she found herself reading instead of working on her project. Again glad that her space was empty, she wanted someone to fill it. She lifted herself and threw her frame into her workroom, intending to begin the new project. Again, her door-klang sounded.

"Brrrahht."

Brazil responded with a greeting, but received no response. She heard nothing on the autumn-filled street, though her window remained open and the noises of cars and pedestrians regularly entered her apartment. She returned to the back room and "Brrrahht" once again. Weary of the game, Brazil brought herself out of the complex and sat on her neighbor's porch, watching. She brought with her a book for reading and found herself interested in a new tone of green discovered by accident, like an earlier blue. It was quite vibrant. She was anxious to obtain it. After a half-hour had passed she was prepared to re-enter her apartment. She walked toward her building, thinking again about how Xenis had returned after a long absence. Perhaps he would return again. It had been so surprising and annoying too. Still, more surprising in the pleasant way. As she approached the door to her place, a short, thin child of ten or so years ran up to the door, pressed her apartment button and dashed away with incredible alacrity. Brazil stood and stared at the child, almost in disbelief. Some part of her wanted to delete what had just happened. She leaned against the building and attempted to restrain tears, but they fell anyway. One or two passing pedestrians seemed intent upon asking her for her trouble, but said nothing. Her ascent back up the stairs came slow and tiresome, and the rest of that evening she wanted to do nothing, not read not sculpt not watch video not move. She meandered about from task to task, sometimes forgetting that she had been in the middle of loading the wash machine when writing an email to her patroness and sometimes recalling she needed to fill a prescription when in full middle of crafting the missive. Her mind seemed to jump about, concentrate on one thing or another, then realize it wanted or needed something else. Still, all of her work came accomplished and she dragged her swollen shape around her four rooms, the one Xenis once occupied remaining empty. The next month consisted of the same sort of living.

She tried to think less about Xenis, and she was successful in a long way. She cleaned her front room, which needed tending badly, and in a pile of neglected bills and leftover art promotionals and credit-card solicitations she found a search she had purchased about Dean Fromm. She examined his history, including the birth and death dates of his parents.

"It's so odd."

Her thoughts began to run along the life of Dean Fromm who for her became more curious and still more enigmatic.

NICHTS

Hip-trop, trip-pop they spread out along the now-tawny grass. No ocher did they produce – though some suspect it – crawling up hills along the inclement plain they stood heavy in the urban soil. Rivals and mates of is, they assembled where what comes. Intimate of each element, they let not the minutest of particles escape and they were enormous, no collection of is escaping. They rode along the sliver of gold that crawls through rock and terra beneath the surface of the plain; they made electricity that guides thoughts which produce psyches of erect beings walking atop prodigious hills with flocks of wool-producing bleeters. They rode in iron trains along dark mountainous paths in masses and within bunches of anything. They have no number and cannot be taken as one, fraction or many – though one counts their species. They marched and did not move, made glory and produced earth and were none of these things. When talking they produced descriptive sounds that gave presence to the light of things, but they themselves cannot be described. Just so, they cannot walk or run, and so they did not crawl, did not die, and one cannot call them immortal, them having no life ever-undying. They did nothing and unified with death, life-giving portion. They glided in proportion and shaped the whole of a man with sable features, penetrating eyes and raven hair. They partook of his making and did nothing while he changed one state for another. Wrapped around his presence, they kept wood from being glass and allowed him rest.

www.ingramcontent.com/pod-product-compliance
Lightning Source LLC
Chambersburg PA
CBHW071004280626
47160CB00016B/2171